"Thank you," she said in a loud whisper. **"I don't know how I'll ever pay you back for your kindness."**

Palmer startled, words caught deep in his chest, his skin burning hot from her touch. "You don't owe me anything," he muttered.

"But I do," Soledad responded. "You don't know how much everything you've done means to me."

Palmer smiled. "You shouldn't have any problems while I'm gone. Just stay inside, please. Away from the windows. I won't be gone long." He pointed toward the guest bedroom. "Lock the door," he said as she turned, headed for the back of the house.

He stood watching as she adjusted Lyra against her shoulder and grabbed the laptop. She tossed him one last look as she walked away, the sweetest smile filling her face. Jack followed them, then lay outside the door after Soledad had closed and locked it. Palmer closed his eyes and took a deep breath. He reached for the side of his face and pressed his palm to his cheek, his fingers trembling ever so slightly.

* * *

The Coltons of Grave Gulch: Falling in love is the most dangerous thing of all...

* * *

If you're on Twitter, tell us what you think of Harlequin Romantic Suspense! #harlequinromsuspense

Dear Reader,

What an emotional journey this writing year has been. Although I genuinely love what I do, there have been times when finding the right words to convey a story just wouldn't come. A year of pandemic has made many things seem impossible. But being a part of the Colton author family and breathing life into Palmer and Soledad's story has just been the best cure!

Palmer and Soledad made my heart sing. Seeing them grow and blossom as they find love was simply heartwarming. Their ready-made family as they find themselves parenting little Lyra sometimes seemed impossible, but when it didn't, it felt all kinds of right.

Thank you so much for your support. I am humbled by all the love readers continue to show me, my characters and our stories. I know that none of this would be possible without you.

Until the next time, please take care and may God's blessings be with you always.

With much love,

Deborah Fletcher Mello

www.DeborahMello.org

RESCUED BY THE COLTON COWBOY

Deborah Fletcher Mello

Special thanks and acknowledgment are given to Deborah Fletcher Mello for her contribution to The Coltons of Grave Gulch miniseries.

Recycling programs for this product may not exist in your area.

ISBN-13: 978-1-335-75934-4

Rescued by the Colton Cowboy

Copyright © 2021 by Harlequin Books S.A.

This edition published by arrangement with Harlequin Books S.A.

For questions and comments about the quality of this book, please contact us at CustomerService@Harlequin.com.

Harlequin Enterprises ULC
22 Adelaide St. West, 40th Floor
Toronto, Ontario M5H 4E3, Canada
www.Harlequin.com

Printed in U.S.A.

A true Renaissance woman, **Deborah Fletcher Mello** finds joy in crafting unique story lines and memorable characters. She's received accolades from several publications, including *Publishers Weekly*, *Library Journal* and *RT Book Reviews*. Born and raised in Connecticut, Deborah now considers home to be wherever the moment moves her.

Books by Deborah Fletcher Mello

Harlequin Romantic Suspense

The Coltons of Grave Gulch

Rescued by the Colton Cowboy

To Serve and Seduce

Seduced by the Badge
Tempted by the Badge
Reunited by the Badge
Stalked by Secrets

Colton 911: Grand Rapids

Colton 911: Agent By Her Side

Harlequin Kimani Romance

Truly Yours
Hearts Afire
Twelve Days of Pleasure
My Stallion Heart
Stallion Magic
Tuscan Heat
A Stallion's Touch
A Pleasing Temptation
Sweet Stallion
To Tempt a Stallion
A Stallion Dream

Visit the Author Profile page at
Harlequin.com for more titles.

To Carly Silver, the best editor in the whole wide world!

You pushing me out of my comfort zone has made my writing better.

Your patience with me has been affirming. One day, I'll get POV right!

You make me want to keep writing, and for that, I thank you!

Chapter 1

Soledad de la Vega brushed her palms against the front of her bib apron, then reached around her waist to undo the ties that wrapped it around her body. As she pulled the twill garment over her head, she stole a quick glance at the smartwatch on her wrist. It was almost midnight and her stomach did a flip, as if the prosciutto and cheese she'd snacked on earlier might come back up.

Working in the bakery after closing rarely unnerved Soledad. Downtown Grave Gulch, Michigan—where her business, Dream Bakes, sat—had always felt safe and she had never given any thought to anyone trying to do her or any of her employees harm. Tonight, though, her anxiety was at an all-time high. She took a deep breath to still her nerves.

She wiped the last remnants of flour from the counter

and covered the yeast rolls that needed to rise before going into the oven. She pushed the oversize tray of rolled dough into the center of the table. The morning crew would brush butter across the tops and dust them with sesame and caraway seeds before they baked. Her small staff would hold the bakery down until she returned, and for the first time since starting her own business, Soledad wasn't sure when that would be.

The night wasn't like her usual nights. She wasn't headed home to Melvin, her overweight tabby cat. There was no plan to finish the book on top of the stack that decorated the nightstand next to her bed, no cup of warm tea to soothe her to sleep. In less than an hour, she would be driving her best friend, Annie, to safety. The two had planned every detail of Annie's escape from her abusive husband, Gavin, and Soledad was only minutes from rendezvousing to whisk her and her baby girl, Lyra, away.

She looked at her watch a second time, then reached for the cell phone on the counter behind her. There was no message saying their plans had changed. Making one last sweep of the space to ensure all the ovens were off and the food was put away, she then shut off the lights, exited the building and headed to her car.

Minutes later, Soledad sat in the cul-de-sac near Annie's home with her car running and the headlights off. She had pulled past the driveway and was parked under a massive oak tree. The quiet neighborhood was one of the more prestigious in Grave Gulch, and both she and Annie knew that the security officer who patrolled the neighborhood wouldn't make his next round past the home until twelve thirty. Still, Soledad was praying steadily, every nerve and muscle in her petite body twitching with nervousness. She was scared, everything that could go wrong playing out in her head. Her biggest fear was that Gavin would wake before Annie could sneak out of the house and their window of opportunity would be lost.

Soledad and Annie had met in high school, the two girls running together on the long-distance track team. They'd been polar opposites, Annie's blond pixie cut, blue eyes and fair skin contrasting starkly with Soledad's blue-black strands, black eyes and olive skin tone. Soledad had been bubbly and effervescent, one of the more popular girls, while Annie had been more reserved and studious. But the two had become fast friends, bonding over the sport, their obsession with boy bands and the soap opera *General Hospital*.

After graduation they'd gone on to Grave Gulch Community College together, Annie wanting to pursue a career in medicine and Soledad unsure of what she wanted to do. It had been Annie who'd encouraged her to turn her love for pastries and baked goods into a career. Annie had pushed her to pursue a degree in business management and Annie had been there with her the day she'd opened Dream Bakes.

Annie had become a nurse practitioner and was considering medical school and pediatric medicine when she'd met Gavin Stone. Gavin, a renowned plastic surgeon fifteen years her senior, had been handsome, charming and obsessed with Annie. So much so that Soledad had gotten a bad feeling about him from the start. He'd been jealous of their friendship, purposely distancing Annie from as many friends and family as he could manage. On their wedding day he'd told Soledad to tell her best friend goodbye, that things would change now that Annie was his. As if Annie were a fragile possession that he planned to tuck away in a drawer far from public view. Soledad had wanted to warn Annie but wasn't sure what to warn her about. And she'd been happy. So much so that Soledad hadn't wanted to do anything to spoil her day or put a damper on the future Annie had seen before her. Soledad had kept her concerns to herself, instead making sure Gavin knew that nothing and no one would ever break the bond the two women shared. No matter how hard he tried.

Gavin's abuse had started slowly, emotional at first and then turning physical. Annie had been made to quit her job at the hospital, Gavin controlling their finances. He told her what she could and could not do and who she could and could not see. He rarely allowed her out of his sight, and even when he was at the hospital working, he would call with regularity to ensure she was home, abiding by his lengthy list of rules. The name-calling had gone from the occasional nasty slur to spitting rages that left Annie in tears. Open-palmed slaps when she had tried to defend her position or said something he didn't like became closed-fist punches that had left her bruised and battered. And each time Gavin had hurt Annie, Soledad had been furious.

With haunting regularity, Annie had cried on Soledad's shoulders, the weight of her problems feeling like a boulder that neither woman could move. Frustration that there was nothing Soledad could say or do to distance Annie from the situation had been devastating. Soledad's suggestions to call the police and report him had fallen on deaf ears, Annie petrified that outside help would only make things worse. She'd been devastated when she'd discovered she was pregnant but had hoped the birth of their child would push Gavin to be a better man. Instead, he'd been furious that their first child together would be a girl when he only wanted a son. He'd proclaimed it Annie's fault, just another in a long list of wrongs he attributed to her.

Soledad's apartment and Dream Bakes had become Annie's sanctuary, the only places where she could run and hide when the abuse became too much. Gavin had tried only once to stall his wife's lifelong friendship with Soledad. It was one of the few times Annie had openly gone toe-to-toe with him, threatening to publicly expose him if he dared impede their bond. Soledad had stood arm in arm with her, ready to show him a world of hurt to protect her friend. Gavin had backed off, but not before leaving Annie with a black eye and bruised clavicle. But Annie had gone back to being a dutiful wife and Soledad had become her refuge. Too often, Soledad had been angry with the world, that Annie was unable to see herself free of the man, and she'd been riddled with guilt that there wasn't something more that she herself could do for her friend.

After the birth of Lyra, Annie had finally agreed to get out of her situation. Soledad knew that the first step was to take Annie as far from her husband as she could run. Therapy and support would follow, and Soledad had put everything in place to ensure as smooth a transition for Annie as she could muster.

Together, they had dedicated weeks to planning each step, considering every fathomable possibility until every detail of Annie's escape plan was committed to memory. Once Annie and the baby were safe inside her Toyota Camry, Soledad would drive them both upstate to a shelter for battered women. The drive would take a few hours and put them at the front door. From there, mother and child would be escorted to their new home and Soledad would be sent on her way to worry about her friend from afar. Cell phones were prohibited, but Annie would be able to call Soledad weekly from a private line in her counselor's office.

Soledad couldn't know her friend's final destination and Annie would be forbidden to disclose her whereabouts, lest she put other sheltered women in danger. Telling anyone of her whereabouts would get Annie evicted from the shelter and the program's many protections. But more important, Gavin wouldn't be able to find her until Annie was ready to be found.

Soledad tapped her hand nervously against her leg, her anxiety beginning to reach peak levels. Annie was ten minutes late. Soledad was tempted to sneak up to the home to peek into the windows, but she didn't want to risk setting off the sensor lights Gavin had installed around the property. They didn't have much time before the security car would make its regularly scheduled drive-by. But there had been contingencies for that, too. Soledad just prayed they wouldn't be necessary.

Panic was just about to set in when the rear passenger door of her car was thrown open and Annie slid inside. She carried little Lyra against her chest and had a designer baby backpack hoisted over her shoulder. She looked like Soledad felt. Scared!

"Drive!" Annie ordered as she slammed the door closed. "Go! Now! Drive!"

Soledad shifted the vehicle into gear and pulled from the makeshift parking space onto the cul-de-sac. Behind her, the Stone family home was suddenly awash with light, looking as if every bulb in every room had come to life. Instinctively knowing that wasn't a good thing, Soledad turned her eyes to the road, hit the gas and peeled off as if someone were already chasing them.

"We're going to stay off the main road until we get into the next county," Soledad said, glancing into her rearview mirror to the back seat. "Hopefully, Gavin will get lost trying to figure out what direction we're headed."

Tears were streaming down Annie's face. It was one of the few times her friend had allowed her vulnerability to show. She looked lost and frightened.

Annie shook her head. "He's going to find us," she whispered.

"He's not," Soledad said firmly. "We won't let him. Did you toss your cell phone?"

Annie nodded. "I left it in the dog food bag."

"Then we're good. Because I wouldn't put it past him to have some sort of tracking device installed to keep up with you. In thirty minutes, we'll be far enough away that there'll be no way he can find you."

Annie forced the slightest smile to her face, but Soledad knew her dear friend wasn't as confident.

Soledad shifted her gaze back and forth between her side mirrors, her rearview mirror, the back seat and the road. Annie had drifted into thought, nuzzling six-month-old Lyra gently beneath her chin, her arms wrapped protectively around the infant. The little girl was wrapped snugly in a cotton blanket, completely oblivious to the lengths her mother and Soledad would go to keep her safe. It was bliss, and Soledad wished she could be so lucky to know that kind of peace and be as unaware.

Annie eased the baby into the infant safety seat, latching it securely around the tiny body before tightening her own seat belt.

They drove in silence for a good little while. The local radio station was playing Shy Carter's newest release. Soledad bobbed her head in time to the beat, singing along with the song that had risen swiftly to the top of the country charts. The service roads were dark, lights nonexistent. Barely a sliver of moonlight peeked through the cover of clouds. It had also begun to drizzle, the threat of heavy rain preceded by a trickle of moisture that was most annoying. And the rising fog was getting thicker with each passing minute.

Annie broke the moment of reverie, her usually poised tone a loud whisper that rippled with tension. "I need you to make me a promise, Soledad."

"Anything. You know that," Soledad responded, shooting her friend a quick glance in the rearview mirror.

"If anything happens to me, I want you to promise

that you'll take care of Lyra. I need you to keep my baby girl safe."

Soledad raised her brows. "Don't talk like that, Annie. Everything is going to be fine. You're going to—"

Annie interrupted her, her voice rising ever so slightly. "Promise me, Soledad. I need you to promise!" Annie's stoic expression was disconcerting, the determination in her eyes feeling almost final.

She nodded. "Whatever you need. You know that!" And Soledad meant that with every fiber of her being as the words slipped past her lips. Soledad understood the fear that gripped her bestie because it rippled down the length of her own spine. It felt corporeal, a thick, viscous energy with the stench of doubt and anger wrapped around it. Stepping into the unknown came with its own set of consequences and proved formidable when you had to worry about someone other than yourself. Annie had her daughter, and fearing for herself was nothing compared to fearing for her child. Soledad was scared for them all.

"I need you to make sure nothing happens to Lyra. That she grows up to be a happy, healthy little girl and a confident young woman. I need you to make sure Gavin doesn't ever get his hands on her. So, please, promise me. I need you to say it!"

"I promise, Annie. I would never let anything happen to Lyra. I'd protect her with my own life!"

"Good," her friend said. "Because I went to see my attorney this week. I left a letter with him to be opened if something happens to me. It details all of Gavin's abuses and points at him if I'm killed. It also names you as Lyra's legal guardian. I've left you two insurance policies, also. One that should be put into trust for Lyra's care. I imagine you'll have to use the other to fight Gavin if he tries to take Lyra from you. It should be more than enough for legal fees or whatever else you might need."

Soledad rolled her eyes skyward to help defuse the tension. "First, please stop being morbid. Things will never get to that point. Nothing is going to happen to you. And, second, you need to stop worrying. I will never let anything happen to my goddaughter. I promised you that, and I will keep that promise."

Annie seemed to breathe a sigh of relief as she gave Soledad a nod. Her eyes shifted to stare out the window at the rain that had started to drop heavily. Another quiet moment passed as Soledad slowed her speed, fighting to see the road that lay ahead of them.

"What happened back at the house?" Soledad asked, her voice rippling through the silence like a pebble skipping across a quiet pond of water.

Annie took a deep breath. Lyra had begun to stir, the faintest squeak rising to a crescendo wail. "She's hungry," her mother muttered softly.

Soledad eyed them in the mirror as Annie lifted the baby from the car seat and undid the top buttons of her blouse. She discreetly covered herself with a blanket as Lyra latched on to her breast to nurse.

"I think he knew," Annie finally said. She shifted her body around to extend her legs so that baby Lyra rested comfortably against her chest. "He'd been ranting all evening about what he would do if I ever thought about leaving him again. He said he had two bullets with my name on them. He said he'd make sure Lyra never knew who I was. That he'd find her a new mother."

"Did you put the sleeping pills in his coffee?"

Annie nodded. "Just like we planned. I made his regular cup after dinner, like I always do. But he barely drank it. When I cleared the dishes away, his cup was still half-full. He was drinking bourbon instead, and you know he rarely drinks. I thought the alcohol affected him harder than I realized, because he fell asleep sooner than I anticipated. I figured he was just drunk enough that he'd be out of it long enough for me to stick to the plan. Once he was snoring, I threw on my clothes, grabbed the diaper bag and Lyra, and sneaked out of the house. But just as I disengaged the house alarm, he was screaming my name. I just ran!"

Soledad realized Annie was crying again, her tears falling on the blanket wrapped around the baby. Annie had tried leaving Gavin once, before Lyra had been born. She'd packed her things and had gone to her mother's, determined to make a go of it without the husband who had promised her the world. Gavin had been relentless in his efforts to get her back. There had been promises of being a better man and trying harder. Assurances they would go to counseling to resolve the problems in their marriage. Every pronouncement had included some lavish gift: huge bouquets of Annie's favorite white roses, gold and diamond baubles, and an excursion to Paris to profess his love. Promises that had held no weight once

Annie had given in and gone back to him, every pledge a well-tuned lie.

Despite Soledad's admonishments for Annie to not trust Gavin, nothing she said could convince her friend the good doctor wasn't good at all. Annie desperately wanted to believe him, and Soledad's frustration with the situation increased tenfold. That frustration had been so tangible that Soledad had actually feared the potential demise of their friendship.

Weeks after their reconciliation, Annie discovered she was pregnant. Eight months into her pregnancy, she'd walked in on Gavin and one of his many mistresses in their marital bed. Lyra came days later, and it was as if a perfect storm had converged on her best friend's life. Postpartum depression, a colicky baby and Gavin's emotional battering had left Annie bruised and broken. When Soledad had stepped in with a game plan, pleading with her bestie to choose herself and her daughter, Annie hadn't hesitated. Now here they were, both women questioning if they'd be able to see those plans to fruition. Neither wanting to voice their concerns aloud.

Because Soledad had concerns, starting with the headlights that had been following them for the last few miles. She'd chosen this road because traffic was minimal at that hour. The vehicle behind her tonight, though, seemed to mimic her moves—slowing when she slowed, speeding when she sped. She didn't recognize the vehicle, the car looking like a late-model sedan, a Cadillac, maybe even an Audi, and she was fairly certain it wasn't Gavin. But fairly certain wasn't certain enough. Under any other circumstances, she wouldn't have given it a second thought. However, she knew what they were up against, and whoever followed behind them had her suddenly feeling anxious. Then, almost as if she'd spoken out loud, the distant lights disappeared from her view.

A wave of relief flooded Soledad. Outside, the rain had finally stopped. Lyra had drifted back to sleep and her mother was no longer shaking. They had only been driving some thirty minutes, but it felt like hours had passed.

"We'll be out of the county in a few minutes," Soledad said. "Now that the rain isn't coming down in buckets, I can pick up the speed."

"Don't get another ticket, Soledad."

Soledad joked, "I like my bad driver certificates."

"Well, the state is going to like taking away your license if they have to give you another."

The two women laughed, seeming to relax for the first time since their night had started. The local radio station was digging through its oldie-but-goodie song box, playing Rissi Palmer's popular "Country Girl." By the second verse, they both were singing loudly together, the baby lulled back to sleep by their voices.

For the briefest moment, it felt like old times, lost in a good time. For a split second, Soledad had not a care in the world, letting herself forget why they were traveling in the middle of the night, fleeing from a past that threatened a joyous future. Laughter rang warmly through the space. Then, just like that, their moment was stolen from them.

Chapter 2

The oversize SUV came from out of nowhere, its high beams shining into the back window of the Toyota. The intensity of light was glaring. Soledad depressed her brake, blinded by the onslaught of brightness reflecting off the rearview mirror and into her eyes. When the vehicle behind them slammed into the back of her car, she felt the steering wheel jerk out of her hands as the Camry spun out of control on the wet road. Soledad felt her stomach pitch with fright as she wrestled for control of the steering wheel. She wanted to scream, panic washing over her like a tidal wave, but no sound escaped her lips. Everything inside the car tossed from one side to the other and back again. Annie cried out loudly and the baby began to whimper. The moment was surreal and Soledad held her breath waiting for it to be over.

Gunshots suddenly shattered the rear window. She would never know which shot struck Annie, just that she heard her best friend scream a second time, the harsh sound cut off abruptly and replaced by Lyra's pitiful wail. Even as it was happening, all she could think of was getting them away, needing to protect Annie and Lyra from the danger on their heels. Never in her wildest dreams could she have imagined that she wouldn't be able to do that. Panic gave way to determination. Glancing at her side mirror, Soledad saw Gavin exit his vehicle, advancing on them, his gun raised.

Without a second thought, Soledad threw the car into Reverse and gunned the engine. She knocked him off his feet, then shifted the car into Drive, determined to put as much distance between them as she could muster.

Another round of shots rang out as she pulled away and the engine sputtered and stalled. The Camry rolled off the side of the road, heading for the tree line before slamming into a tall pine and coming to a full stop. Soledad's survival instincts kicked into high gear, her reflexes shifting into overdrive. Stealing another glance behind her, Soledad watched as the man on the ground struggled to get onto his feet, falling on his back as he fought to catch his breath.

"We're going to have to run," Soledad said, turning to eye her friend. But Annie never heard her.

The moment felt like forever as realization settled over her. Soledad felt as if time had come to a standstill, everything spinning in slow motion. Annie was slumped forward, blood streaming down the side of her face. One hand lay protectively over the baby, the cotton blanket clutched tightly between her fingers. Soledad scrambled out of the car and flung the back door open. She muttered her friend's name over and over again, the mantra a loud, pitiful whisper.

"Annie, Annie, Annie, Annie, Annie!" she cried, tears streaming down her face. But Annie was gone, having taken her last breath. Her eyes were open, but the light that had shimmered in the oceanic orbs was gone. "Oh, Annie!" Soledad wailed, her fingers pressed to the dead woman's cheek. She could never have previously imagined the level of hurt that suddenly consumed her now, every ounce of it slicing through her heart like a hot knife through butter. It flooded every vein and blood vessel in her body, like a virus gone awry. She had failed her best friend and she would never again be able to make it right between them. Soledad stifled a sob.

Knowing she had no time to grieve her loss, Soledad snatched the ergonomic baby carrier from the car's floor and wrapped it around her torso. She reached to lift the baby from the car seat and settled the child against her chest.

Gavin's deep baritone suddenly rang out in the darkness. From the corner of her eye, Soledad could see that he'd finally made it onto his feet. His legs were still shaky, but he was snarling like a wounded animal as he stumbled in her direction.

A single gunshot whizzed by Soledad's head, barely missing her as she held tightly to little Lyra. Gavin fired a second and a third shot in her direction, loudly bellowing each time he pulled the trigger. Grabbing the diaper bag, Soledad paused for the briefest moment to squeeze her best friend's hand one last time. Then she took off running into the trees, knowing their lives depended on it.

Behind her, Gavin was still shouting profanities. His rage filled the late-night darkness, haunting the stillness of the cool air. He screamed, his voice eventually fading with each step Soledad put between them. But his final words sent a chill up her spine.

"I'll find you, Soledad! I will find you, and when I do, I'm going to kill you!"

Soledad knew enough from her days as a junior Scout that she was headed north. Beyond that, she didn't have a clue where she was going, but desperation and terror kept her moving forward. Her heart was beating rapidly, feeling like it might burst from her chest, and she sucked in air as if it were her last breath. Tears rained from her eyes and her whole body shook with disbelief and sadness. She felt alone and scared and angry that Gavin had not only taken her best friend from her, but he now had her literally running for her life.

The clouds had cleared, and the stars were shining brightly. The boundary of thick trees began to fade, leading to an open clearing that seemed to go on for miles. With the full moon overhead, there was just enough light that she knew she'd reached farmland.

She slowed her pace, still cradling the baby closely to her. Surprisingly, the steady rhythm of her running had apparently lulled Lyra back to sleep. The infant was out like a light, oblivious to the fact that her whole world had just been ripped to shreds. She would never know her beloved mother, save the stories Soledad would one day share with her. And she'd be sure to also tell her about how Annie could sleep through a storm and never flinch, too.

She couldn't help but wonder what she would tell Lyra about her father. She only hoped that when that time came, Gavin was six feet under or doing a life sentence with no possibility of parole.

Soledad pulled her rain jacket closed, zipping it around herself and her goddaughter. The temperature had dropped considerably with the storm, and the chill in the air felt bone deep. Soledad knew she needed to find refuge to protect Lyra, and herself, from the late-night elements. Off in the distance, Soledad noticed a light—and a light could mean shelter. She snuggled Lyra one last time, took a deep inhalation of air and began a slow jog toward help, praying that assistance would be available when she got them there.

Palmer Colton slipped his size-twelve feet into his favorite pair of rubber boots, the well-worn footwear years old and as comfortable as walking on air. The storm had finally passed, the downpour gone as quickly as it had risen. He had to make one last check on the animals, most especially Pharaoh, the young Arabian he'd recently acquired. He had purchased the horse to show, Pharaoh's versatility and intelligence making him a natural at a variety of equine sports. Palmer had seen a bright future for the animal, and then Pharaoh had been diagnosed with a case of equine flu, a contagious viral infection. The colt had been quarantined, and Palmer imagined that between the move and now being ill, Pharaoh might be having some difficulty adjusting. He hoped a kind voice and gentle hand would ease the animal's transition to his new home.

Jack, his Bernese mountain dog, suddenly nuzzled his palm and barked.

"What?" Palmer chuckled. "Am I not moving fast enough for you?"

The dog barked a second time.

"Okay, okay. I'm coming!" Palmer said as he stood upright and reached for his jacket.

Jack spun in a circle, his tail wagging excitedly.

Outside there was a distinct chill in the air, the evening temperature feeling more like fall and winter instead of the middle of the summer. There was a full moon, and even in the darkness, Palmer could see farther across the vast expanse of fields than usual.

Jack took off behind the large farmhouse, running at warp speed toward the line of trees that bordered the property. Palmer stared after him, thinking he saw something move in the distance. It was the briefest blip in the dark before it faded into the wave of shadows that danced over the landscape. More than likely a family of white-tailed deer roaming across the land, he thought.

Palmer walked to the barn, turned on the lights. Inside, he moved to the stall where Pharaoh stood, his head hanging just slightly over the stall door. He neighed when Palmer approached and ran his palm down the Arabian's arched neck.

"Hey, big guy. Are you feeling any better?" Palmer said as he stepped inside the stall to give the colt a quick once-over. His nose was running, but the discharge had thinned considerably since his diagnosis. His breathing was only slightly labored, and he had a sporadic cough, his body's natural reflex to the inflammation in his airway. The infection was viral, so there was little that Palmer could do other than keep the animal comfortable and let him get plenty of rest. The vet was scheduled to come back to check on him, so until then, it was a waiting game.

Palmer adjusted the gray blanket he'd thrown over the horse's broad back the night before. "You're going to be just fine," he said, stepping out and securing the stall door behind him.

Pharaoh whinnied again as if in agreement.

A noise at the barn doors suddenly pulled at Palmer's attention. Jack stood there, panting softly.

"Why do you look like trouble?" Palmer questioned, patting Jack's head as the dog moved to his side and lay at his feet.

A bolt of lightning suddenly rippled across the night sky. The rain had returned, beginning to fall steadily. Storms rarely bothered Palmer, but something about the change in the air felt ominous. Things didn't feel right, and he couldn't begin to put his finger on it. Something was coming, but he didn't know what the premonition meant.

"Jack, head to the house," Palmer said, pointing his index finger.

Jack jumped and bolted out the door, heading for the home's back porch. Palmer gave the horse one last pat, wished him a good night and then followed his four-legged friend.

* * *

Fear rippled deep in Soledad's midsection as she paused. She came to an abrupt stop when she encountered the family of deer standing still, her presence having interrupted their midnight meal. She hadn't stopped to consider the wild animals that might be in her path as she fled. In fact, there was little she was able to focus on—other than putting distance between them and Gavin. The sounds that emerged from the darkness suddenly felt like a horror movie waiting to write itself.

The dog, though, had been unexpected, a large furry bear of an animal with a tail that wagged nonstop and a tongue that hung lopsidedly out of its mouth. It had come barreling at her, and Soledad had stood defensively, ready to kick if it lunged. Her arms were wrapped protectively around the baby and the carrier, her stance defiant as she presented Fido with her side and back.

The dog had run around her twice, then sat, panting softly, its head cocked to the side as it stared at her. Soledad wasn't sure whether to step or not, but when the large bundle of fur didn't growl or attack, she kept nudging forward, talking to it as it moved in step with her.

"You must be the welcoming committee," she said sarcastically. "I hope your humans are just as kind."

Its tail wagged briskly.

"Do you have a name?" Soledad asked, the question coming as if the animal might actually answer.

The dog suddenly bolted in the direction they'd just come from. Soledad turned to look where it ran but couldn't see.

Lyra suddenly stirred against her chest and Soledad patted her back gently. "We had company, Lyra," she whispered loudly to the little girl. "I'm not sure where it's run off to," she said. "But you just go back to sleep, baby girl."

Lightning suddenly lit up the dark sky and rain began to fall again slowly. Soledad cursed. "Damn it!" she said as she tucked the blanket and her jacket closer around the baby's body. "I need to find us some shelter before we both catch pneumonia out here in this weather. Or your father catches up to us and keeps his promise to kill me." She began to jog again, the light in the distance much closer. Then, above their heads, the sky opened with a vengeance.

Minutes later, Soledad passed a stone wall that bordered a small garden. She picked up her pace until she reached a large barn. There was a farmhouse a short distance away, but not a single light shone through the windows. From what she could tell in the darkness, the outside of the barn was weathered, reminding her of the old tobacco outbuildings found in the Carolinas. It was rustic and aged, and looked aptly dry.

This will work, Soledad thought. At least until someone found them there. She only hoped whoever that might be would be a friend, and definitely not Gavin. Worst-case scenario, she mused, they would call the police and have her arrested. Best case, she'd be able to get a few minutes of rest so that she could think about what to do next.

Soledad eased the barn door open and slipped inside. Toward the rear of the structure, a single bulb burned from the ceiling, emitting just enough light to hold the darkness at bay. Bales of hay lined one wall, facing four empty stalls. A large black horse stood in the fifth stall, seeming to eye her warily.

"Sorry to be trespassing," Soledad muttered. "But it's an emergency." She wanted to reach out a hand to stroke the horse's neck, but she didn't know the animal and it didn't know her. She also sensed that it might not be well.

She felt like she'd struck gold when she discovered a wooden cabinet filled with blankets, thick and heavy wool coverings to wrap herself and the baby in. She took off her rain jacket and flung one around her shoulders. The baby was still sleeping as if there were nothing in the world for her to worry over, and Soledad was grateful for that small blessing. Preparing a makeshift pallet, she laid Lyra down, ensuring the child wouldn't roll away and hurt herself. She searched the diaper bag and found clean clothes and diapers, as well as a copy of the little girl's birth certificate and other documents Annie had labeled important, and a stack of unopened mail.

Soledad could have kicked herself for not grabbing her cell phone and purse, both now lost in the wreckage of her car. Not that there was anyone she would call under the circumstances. No one she dared put at risk. She'd been thinking about the police, but something told her there was nothing they could do to protect her and Lyra from Gavin. He was intent on doing them harm, and while the law investigated his crimes, he'd be committing just as many more. She wasn't interested in being a casualty of his transgressions. She was safer, she thought, figuring out her next moves on her own, hidden away where Gavin couldn't find her.

But in that moment, she truly wasn't sure she could think straight. The adrenaline that had been fueling her steps had dissipated like air from a popped balloon. She could feel her body beginning to fail her, her eyes wanting to close, sleep anxious to claim her. Her legs had begun to tighten, the muscles fatigued. Her feet hurt; the canvas-bottomed sneakers were not the best running shoes. It was becoming harder to focus and her head hurt, pain throbbing like a drum line behind her eyes.

Soledad leaned back against the bale of hay and pulled at the blanket covering her. Then she saw the blood that saturated her T-shirt and realized for the first time that she'd been shot. She gasped as sanguine fluid gushed over her fingers. That adrenaline had kept the pain at bay, but suddenly it hurt like hell, bringing tears to her eyes. Rising, Soledad went back to the cabinet to grab a roll of gray duct tape from inside it. Back behind the hay bale, she took one of the clean diapers and pressed it tight against the wound. To keep the pressure on, she tightly wrapped the tape around the diaper pressed to her waist and a second against her back where the bullet had made its exit.

Soledad suddenly wanted to cry. Her entire body felt like she'd been hit by a bus and her heart was shredded over the loss of Annie. She patted the baby against her back as she struggled not to sob. She wanted to scream and pull her hair, but she couldn't. She could hear Annie in her ear, reminding her that she had more important things to consider and her pity party would have to wait for another day.

Things weren't looking good and she needed to get herself and Lyra out of the mess she'd dropped into. Trespassing on private property wasn't going to help her situation and keeping Lyra safe would take more than running from the problems she was facing. She needed a plan, but one wasn't coming easily through her fatigue. With a heavy sigh, she pulled the blanket up and around her shoulders. Leaning her head close to Lyra's tiny body, Soledad closed her eyes.

Jack pawed at Palmer's leg. He ran in a small circle beside the bed, his exuberance at an all-time high for the late hour. It was close to three o'clock in the morning and not like the animal to be wide-awake and so perky. Palmer opened one eye to stare at the dog. Jack barked and jumped up to paw at him a second time.

"What, Jack? Go to sleep. It's late." He rolled onto his side, his back to the dog.

Jack barked again and ran to the door.

Palmer sighed and rolled to the other side of the bed. He threw his body upward and swung his legs off the side of the mattress. "You've been out all night, Jack. You were acting strange then. What's going on with you, dog?"

Moving down the hall to the front foyer, Palmer slid on his boots. He swung open the front door and took a look out into the dark night. Outside felt like it had dropped another ten degrees, the temperatures clearly out of sync for the time of year. He reached for a jacket and slipped it on. Instinctively, Palmer knew something was amiss as Jack barreled toward the barn, his determination to get inside warning that something wasn't right. Palmer moved down the short flight of steps and followed Jack, suddenly worried that something might be wrong with Pharaoh.

Opening the large doors and stepping inside, Palmer paused to listen, his eyes skating back and forth across the space. Jack sniffed the floor, his tail wagging excitedly, and that was when Palmer noticed the dark spots that trailed across the barn floor. He knelt to take a closer look and saw that it looked like fresh blood. Jack rushed to the back side of the hay bales, but Pharaoh wasn't making a sound, his hindquarters frozen as if he were ready to lurch at something.

Palmer slowly eased toward a corner cabinet and the rifle he kept stashed there for emergencies. He pulled the weapon from inside and slid the bolt back to ensure there was still a round in the chamber. If it were an animal bleeding out, it might feel threatened and attack, so he wasn't going to take any chances. But Jack had taken a seat, seeming unnerved by whatever it was he was staring at.

Easing behind the dog, the barrel of his rifle lifted just in case, Palmer peered around the side of the haystack. His eyes widened in surprise as he was filled with shock and blinked to make sure he wasn't dreaming. Recognition hit him like a sledgehammer slammed against concrete. Palmer knew the woman huddled in the corner of his barn. He knew her and her family. Jack suddenly barked and lunged forward, waking

Soledad de la Vega—who was for some reason slumbering peacefully in his barn.

Soledad's eyes shot open, startled from the beginnings of a deep sleep. The dog from earlier was licking her face and sniffing at the wound on her side. He jostled against her, his exuberance palpable, before shifting his attention to Lyra, who'd started to whimper softly.

Instinctively, Soledad pushed to her knees, shooed the animal back and slid her body between the two. The gesture was protective as she threw her arm across the baby's body. Her eyes rose to the handsome man who was staring at her. Shock and awe painted his expression, his eyes wide and his jaw slack.

Soledad was still groggy as she assessed the man and the way he was staring at her. She'd been praying for someone to find them, and now that someone had, she wasn't sure it was a good thing. She realized he might call the police, and she found herself questioning if that was really a good idea.

"You're bleeding," he suddenly said.

She nodded. "I've been shot."

The man took a step forward, his brow furrowing with concern. "Shot?"

"And my best friend was killed," Soledad continued. Her story came quickly. She talked softly and fast, her words emanating from a deep breath that she seemed to be holding in her lungs. They surged like a tidal wave hitting a shoreline, spewing into the late-night air with a vengeance. And when she finished, tears had begun to rain from her eyes, falling against her cheeks. Catching herself, Soledad wiped her eyes with the back of her hand.

"We need to call the police," he said.

Soledad shook her head vehemently. "Please, don't. Don't call the police. I'm begging you!"

"You can't just bleed out in my barn," he said, his tone matter-of-fact. "I could call for a doctor."

"It's a flesh wound. I'll be fine."

"How do you know that? Do you get shot often?" Palmer questioned, a hint of snark in his tone.

"I just know," she replied, not amused. "And you can't call the law. Not until I've figured out what I'm going to do—please!" Soledad pleaded. "Because if her father finds us, he will kill me, and I don't know what will happen to Annie's baby. Please."

Soledad lifted Lyra into her arms and hugged the now awakened little girl close. The baby stared up at Soledad and then in the direction of the man. Her attention dropped to the dog, who was gently nuzzling her little foot. She suddenly laughed, stretching her fingers toward the animal who licked them eagerly.

"Her name's Lyra," Soledad said as she rose. "And I'm Soledad. Soledad de la Vega."

"I know," the man responded. "I'm Palmer. Palmer Colton." He gestured at the dog. "And that's Jack."

Soledad's eyes narrowed ever so slightly. "Colton? Are you related to Stanton Colton?"

"He's my cousin. Our fathers are brothers. He's engaged to your sister."

"Dominique, my twin," she said with a nod of her head.

"We were both at their engagement party last week. You probably don't remember me."

Soledad's eyes skated from side to side as she thought back to that party, remembering her sister's joy. It had been a good time.

Recall suddenly came swiftly and she nodded again. "I do remember you," she said, looking up to meet Palmer's stare. He'd been the most handsome man in a room full of good-looking men. His silk suit had fit him well, despite his apparent dislike of the necktie that he'd kept pulling at awkwardly. There had been a failing effort to tame his tousled blond hair and she'd thought the barest hint of a beard had been sexy as hell. He'd been kind, and polite, and very much a gentleman. The kind of man grandmothers adored and mothers wanted you to marry.

He'd had an intensity about him that had made him quite popular with many of the women. Every single female hedging her bets for a husband had chased him, but it had been obvious to anyone paying an ounce of attention that he wasn't interested in being caught. And Soledad had been paying attention.

She thought back to how she had caught him watching her intently but hadn't made any effort to speak to her. The intensity in his emerald green eyes had been heated. They'd crossed paths a few times that night, but had ignored each other, barely bothering to exchange warm hellos. The little conversation they had shared had been casually polite at best. Each pretending not to notice the other, despite eyeing one another keenly. Heat suddenly flushed her face and warmed her cheeks.

"We need to move you to the house," Palmer said, changing the subject. "I should check out that wound and get you bandaged up properly."

"But you won't call the police, right? If you do, I'll have to leave." There was a hint of attitude in her tone. Just enough to let him know that she meant what she said—that she would not be moved from her decision.

Palmer stared at her, seemingly contemplating how he would make that call without her knowing. How the smart thing for them both to do would be to involve law enforcement if someone was truly intent on harming her. She had been shot, for goodness' sake.

He shook his head. "I won't tell them you're here," he finally said, "but we need to report the accident so they can at least find your friend's body and start investigating the case."

Soledad took a deep breath. She was just about to respond when they heard a car rumble up the length of road that led to the house.

"Are you expecting someone?" Soledad asked.

"No," Palmer answered. "Not at this time of night."

Soledad took a step back, moving into the shadows, out of sight.

"Stay here," Palmer said. "I'll see who it is."

Soledad nodded and cradled the gurgling baby closer. As Palmer moved to the door, Jack on his heels, she called after him.

"Yes?"

"Thank you," she whispered loudly. "Thank you."

Chapter 3

Palmer peeked out the barn door, watching a man standing outside a black SUV and looking toward the house. He appeared disheveled, as if he'd been run over by a bus. His hands rested on his hips and he was leaning to one side as if his knee or leg hurt.

The man closed his suit jacket, trying to neaten his clothes. Even though it was pitch-black out, save the glow of lights from the house, he pulled a pair of sunglasses from his pocket and put them on his face. He was heading for the home's front porch when Palmer exited the barn, still holding tight to his rifle.

"Can I help you?" he asked, eyeing the man suspiciously.

"My apology for the intrusion, Mr....?"

Palmer didn't bother to acknowledge the question.

"This is private property. So I'll ask again—can I help you?"

The intruder bristled, posturing ever so slightly. He reached into his breast pocket and flashed what appeared to be an ID card in Palmer's direction. In the dark, the gesture was more for show than anything else. Palmer dismissed it as he continued, "My name is Detective Gavin Stone. I'm with the Grave Gulch Police Department. We're looking for a murder suspect. A woman named Soledad de la Vega. We believe she's here in the area and she may have an infant with her."

Palmer recoiled. It didn't take a brain surgeon to know that this was the man Soledad was running from. Him saying her name as he clearly lied had Palmer suddenly on edge. His posture stiffened and he tightened his grip on the rifle. "It's kind of late to be going door to door searching for someone, isn't it?"

Gavin took a deep breath. "We had a tip that she was seen in the neighborhood and we wanted people to be aware that she is armed and dangerous. Fortunately, there aren't a lot of private homes out this far, so I won't be disturbing too many people at this hour."

"Who'd this woman kill?" Palmer questioned.

Gavin's gaze narrowed. He shook his head. "I'm not at liberty to say. Have you seen anyone strange in the area tonight?"

Palmer shook his head. "Just you. There's been no woman here. If there had been, either I or one of the men who works for me would have seen her. We don't usually get a lot of random strangers out this way."

"Are you usually up at this late hour?" Gavin eyed him curiously.

"No. One of my horses is ailing. I came out to check on him."

"There in your barn?" Gavin asked, taking a step in that direction.

Palmer took his own step, blocking the man's way. "Detective Stone, is it?"

"Yes, that's right."

"I haven't seen anyone wandering out here on my property. And definitely not a woman with a baby. But if I do, I will reach out to the police department." But it was more likely he'd call one of his family members at the GGPD to check out Gavin Stone, Palmer thought to himself.

"I'll need to search your barn. In case she may be hiding there." Gavin's pronouncement came with such conviction that Palmer felt himself bristle with indignation. His muscles tensed and his grip tightened around the rifle.

A pregnant pause rose full and thick between them. Unspoken words danced harshly through the late-night air. Both men clearly had things they wanted to say, but neither spoke, waiting to see who would jump first. Palmer suddenly stepped aside and gestured with his free hand. He had learned early in life that the best defense was a good offense, so he was willing to call the man's bluff, knowing he'd never get past his guard dog.

"Help yourself."

Gavin made it as far as the barn door. Jack sat in the

entrance, and as Gavin approached, the dog snarled and then snapped.

"Nice doggy!" Gavin said, extending a nervous hand.

Jack growled a second time, his bark threatening.

"He doesn't do well with strangers," Palmer said. "So, like I told you, it's doubtful any woman with a baby is hiding out anywhere around here."

Gavin took two steps back. He gave Jack one last look and headed slowly toward his SUV.

"If I see this woman, I'll be sure to dial 9-1-1 and get the Grave Gulch police right on out here," Palmer said, working to keep his expression stoic.

Gavin nodded. "I appreciate your time," he said as he slid back into the driver's seat and started the engine. He reversed onto the grass, then pulled forward to head back in the direction from which he'd come. As he pulled off, there was no missing the damage to the front end of his vehicle.

Palmer stood watching until the stranger was out of sight, his taillights disappearing in the distance. A good few minutes passed before he moved. Whoever that man was, he wasn't with the Grave Gulch Police Department. With so much of Palmer's family in law enforcement, there wasn't an officer with the department that he didn't know personally—and there was certainly no Detective Stone. The stranger had lied too easily. Obviously focused on finding Soledad, his intentions had clearly not been in her best interest, just like Soledad had told him.

When Palmer had first laid eyes on her, there had been sheer terror on her face. She'd been petrified and her fear had gleamed from her eyes in a way that tugged at his heartstrings. Despite the story she had told him, he couldn't begin to imagine everything she and her friend had gone through. But he was determined that she would not have to endure any more hurt if he had anything to do with it. He'd initially seen her plea to not involve the police as irrational. And, realistically, it was. But he now had better understanding and her request was making far more sense to him. He blew a loud sigh and turned back toward the barn.

Soledad was shivering, fright overriding the cold. The entire time Palmer had stood outside the barn with Gavin, she'd been scared to death Gavin would find her. The conversation between the two men had seemed tense. Wanting to see what was going on, she'd scaled a ladder to the barn's loft, peering out an upper window.

She'd quickly discovered that keeping herself hidden and Lyra quiet was a bigger challenge than she'd anticipated. The baby had been anxious for attention and gurgled constantly. She was a chatterbox without the words to explain herself, but didn't let it slow her down. Soledad had pulled out every trick she knew to keep Lyra quiet, grateful that the little girl was not a crier. It had been nerve-racking at best, to say nothing of the fact that Soledad felt horrible to be putting her through such turmoil to begin with.

She was climbing back down the wooden ladder when Palmer reentered the barn. She noted the quizzical look on his face as he watched her ease down to the main floor, so she gave him the faintest smile.

"We need to move you and the baby to the main house," he said.

"What did Gavin say?"

"Are you certain that was your friend's husband?"

Soledad nodded.

"He asked a lot of questions. Something tells me he didn't get the answers he was hoping for, so he may come back. Then again, he might not. We just need to make sure we're ready if he does. For the time being, though, we need to take care of that wound and then try to figure out what's next."

"I really could use a shower," Soledad said. "And this bundle of joy—" she kissed Lyra's cheek "—needs a diaper change and a bottle."

Palmer nodded. "If it were daylight, I'd probably hide you away in the horse trailer and drive you to the back of the house, so no one sees you."

Soledad shrugged as she considered his comment. She was grateful for his help because he didn't have to be bothered. "Do you think anyone is up this time of the night who might see me?"

He shook his head. "No, and I'm fairly sure your friend is gone. But I'm going to shut down the lights to the house just to be sure. Jack will also give us a heads-up if anyone is out there. Just walk straight ahead. There should be enough moonlight for you to see your way."

"I'll be fine," she said.

Standing in the entrance, he gave a low whistle and Jack shot past him into the darkness. Palmer hesitated momentarily, as if listening for Jack to give him a signal. When the dog didn't return or bark, he gestured for her to follow. Leading the way, he moved swiftly across the property to the path that led straight to the family home. When they reached the front steps, Palmer tossed her a look, concern seeping past his thick lashes.

"Watch your step," he whispered loudly.

"I'm good," Soledad whispered back. She flashed him a grateful smile.

As she took the first step, Palmer eased a protective arm around her waist, his hand resting lightly against her hip, the other cupped under her elbow. His touch was warm, and she was suddenly at ease, comfort washing over her spirit. Soledad hadn't anticipated such a thing ever happening again. The feeling was unexpected, and her stomach did a slight flip. Then her knees began to quiver and her whole body began to shake, threatening to drop her back down to the ground. She held Lyra tighter.

"Are you okay?" Palmer questioned as he pushed open the front door and guided her inside.

Soledad nodded, words stuck deep in her throat. She couldn't bring herself to explain. Despite everything that had happened, feeling like all was lost, being with this man she knew nothing about had her feeling like everything could be well again if she just gave it some time.

"Soledad?"

She lifted her eyes to meet his. He was staring intently, his gaze searching hers, concern seeping from his eyes. Soledad clutched the baby just a little tighter, then dropped to the slate floor and sobbed.

* * *

Lyra lay in the center of the queen-size bed, pillows propped on either side of her to keep her from rolling off, later that evening. She was warm, her belly was full, and once again she was sleeping as if she didn't have a care in the world. Soledad, on the other hand, looked like she'd taken a swift trip to hell, stopping to battle in the next world war before making the trip back home. She could only imagine what Palmer had thought.

She stared at her reflection in the full-length mirror that decorated the door leading into the private bathroom. Dried blood was splattered in her shoulder-length hair and her tears had left deep streaks in the dirt that painted her face. Her clothes were tattered from the thorny branches they'd caught on and mud caked her shoes and pant legs. She looked wretched and it was a wonder the man hadn't been frightened away by the sight of her. But he hadn't looked at her with fear, just compassion and kindness. And something else that she couldn't quite discern. She only knew that she instinctively trusted it, and him.

Moving to the bathroom, she dropped her top, pants, bra and panties to the tiled floor. She turned on the shower, and when the water was nicely heated, she slid beneath the spray. The warm liquid was a balm to her skin, and she could feel every muscle easing into the comfort of it. She would never have imagined anything being so exhilarating to her spirit, but this was like angels singing in her ears, she thought. Soledad tilted her face into the flow and let it rain over her shoulders and saturate the length of her hair.

As she lathered the strands, she thought about Annie. How Annie would have teased her about always running into a man when she looked like she'd been dragged around and abandoned by a neighborhood cat. Usually, it was baking flour that clung to her clothes and a spattering of chocolate or butter in her hair, depending on whatever she'd put into the ovens at the bakery. Annie would have doubled over with laughter if she'd been there to hear Soledad tell her about being in Palmer's barn. Soledad wasn't ready to laugh about it just yet.

With no sense of time, she stood beneath the warmth until the water began to run cold. The chill was just enough to pull her from the reverie she'd fallen into, thinking about the past and pondering the future. A future that suddenly included a six-month-old and the fight to keep her safe from her father. Motherhood hadn't been on Soledad's to-do list. Not that she didn't want to be a parent. Because she did. But she'd planned on having a husband and father for her child first. She'd been more than satisfied with the role of godmother, able to spoil Lyra senseless. Her sister, Dominique, was also planning to be pregnant as soon as she and Stanton made it down the aisle, so she'd be an auntie sooner than later.

She'd had plans for them that involved excursions for ice cream and visits to the toy stores before returning to their respective parents. Now, assuming she'd get legal custody of Lyra, per Annie's wishes, Soledad had to consider day care and dance classes, doctor's visits, Girl Scouts and whatever else little ones did these days. The fact that Soledad didn't have a clue spoke volumes. She was going to need help with poor little Lyra, she thought.

Stepping out of the shower, Soledad reached for the oversize white towel Palmer had left for her. He'd been overly concerned with her being comfortable and she appreciated his efforts.

She paused to examine the wound. It looked worse than it was, the abrasion superficial. The bullet had gone in and out, not hitting anything internal or doing any major damage. She'd gotten lucky and she whispered a prayer of gratitude that it wasn't worse. The bleeding had stopped and the wound had looked ghastlier than it was. Admittedly, it had scared her at first, and she realized it had unnerved Palmer, as well. She was just grateful the shots had missed Lyra, Gavin not at all concerned about his child with his felonious behavior. He was lower than graveyard dirt, she thought, knowing she'd never be able to rest well until he was behind bars. She took a deep inhalation and held it for a moment before slowly blowing it back out.

With one last glance in the huge mirror, Soledad made her way from the bathroom back to the bedroom. She suddenly came to an abrupt halt, panic delivering a deep gut punch to her midsection. The bed was in disarray and Lyra was gone.

It had been crying, little face beet red as it gasped for air to bellow back out. Palmer had gone to check that both were well when he heard the baby crying and the shower running. He'd hesitated, not quite sure what to do, but then realized Soledad probably couldn't hear the child wailing if she were in the shower. And now it lay in his lap, staring up at him, pale blue gaze eyeing him warily.

Palmer kicked himself for referring to the baby as an it. Even if only in his own head. *It* was a girl. Her name was Lyra. And she wasn't crying anymore. Now she just smelled bad. Like the cow pasture multiplied by ten. He couldn't begin to fathom how such a tiny person could smell so foul. But she reeked, and for the last ten minutes, he'd been trying to get past the stink to put a clean diaper on her bottom.

Palmer had no children, and for the most part, kids were an anomaly. He had friends who had them and, more times than not, he ignored them. His sister had a son, the toddler holding a permanent place in his heart. But he was not a favored godfather or uncle and had never given any thought to being a parent. Fatherhood had not been anything he'd wanted for himself, most especially when he considered the state of the world. His past had also left him jaded when it came to love and family, not that he was interested in rehashing his bad experiences while trying to get beyond toxic sludge oozing past the thigh line of Lyra's diaper. He gagged, fighting not to hurl whatever he'd last eaten onto the floor.

Soledad suddenly barreled into the room wearing nothing but a towel. Her hair was soaked, water trickling down her ringlets. Her warm complexion was pale with fear and fury, the emotion like a stark tattoo across her forehead. Palmer's eyes widened at the sight of her, skating over the curve of her bare shoulders down to the taut muscles of her legs. She was gorgeous, and she took his breath away, even if he did sense a tongue-lashing coming his way.

"What are you doing with her?" Soledad snapped, clutching at the towel she was holding precariously around her lean figure.

He picked up the clean diaper and waved it at her. "She was screaming her head off while you were in the shower. I thought I might be of some help, but it's not going well." Wrinkling his nose, he lifted Lyra up and held her and the diaper at arm's length.

Soledad looked from him to the baby and back again. The wealth of emotion that had led her into the room suddenly dissipated, rising like a morning mist to expose a sky full of sunshine. A smile suddenly pulled at her mouth and she bit her bottom lip to stop herself from laughing outright.

Palmer shook his head. "It's really not funny. What the hell did you feed her?"

Chapter 4

Lyra gurgled contentedly, her little arms flapping at her sides. She sat propped against a fortress of pillows on the family room floor. Jack lay beside her, seeming to ignore the occasional ear pull or kick to his side.

From where he stood in the home's kitchen, Palmer could easily watch them both and finish the meal he had started making. Usually, he would have grabbed a bowl of hot cereal and kept moving, but he thought Soledad might enjoy homemade banana pancakes with a side of bacon.

She had been exhausted, and when sleep had finally claimed her, she hadn't wanted to let it go. After the late night they'd all had, he'd appreciated the few hours of slumber he'd garnered, as well. Lyra's schedule seemed to mimic his own, the little girl waking with the morning sun. Soledad had been grateful when he had offered to take the child with him so she could rest a few more minutes. Now he was watching Jack watch her watching him and, despite the absurdity of it all, was feeling far more comfortable with the situation than he was willing to admit.

Jack shifted his body to lie beside the baby, his tail like a windshield wiper gone awry. He swatted the infant once and then twice, then suddenly yelped when Lyra grabbed him and pulled. The little girl laughed heartily, the wealth of it like the sweetest balm to his heart through the morning air. Jack barked.

"Good dog," Palmer muttered. "Don't take any crap from her. She's trying to steal your heart, pal. Don't let her."

A warm alto responded from the doorway. Palmer turned as Soledad stepped through the entrance. She looked relaxed. Her hair was down and loose, the blue-black strands framing her face. She wore one of his T-shirts and an old pair of shorts he'd found in a closet. Left by one of his sisters, probably Grace, they fit her nicely. Barefoot and comfortable, she was the most beautiful woman he knew, if you excluded his mother, of course. He blushed, feeling his cheeks warm with color.

Soledad laughed. "Really? That's a little cynical, don't you think?"

Palmer had looked up sheepishly as the sound of her voice drew his attention. He felt a wide grin pulling across his face as amusement filled him. "Good morning. I didn't see you standing there."

"Obviously!" She giggled softly. "Good morning to you, too. Lyra wasn't any trouble, was she?" she asked as she moved to the baby's side, a finger tickling her chubby cheek.

He shook his head. "She's been good. No massive explosions. No tantrums. She took a bottle and she's been content lying there ever since. Jack's been in charge, so we've had the situation under control."

Soledad nodded. "Well, thank you." She gave him her own bright smile. "You're good with her," she said as she eased to the center island and took a seat on one of the bar stools.

He ignored the comment, the compliment making him feel uncomfortable since being good with anyone's baby wasn't in his game book. "Would you like a cup of coffee?" Palmer questioned.

"I would love some coffee. And eggs and toast, if you have them."

"I can make that happen. I also have some banana pancakes here. Would you like bacon, too?"

"You must be reading my mind. I'm famished, and those pancakes smell divine."

"You should be. I hadn't realized how far you'd run last night. You were on the south side of my ranch. That's almost ten miles by foot, and most of that property is heavily wooded. How long were you running?"

"I was pacing about ten minutes per mile. Maybe eleven. The added weight slowed me down some." She gestured toward the baby, who was beginning to nod off, her eyes closing and opening and then closing again.

"You're a runner?"

"Since high school. Lyra's mother and I ran track together. That's how we became friends."

"You're lucky you didn't get lost in those woods."

"I was more afraid of the man chasing us than I was a few trees."

Palmer nodded as he cracked half a dozen eggs into a stainless-steel bowl and began to whisk them with salt and pepper and a splash of milk.

"There's a heavy police presence there right now. When I made my morning rounds earlier, I drove past to see for myself. I'm sure it'll be on the news before too long if it isn't already."

"Do you have a remote to that television?" Soledad pointed to the fifty-inch Sony that hung on the family room wall.

Palmer gestured to the corner of the counter, the device resting beside a stack of cookbooks.

Reaching for it, Soledad hit the on button, then sat back against the counter as she flipped the channels to the local news station. There was the briefest commercial and then a familiar newscaster's face filled the screen.

"The big story this morning—an Amber Alert issued for a missing baby and the mother's body found in an abandoned vehicle on Highway 55. The station's Diane Albert reports."

The camera shifted to the roadside where Soledad's white Camry was being pulled out of the ditch by a tow truck. The woman named Diane stared into the camera.

"There is still a lot about this case that detectives are not telling us," Diane said. She was a tall, thin woman, with sharp features, lengthy blond extensions and a hungry glint in her eyes. "What we do know right now is that a young mother is dead, her six-month-old daughter is missing, and the woman's husband and best friend are persons of interest."

Soledad bristled. "A person of interest? How could they think I hurt Annie? Why am *I* not a missing person, too?"

Palmer reached for the remote and turned off the television. The situation was depressing enough without the two of them scrolling for news that would only make things feel worse. For a split second, Soledad looked as if she wanted to argue. Then she didn't, her shoulders rolling forward as she seemed to sink lower in her seat.

Concern seeped out of Palmer's eyes as he stared at the woman. Sadness had washed over Soledad's face. She took a deep breath and exhaled slowly.

Palmer felt the melancholy that tugged at her spirit. It was corporeal, feeling like clabber and just as foul. He slid a mug across the counter toward her, the warm aroma of Colombian coffee beans wafting through the room. "It's going to be okay," he said, although he wasn't wholeheartedly convinced of that himself. "We're going to figure out what to do. We'll make this right. I promise."

There was something about how he said "we" that lifted Soledad's smile back to her face. Despite the gravity of her situation, she felt comfort in knowing that she wasn't alone. That Palmer Colton, who didn't know anything about her, was willing to promise his assistance and stand by her side meant everything to her.

She tossed a look in Lyra's direction. The child was sleeping soundly, and Jack lay with his head in the baby's lap, her fingers tangled in his fur. She changed the subject. "So, do you have any children of your own, Palmer?"

He tossed her a look before turning to the stove and the pat of butter that had begun to sizzle in the frying pan.

"No. I have neither the time for kids nor the interest in them. I've never wanted to have any."

"Ouch!" Soledad said, her eyes flaring at the comment. Surprise showed on her face, warming her cheeks and furrowing her brow. "That was harsh. Why don't you want kids?"

"I just don't," he said emphatically.

There was a moment of pause as Soledad waited for him to elaborate, but when no explanation came, she persisted. "Do you not like them?" she asked.

"I don't dislike them. I just…well…" He hesitated, visibly thrown off guard as he seemed to search for the right words to explain himself. "I like them well enough," he muttered. "I just don't want my own."

Soledad paused, eyeing him curiously. She finally took a sip of the hot coffee. The silence in the room was thundering, both clearly feeling ill at ease. The moment was awkward, as if neither was sure how they'd gotten there or how to move themselves past it.

Palmer suddenly heaved a heavy sigh. "I'm sorry. I

didn't mean to kill the mood," he said, forcing a smile onto his face.

Soledad smiled back, shrugging her shoulders dismissively. "It's all good," she muttered softly.

Palmer turned his back to her to plate the morning meal. After he loaded the dishes with crisp bacon, pancakes and scrambled eggs, he moved around the counter to take the seat beside her. He watched Soledad take her first bite, her eyes closing as she chewed.

She purred, the low hum moving Palmer to grin broadly. He dropped his eyes to his own plate and began to eat.

"This is so good!" she exclaimed as she took a second bite and then a third. She shifted her gaze to meet his. "You've got skills in the kitchen."

Palmer chuckled. "Thank you."

For the next few minutes, the two ate in silence, nothing but the sound of gnashing teeth and the occasional hum bouncing off the four walls. A grandfather clock ticked loudly from the foyer hallway, and Jack and Lyra were both snoring.

Palmer suddenly broke through the silence. As he began to speak, Soledad lowered her fork and turned to him to listen, giving him her full attention.

"I was adopted into the Colton family. My biological parents had addiction problems and they both died from overdoses. The first time I was removed from their custody, I was two years old. I don't remember a lot from back then, but I do remember constantly being hungry and not always having a bed to sleep in. My mother died when I was three. I had only been back with her for a few weeks when that happened. My father wasn't fit to care for me, and I was put in foster care. Most of the families were decent, but there is always one that gives the system a bad name. I was with that family for two months too long." He took a deep breath, seeming to push the unwanted memories aside. The moment was suddenly awkward as he realized he was sharing more than he'd planned. But he felt an overwhelming sense of ease with the woman who was staring intently in his direction.

A slight grin pulled at his mouth as he continued. "Leanne was volunteering in the last group foster facility I'd been placed in. I thought she was an angel. She was young, only nineteen at the time. And she was beautiful and kind, and she made me feel incredibly special. My first name was her maiden name, so we had an instant connection. I was slightly desperate for attention and would follow her around the home. And she let me. She became *my* angel. I was five when she adopted me. When she married my dad, he adopted me, too."

"Your father's Geoff Colton, right?"

Palmer nodded. "He is."

"I've met him. I sometimes supply fresh-baked bread to Grave Gulch Grill. He has always been genuinely nice to me."

"Dad's a good guy and that restaurant is his pride and joy." He smiled, thinking about his parents bringing him immense joy.

"My past is why I don't want kids, Soledad," he continued. "I've seen the worst of what can happen in families and how children are affected by bad behavior and actions they have no control over. I can't imagine myself putting any child at risk of that."

"But you aren't your parents. And you're not an addict, are you?"

"No, of course not," he said, annoyed at the question. "But we don't know what the future might hold for us. Look at Lyra. Most people would have assumed she had the perfect life with a bright future. Two parents in a beautiful home and a host of possibilities ahead of her. Had her mother anticipated her father turning on them, she surely would have never put her daughter through that. Never!"

"So, you're afraid you'll turn on your family if you have one?" Confusion furrowed Soledad's brow. She sat straighter in her seat as she looked at him intently.

"I'm afraid that life will throw me a curve that I can't control. I wouldn't ever want a child of mine to become lost in the foster system. It's not a pretty place for any kid to be, despite the many professionals and families who care about them and make every effort to make them feel loved."

"That's a bit irrational, don't you think? Especially because I have no doubts that your family would step in to take your kids. Your brother, sisters, even one of your cousins would make sure they weren't put in the care of strangers. Right?"

"I'm sure when your friend had Lyra, she wasn't thinking her daughter would be in the position she's in now."

"Lyra will never go into foster care," Soledad said

insistently. "Not as long as I live and breathe. I promised Annie that I would look out for her and I fully intend to keep that promise."

"And that's admirable. But what happens if something happens to you that you can't control? Then what? You can have the perfect family, trust the best people and things still not work out the way you want them to. That's just life, and it will throw you a curve when you least expect." He shrugged his broad shoulders, the gesture dismissive. "Maybe I do sound irrational, but it's how I feel."

Soledad gave him a slow nod. "It's a bit of a reach, but I respect that you've given it so much thought."

"Growing up, it's all I ever thought about. I didn't want any kid of mine to go through a minute of what I went through. Feeling unwanted. Worrying about where my next meal would come from. Desperate for my parents to love me. Then feeling lost when they died and being scared because I didn't have anyone. It was a lot. Granted, I was one of the lucky ones. But there are thousands of kids in the system who'll never get as lucky as I did. And there are twice as many who'll go to hell and back just trying to survive."

Soledad stared at him. There was intensity in his tone, the wealth of emotion wrapped so tightly around his words that she could just imagine the pledge he had made to himself as a boy. He'd reiterated those words his entire life, until they were so ingrained in his heart that there would be no moving him from his convictions. Tears suddenly formed in her eyes, her own emotions on overload as she imagined the wealth of pain that could have laid that on his spirit.

Soledad had never imagined herself without children. Although there had been no potential father on the horizon, she genuinely believed in the fairy-tale ending. She knew that one day the perfect man would come at the perfect time and, after the perfect engagement and a Disney-worthy wedding, there would be kids. Perfect or imperfect, they would have been hers. Two boys and a girl, and maybe even a beagle named Charlie. She wanted for her own family what she'd had as a girl, she and her sister blessed with an abundance of love and attention from parents who loved each other fiercely and loved their daughters even more.

Now, as she considered the future she hoped to give Lyra, that fairy tale suddenly had an alternate ending she hadn't prepared for.

"I'm sorry," she whispered. "I'm so, so sorry." She fought the sudden urge to reach out and hug him. Instead, she folded her arms across her chest and tucked her hands beneath her armpits. She bit down against her tongue. Hard. Hoping the gesture would stem the rise of feeling that pulled at her.

Palmer shook his head and shrugged.

Another moment of pause rose thickly between them, both refocused on their plates and the last bites of their morning meal.

Soledad found herself thinking about what he'd said, wondering what might happen to little Lyra if something did happen to her. Her emotions were on edge yet again. She took a deep breath and held it deep in her lungs.

Palmer finally spoke, his deep baritone sliding through the silence. "I know how it sounds," he said as he cut his eyes in her direction. "Although I try to be more pragmatic about things, that's the one thing that's like a burr in my side. I hate feeling that way, but it is what it is."

Soledad smiled. "You only sound a *little* off-kilter."

He laughed, a wave of ease washing over him. "I'll take that."

Minutes passed as their conversation shifted gears. Soledad asked questions about the ranch, wanting to know more about the expanse of property. As he answered her questions, pride gleamed from his eyes.

"Colton Ranch is over eight hundred acres of highly productive pasture farm, and I have a great team that helps me manage the property. There's also a good sixty acres of hay fields that we maintain. You ran through the hay fields last night. We have a four hundred cow-and-calf operation, supplying milk around the state. We have a few hundred sheep that we raise for their fleece, their milk and for meat. Our eggs this morning came from my chicken coop, and the hens lay prodigiously, so we eat a lot of them around here."

Soledad laughed. "Your cholesterol levels are probably off the charts."

He shrugged as he continued. "We're pretty self-sufficient. There are also three fully stocked ponds, if you like bass or catfish. We eat a lot of fish, too. And during the fall and winter, you can hunt turkey and white-tailed deer."

"You don't eat Bambi, do you?"

"Why else would we hunt deer?"

Soledad rolled her eyes skyward. "And here I thought you and I could be friends."

Palmer smiled. "It's country living. You spoiled city girls don't know anything about that."

"Spoiled? Obviously, you didn't meet our father. We de la Vega girls were hardly spoiled."

Palmer laughed heartily. Because he had met her father and knew him fairly well. Rigo de la Vega was exceptionally protective of his daughters, wanting nothing but the absolute best for them. When Soledad's twin sister, Dominique, was being threatened, the patriarch had hired Palmer's cousin Stanton to be her bodyguard. There was little their father would not do for them or give to them. They'd been spoiled in the absolute best way, and he imagined her desire to have kids was her wanting that for her own family.

Rising from her seat, Soledad reached for his empty plate. "I'll do the washing up," she said.

"No, you won't," Palmer responded, pulling the dirty dishes from her hands. "You're a guest. Besides, we need to make plans. They'll be looking for the two of you."

For the briefest of moments, Soledad hadn't thought about her predicament, and she'd been grateful for the reprieve. She'd been enjoying his company. She sat, feeling like a ton of weight had been dropped back onto her shoulders. Across the room, Lyra still slept soundly. She sucked her tongue in her sleep and her expression was angelic. The dog hadn't moved, lying protectively beside her. Occasionally, he would lift his head before dozing off.

As Palmer rinsed and loaded the dishwasher, Soledad nosed around the home. The country farmhouse was sizable, almost four thousand square feet of meticulously designed space in a very private setting. The windows were expansive and afforded wonderful views of the pasture, the cattle and the wildlife. The open floor plan included the chef's kitchen and an exceptionally large master suite. There were four bedrooms, each with its own fireplace, six bathrooms total, and Soledad imagined the cream-tinted walls with the pitched ceilings and hardwood floors held many cherished memories of his family's gatherings. She couldn't help but wonder if there'd been someone special who'd been part of the plans for a home so large. A home fit for a family with children and pets.

She liked Palmer. Yet there was something about him that gave her pause, and she found herself wanting to know even more. She was curious about his likes and dislikes and his dreams and goals. She had questions about the women who were important to him, wanting to know more about his mother and sisters and half siblings. She wondered about his past relationships, whether there was someone important in his life who might not be happy about her finding shelter in his family home. She had a multitude of questions, but wasn't sure she should even ask or if she'd ever get the answers.

Soledad was heading toward the family room when she saw a large shadow pass by the front window. Her heart began to race, her breathing suddenly labored as she gasped for air. She sprinted to where Lyra lay, snatching her up so quickly that Jack jumped in alarm and grabbed her by the arm with his teeth. The dog growled. Soledad's eyes widened with fright.

"Jack, no," Palmer said sternly, moving swiftly to her side.

The dog released his grasp and whimpered softly. He sat and then settled at Palmer's feet, his eyes still on the baby as if he dared Soledad to try and run.

"What's wrong?" Palmer questioned, his large hand gently caressing where the dog had just vised her arm in a toothy grip.

"There's someone sneaking around the house," Soledad whispered loudly. "I saw them pass by the front window."

Before Palmer could answer, there was a knock on the kitchen door. His heart was suddenly beating as spastically as he imagined hers was, the intensity surprising him. He took a deep breath and pointed to the back of the family home and the master bedroom. "Hide in my bedroom. I'll see who it is," he said firmly.

With a bob of her head, Soledad scurried down the hallway. Palmer watched until she'd closed and locked the bedroom door after herself. Jack had followed Soledad, visibly unhappy when she closed the door in his face, not allowing him into the room with her and Lyra. He lay at the threshold, determined not to be moved.

Palmer walked swiftly to the door, someone knocking a second time for his attention. When he pulled it open, Noé Maldonado stood with his hat clutched in both hands. He was a slim man with a head of jet-black curls and a sepia complexion. The farmhand had been with Palmer for a few years.

"Noé! What's up?" Palmer said, his eyes dancing swiftly across the landscape behind the man's shoulders.

Noé grinned warmly. "*¡Buenos días, jefe!* I'm sorry to interrupt, boss," he said, his accent thick and as rich as warm molasses.

"Not a problem, Noé. What do you need?"

"Just wanted you to know I need to take the big truck into town to pick up supplies. They're behind with the deliveries and we need that last order."

Palmer nodded. "That's not a problem. Who's working the ranch today?"

"It's a small crew, jefe. I have four men working that northern pasture. The fence came down and needs to be replaced. They will not be a problem to you."

"I wasn't concerned," Palmer said. "I know you have it under control. I'll be inside most of the day. I have some paperwork to catch up on. Just call me if you need anything else."

"Yes, sir. Thank you, jefe." Noé backed his way out the door, sliding his hat onto his head. He suddenly hesitated, as if there was something he'd forgotten.

"What is it, Noé?" Palmer asked. "Is something wrong?"

"There was a man on the property earlier. Down by where the horses were grazing. He said he was police, and was asking questions. Said he was looking for a woman. That she had run off with someone else's baby. We told him we hadn't seen anyone, but he said he did not believe us. He said her GPS showed that she was here. When we couldn't tell him anything, he threatened to call ICE on us. But we didn't have anything to tell him, jefe! I told him again that we had not seen any woman and to come talk to you. He said you told him to come talk to us. He made the men nervous. None of them wants any trouble. They are good men, jefe."

"That man lied. I would never send anyone to talk to you or the men, and I certainly wouldn't let anyone threaten you." There was an edge to Palmer's tone, every word wrapped in annoyance and rising rage. Knowing Gavin had violated his property and purposely tried to intimidate his employees had him spitting mad, the emotion wrapped in swells of barbed wire.

"I know, jefe. But not all men are good like you."

"If you see this man again, you call me immediately and I will come to you. And you tell the others they have nothing to be afraid of as long as they are working for me."

"Gracias, jefe," Noé said. "Thank you very much."

Palmer watched until Noé had climbed into the cab of the Ford F-150 and started the engine. Then he closed the door.

He stood quietly for a moment, reflecting on the conversation. Clearly, Soledad's problem was not going to go away, and Lyra's father was laser focused on finding them both—there on the ranch. Palmer had to question why this location and then remembered something

Noé had said. Gavin had told him her "GPS" had put Soledad's location there on the farm. What had Gavin been talking about?

Chapter 5

When Soledad felt safe enough to return to the family room, she found Palmer sitting at the kitchen counter. Lyra's diaper bag lay before him, the contents strewed across the sofa and floor. Concern pulled at the muscles in his face, his brow creased. He lifted his eyes to hers as she entered the room and suddenly Soledad's stomach pitched with fear.

"What?" she said, eyeing him anxiously.

Palmer lifted a small black box from the countertop. It was no bigger than a digital watch face and fit neatly into the palm of his hand. It was nothing Soledad recognized. She gave him a questioning look, asking what it was and why he looked like the world was coming to an end.

"It's a tracking device. It was sewn into the lining of the baby's diaper bag."

Soledad's eyes widened. She had wondered how Gavin had known where they were to pull up on them like he had. She and Annie had considered he might track her through her cell phone, which was why Annie had left hers behind. Neither had considered he would use Lyra to track his wife's whereabouts, much less put a tracking device on anyone. Knowing how abusive he'd been, it shouldn't have surprised her, but Soledad was thrown off guard.

"He knows we're here," she breathed loudly.

Palmer nodded. "It's why he came last night. It's also why he came back this morning."

"He came back?"

"That was one of my ranch hands at the door. He came to tell me that your friend's husband was asking the men questions about you and Lyra. But they didn't know anything and couldn't give him any answers."

Something that felt very much like guilt washed over Soledad's spirit. She suddenly felt responsible for putting Palmer and his employees in harm's way. And she didn't think she could ever forgive herself for Annie's death. Despite her best efforts, she hadn't contemplated every single possibility that could have gone wrong. And the one thing she hadn't considered had gotten her best friend killed.

She hadn't given Gavin's previous bad behavior enough weight. Despite what she did know, she had let her guard down when Annie had trusted her to get it right because she herself had gotten it wrong so many times. Soledad couldn't have been more wrong. She had led Gavin straight to them, and he clearly had no plans to go away until he found her and got his murderous hands on that beautiful baby.

As if he were reading her mind, Palmer shook his head. "This isn't your fault," he said softly, his eyes dancing across her face.

Soledad shook her head, much less confident about him being right. "We need to get out of here," she said, her mind beginning to race. "He can't find us here!" She began to scramble for the baby items that had been tossed to the floor.

Palmer rose from his seat and reached for her, grabbing her arm gently to stall her anxiety. His touch was like an electrical current shooting through her and Soledad's breath caught deep in her chest. She gasped. Loudly.

Palmer snatched his hand away, his eyes wide. "I'm sorry. I didn't mean…" he started, the comment stalling midsentence.

She shook her head vehemently. "No. It's fine. I'm just…"

They were both suddenly stammering, words having slipped into an abyss of emotion that neither had anticipated.

Soledad's heart was beating rapidly. "I'm scared," she whispered loudly, tears welling in her dark eyes. "I've never been so scared."

"It's going to be okay," Palmer responded. He reached for her a second time, his hand gently caressing her forearm. This time she didn't flinch or pull away from him. "I'm not going to let anything happen to you or that baby. But we need to be smart and we need to out-smart him."

Soledad nodded. She felt herself lean into his touch, her knees quivering ever so slightly. She closed her eyes as she considered each word he spoke, feeling her com-fort level beginning to revive.

Palmer continued. "Right now, that little device is telling him that you're here. So, we're going to use that to our advantage. I need to go into town to get sup-plies for you and the baby. When I do, this GPS will put you at the mall, and that's where the tracking de-vice will stay.

"Meanwhile, you need to make some calls. People are worried about you. You need to stay missing, but the authorities need to know you're okay. So, I want you to call my cousin and tell her what happened. You don't have to tell Melissa you're here with me. Just let her know you're safe. Then I think you should call your family. I'm sure they are worried sick."

There was a moment of hesitation as Soledad con-sidered his plan. His cousin Melissa Colton was the chief of the Grave Gulch Police Department. She knew Melissa in passing and had always found her to be pleas-ant and fair.

She also knew that Melissa already had her hands full with an internal scandal that involved GGPD's for-mer forensic scientist, a man named Randall Bowe. Discovering that Bowe had tampered with evidence in several police cases and allowed a serial killer to go free and kill again had eroded the public's faith in the department. There had been calls for Melissa's resignation and protests had become rampant through the city. Soledad understood that, like people in general, not all cops were good and that a few bad apples in the bunch could make life significantly harder for those who only wanted to do their best under harrowing circumstances. She was sure another investigation, finding killer Len Davison, only added to Melissa's lengthy list of problems. An unnecessary missing persons case added to her list would only hinder the work she needed to be doing. But Soledad still wasn't comfortable with reaching out to the police.

"You can trust her," Palmer assured her.

His voicing the thoughts in her head had begun to give her serious pause. He was overly perceptive, reading her emotions as if they were inked across her forehead. She didn't need to tell him that she would only trust his cousin because he did. She was certain he already knew.

"I don't have my phone," she said softly.

"That's not a problem. I have a burner phone you can use."

Soledad blinked, her lashes batting rapidly. "Why do you have a burner phone?"

"I have a few of them. I buy them in bulk. I employ a lot of migrant workers to work the ranch and sometimes I need to contact them. It also enables them to keep in touch with their families. It just makes things easier for all of us."

"That's actually exceedingly kind of you. I'm sure they appreciate your generosity."

Palmer shrugged. There was suddenly a loud wail from the bedroom and his shoulders rolled back, his head tilting slightly. He gave Soledad a look, concern pulling at his expression.

"That sounds like a diaper overload cry," Soledad said. "Someone's awake and in need of some attention."

"Then that sounds like she's crying for you!" Palmer responded. He gave her a slight smile. "You go grab the baby and I'll go grab you a phone. Then I need to ride out and check on my men. I won't be long. You'll be safe while I'm gone."

As he turned, Soledad reached for his hand to stall his steps. She slid her fingers between his and held on tightly as he turned back around to meet her gaze. "Why are you doing this for me?" Soledad questioned, staring deep into the look he was giving her.

"Because you need me," he answered. "And I want to help." He gave her hand a warm squeeze, then gestured toward the bedroom and the pitiful cry fervently rising from inside.

And, as extreme as it sounds, because I need you, he thought to himself as she walked away. *Because I need you, too.*

The drive to the north side of the ranch didn't take any time at all. On the way, Palmer thought about the young woman he was harboring in his home. He didn't know if he would ever have the words to explain what it was he was feeling. Mostly because he didn't fully understand it himself.

Palmer had always enjoyed his life. After his adoption, he had wanted for nothing and what he'd received in abundance was love. Yet, despite everything his parents had done for him, trust had always been a major issue he could never overcome.

As an adult, he was content with his choices. He had never imagined himself in a long-term relationship with any woman. He had no need for a wife and preferred casual encounters over lengthy entanglements. It worked for him, and even when it didn't, there was no stress. Women who became attached usually left with their hearts broken, but Palmer never made any promises he wasn't willing to keep. Forever was not something he had ever promised any woman. He was always direct and to the point. They'd known where he'd stood from the start. That level of honesty had always served him well.

Others worried about him being lonely, but even the solitude didn't bother him. He worked hard, rested well, and had never been unhappy with his choices. Or at least he hadn't thought so before Soledad had come barreling into his life. Something about the beautiful woman was creeping beneath his skin and latching on like a wild ivy gone awry. He was genuinely concerned about her well-being and about the baby's. Those bright eyes and that innocent smile had yanked his heart as hard as the little girl sometimes yanked Jack's tail. Like his dog, Palmer was protective of them both. He would move heaven and earth to keep them safe. He was finding a level of joy with Soledad that he'd never known before, and the feeling both surprised and confused him.

* * *

Soledad snapped the onesie closed around the clean diaper, wriggling her nose at Lyra, who was sucking on her fist. The baby smiled and laughed, and Soledad laughed with her.

She started to sing as she lifted Lyra into her arms. Nuzzling her nose into the roll of baby fat beneath Lyra's neck, Soledad inhaled the scent of baby powder deep into her lungs.

"Do you feel better?" Soledad gushed as she kissed the baby's cheek.

Lyra gurgled, pulling her fist back to her mouth.

"You're hungry. Let's go get you something to eat," she said as she settled the child on her hip and headed for the family room.

The burner phone Palmer had promised rested on the kitchen counter. There was also a note that he had already programmed his number and Melissa's cell into the device.

Soledad sighed heavily. Despite her reservations, she had no reason *not* to reach out to let the authorities know she was safe and well. And she definitely needed to put her father and Dominique at ease. Granted, she was scared that Gavin might find her, but she knew no one could find him if they were focused on her and the baby. But that call would have to wait, she thought. Because Lyra was pulling at her shirt and throwing herself backward for Soledad's attention.

Three jars of baby food rested next to the diaper bag. "Look!" Soledad exclaimed, making a face at the little girl. "You can have pears, pears or pears."

Lyra burbled.

"Pears it is," Soledad said excitedly.

She propped Lyra in the corner of the couch, then popped the top on the jar of food. Sitting herself beside the child, she began to feed her, amused as Jack jumped up to sit beside the baby to watch her eat.

"You're a lucky little girl, Lyra," Soledad said as the infant swirled the puréed fruit around in her mouth. "You have your very own bodyguard. Doesn't she, Jack?"

The dog panted, looking exceptionally happy as he laid his head on Lyra's little legs. The baby giggled, drool sliding down her chin.

Minutes later, finished with her meal, Lyra was chewing on the nipple of her water bottle as she kneaded her fingers through Jack's fur. The dog lay with his eyes closed, not at all bothered by the child's grabby hands.

Soledad loved the bond the two had already formed, thinking that she might have to get Lyra a puppy of her own when they were able to come out of hiding and settle into their fated new life. She was even a little sad that Jack would never have a little person of his own if Palmer stayed true to his convictions about not having children. She couldn't help but hope that he might change his mind. She sensed that he would make an incredible father if he relaxed and just allowed himself to enjoy the experience. He was good with Lyra. She'd even caught him smiling a few times as he'd watched the baby with his dog.

Thinking about Palmer, Soledad had dozens of questions she wanted to ask him, her curiosity increasing tenfold. She wondered about his life between being orphaned and being adopted, and if it were something he ever talked about. It clearly caused him angst.

Appreciating she might better understand if she knew more, she pondered what little she did know.

She assumed from the home's interior decor that blue was his favorite color, shades enhancing the walls, the floor and the furniture. He was also a fan of Western artwork. Paintings of the Wild West decorated the walls. Her favorite was the cowboy and his horse in the home's front foyer. He clearly loved his animals. They were like family to him, especially the horses. She had eyed the pictures of them that adorned his office walls. She hoped one day to be able to travel down to the stables to see them and maybe even ride with him.

Lyra and the dog suddenly growled at her. She rolled her eyes at the two and sneered. Both seemed to remind her that she and Palmer weren't really friends like that, and she shouldn't be planning future days with the handsome man. Not that a random thought meant she was planning anything.

"You two are no help," Soledad muttered. She leaned to kiss the baby and then the dog as the duo kept playing with each other contentedly.

Moving to the counter, Soledad pulled the burner phone into the palm of her hand. She took a deep breath and pushed the button to dial the police chief. It rang once, twice and then three times before Melissa Colton answered.

"Chief Colton!"

A wave of panic suddenly hit Soledad broadside and she disconnected the call without saying anything. Her hand was shaking; she felt like she might be sick to her stomach. Her gaze shifted to the sofa. The dog was teasing the girl, nuzzling her on one side and then the other. Lyra giggled, her little arms and legs flailing as she tried to grab at the animal. Jack was proving himself to be the best babysitter.

After giving it some thought, Soledad knew she couldn't call to tell Melissa her story without breaking down in tears, and possibly changing her mind about hiding out. Despite her best efforts, she was only holding on by a slim thread. Caring for Lyra was a pleasant diversion and Jack was keeping them both entertained. Her attraction to Palmer was a whole other story. She wasn't yet sure if he was the cherry on an extremely sweet slice of cake or just a necessary distraction through this truly hard time.

Soledad took a deep breath and began to text with her thumbs. The message was direct and to the point.

Melissa, this is Soledad de la Vega. I saw Gavin Stone murder his wife, Annie. He shot me, too, but I am fine. He has threatened to kill me and take Annie's baby, Lyra. We are both safe for now, but I know Gavin is searching for us. We will come out of hiding when he has been caught and is in your custody. I don't mean to be difficult, but I can't risk him finding us. I hope you understand.

She took another deep breath, reread the message once and then again, and then she pushed the button to send.

Minutes later, Melissa responded to her message.

Soledad, I really need you to turn yourself in. We need the details of what happened. I assure you we will do everything in our power to keep you safe, but I cannot have you impeding the investigation. You need to tell me where you are.

Soledad texted back.

No. I don't trust that you can keep me and the baby safe. I'm sorry. Find Gavin and I will tell you where I am. But you will need to arrest Gavin first. You also need to contact Davis Fairbanks. He's Annie's attorney. Annie left information with him that may help you.

There was a lengthy pause before Melissa finally responded. Soledad knew the chief must not be happy with her and could only begin to imagine the rant Melissa was currently waging with herself. Almost thirty minutes passed before Melissa's final text message came through.

Stay safe. We're here for you and will protect you and Lyra when you're ready. Until then, please keep this line open in case I need to reach you. Thank you.

Relief blew past Soledad's lips as she released the breath she'd been holding deep in her lungs. She dropped the phone back to the counter. Stepping up to the large bay window, she looked out over the landscape. The views from the window were stunning, everything about the property already feeling like home. The house was set far off the main road, and she appreciated that it would take some maneuvering for anyone to sneak up on them without being seen or heard.

Palmer had assured her that she and Lyra were safe, and she believed him. With no one knowing they were there, they would not be easily found, not even with Gavin's little tracking device. She trusted that once Palmer disposed of it, not even Gavin would be able to find them. Until life went back to normal, Soledad thought, Palmer Colton might be hard-pressed to rid himself of her and the baby.

Palmer stood on the front porch, pausing to reflect before entering. He'd driven the perimeter of the property, checking the fences and double-checking all the gates and entry points. There were cameras at each location, and he ensured each was functioning and recording. If anyone were to trespass, there'd be a video recording of the infraction. He'd also hired a security team to periodically patrol the property. There was no point in taking any unnecessary risks. Any threat to Soledad would be dealt with vigorously. If he knew what was good for him, Gavin Stone didn't want to come back to Colton Ranch to look for her.

Palmer's act of kindness had become an obsession of sorts. He felt responsible for Soledad and Lyra. The thought of anything happening to them on his watch knotted his stomach and set his teeth on edge.

Truth be told, he'd had a crush on Soledad since

forever. He'd often frequented her bakery hoping to catch a glimpse of the beautiful woman as she worked in the back. He was still kicking himself for not taking advantage of the opportunity to speak with her at her sister's engagement party. His brother Troy had teased him about his bachelor lifestyle, encouraging him to go for it, but Palmer had hesitated, fearful of embarrassing himself. Then, just like that, she'd been gone.

Suddenly, with the nearness of her, he found his emotions on overload. Focusing on Soledad's protection enabled him to ignore any other feelings that were trying to surface. Instead of considering what all that sentiment might mean, he focused on keeping her out of harm's way. It was the very least he could do for them both, he thought. If only he could stop himself from wanting to pull her close and kiss her mouth, curious to know how she tasted.

Shaking himself from the reverie he'd fallen into, he reached for the doorknob and stepped inside the home. A bright smile suddenly pulled full and abundant across his face as he took in the view.

Soledad was leading a dance party, twirling the infant around in her arms. She was singing at the top of her lungs, a bad karaoke version of an old Carrie Underwood song sounding through the air. Jack was hopping up and down beside them, an occasional yip thrown in for good measure. The sight of them together seemed to fill his home with joy that he'd only seen on Thanksgiving and Christmas when his sisters had made him host the holiday meal. It was the first time Soledad had looked relaxed since he'd found her hiding in his barn.

She suddenly came to an abrupt stop, spying him standing there watching. She grinned, the wealth of the joy filling her face. Lyra was still laughing excitedly, and this playful Jack was doing more than Palmer had seen Jack do in a very long time.

"Hi," Soledad said, panting ever so slightly. "How long have you been standing there?"

"Not long. Don't let me interrupt. You three look like you're having a grand old time."

"Jack is an excellent dance partner. Isn't he, Lyra?" Soledad nuzzled the baby's cheek.

Lyra yawned in response. Soledad laughed. "That was a yes. He's just worn her out."

"That's Jack."

"Come join us!"

Palmer eyed her with a raised brow. "I think I'll pass. I need to run into town to the store. I figured I'd pick up some things for you and the baby. Since we're not sure how long you're going to be here."

"I appreciate that. In fact, I already made you a list." She gestured toward the counter.

Palmer laughed. "That was slightly presumptuous of you, don't you think?"

Soledad shrugged. "Slightly, but it was either that or Lyra and I would soon be wearing your underwear."

"Makes perfect sense to me," Palmer said with a nod and the faintest of smiles.

He moved to the counter to review her list. It included those things he'd expected: diapers, formula, baby food. As he neared the end of the list, he raised his eyes to hers, a question mark in his stare. Confusion washed over him. "Flour, butter, sugar... What am I missing?"

"I have to bake a cake."

His brows lifted. "A cake?"

Soledad nodded. "I've promised a client a cake, and I need to make good on that promise. My reputation and the reputation of my business is on the line. I've worked too hard to build my business to just throw that away."

"There's no one who works for you that can bake this cake?"

Soledad shook her head. "I have two young women apprenticing with me, but they're not ready for something like this just yet. My other employees are front-end staff. They handle the cash register, bag up the goodies and keep the bakery clean. All of them together can keep things running for a week or so, maybe even two, but it's iffy after that."

"So, you don't think it's going to look strange that the missing woman in a murder and child abduction case suddenly turns up with a cake?"

"I just plan to bake the cake. You're going to get it delivered."

Palmer laughed. "Me?"

"Do you have a better plan?"

"Maybe you don't bake a cake?"

"That's not an option."

Exasperation furrowed Palmer's brow. "Let's be realistic, Soledad. No one is expecting you to bake a cake after everything that's happened."

"No one is going to know I did it. And there's nothing you can say or do that's going to stop me. You're going to make sure it gets there without anyone being able to track it back here to us. I'll let you figure out the logistics of that."

"What if I conveniently forget to buy that half of the list?"

Soledad tossed up a dismissive hand. "Fine. I'll go myself. You stay and watch the baby. If I don't come back, then I'm going to trust you to keep her safe."

A wry smile pulled at Palmer's mouth. His expression was smug. "You are not going to leave that baby. There isn't anyone who knows you who'd believe that."

"Fine," Soledad said defiantly. "I'll take her with me, then."

Palmer rolled his eyes. "I'm missing something. You're really willing to take that risk over some baked goods?"

"I'm willing to do whatever I need to do to keep a promise I made."

"I don't understand." Palmer moved toward her, taking a seat at the counter. He folded his arms across his chest and stared intently. The baby had settled against her shoulder, beginning to doze off. Jack lay with his head against Soledad's foot. Something about the trio made Palmer's heart sing, and he felt a wealth of energy pitch through his midsection, the warmth spreading into his limbs.

"Who did you make a promise to?" he asked. His tone was softer, curiosity tinting his words.

"You're familiar with Randall Bowe and what's going on with the police department, right?"

Palmer nodded. "It's all anyone's talking about. People are even demonstrating downtown in front of the police station. He's made a complete mockery of the judicial system. It's going to take a lot for them to recover from the damage he's caused. But what does all that have to do with this cake?"

"You may have heard about Rachel Montclair?"

His eyes skated back and forth briefly. "I know I've heard the name, but…" He shrugged his shoulders.

"Rachel went to school with me and Annie. She worked as a financial adviser for Grave Gulch Fidelity. Two years ago, she was charged with fraud, theft by false pretenses and embezzlement of funds. She was also charged with the attempted murder of the bank's president. They said she poisoned him when he discovered what she had done. But anyone who knew Rachel knew she didn't rob that bank or poison that man. But she didn't have an alibi the night her boss got sick, nor could she explain her signature being on checks and documents that allowed someone to walk off with a million dollars in bank funds.

"She was convicted on evidence that Randall Bowe manipulated and planted. When they started investigating him, her case came back under review and she was completely exonerated. She's being released from jail tomorrow and I promised to make the cake for her welcome home party. I know I can't be there, but that cake is the least I can do to help celebrate her vindication."

Palmer was still staring at her, noting the strand of blue-black hair that had fallen over her brow and the rise of color that suddenly tinted her cheeks. Her loyalty to her friend was endearing, every ounce of her spirit committed to doing right by those she cared for.

He stood, brushing his palms down his denim slacks. "I don't grocery shop, so we're going to let technology be our friend." He pointed to the laptop that rested on a desk in the corner. "I have an account at Holiday Market. Sign in and order whatever you need. I'll pick it up on my way back. Does that work?"

Soledad nodded. "I can do that."

"There may be a few items already in the cart. It's how I keep up with things I need to remember to shop for. Just add them to whatever you need, please. I know I need cornflakes."

"Cornflakes?"

Palmer shrugged. "I like cornflakes."

Soledad smiled. "Me, too."

"Anything else?"

"You don't have a lot of cookware. I have a business account at the Kitchen Supply House. If I place an order for cake pans, will you pick those up for me, too?"

Palmer gave her a look and shook his head. "Whatever you need," he said, the slightest smile pulling at his lips. "But it might take me a little longer. I'll need to make sure no one is following me. Just in case Dr. Stone gets any brilliant ideas."

"Thank you," Soledad said, nuzzling the baby softly.

"I'll set the house alarm when I leave. Lock yourself and the baby in the bedroom. Just in case. And keep that burner phone close. If there's an emergency, the house alarm will alert me and the authorities. If you need anything, you call me. I'll leave Jack here, too.

He'll make sure no one enters the house who's not supposed to be here."

Soledad eased to his side, her arms still cradled around Lyra. She leaned in as if to whisper something to him, and when he leaned forward, meeting her halfway, she pressed her lips to his cheek in a gentle kiss.

"Thank you," she said again, her voice a loud whisper. "I don't know how I'll ever pay you back for your kindness."

Startled, words caught deep in his chest, he felt his skin burning hot from her touch. "You don't owe me anything," he muttered.

"But I do," Soledad responded. "You don't know how much everything you've done means to me."

Palmer smiled. "You shouldn't have any problems while I'm gone. Just stay inside, please. Away from the windows. I won't be gone long." He pointed to the guest bedroom. "Lock the door," he said as she turned, headed for the back of the house.

He stood watching as she adjusted Lyra against her shoulder and grabbed the laptop. She tossed him one last look as she walked away, the sweetest smile filling her face. Jack followed them and then lay outside the door after Soledad had shut and locked it. Palmer closed his eyes and took a deep breath. He reached for the side of his face and pressed his palm to his cheek, his fingers trembling ever so slightly.

Chapter 6

Soledad and her friend had been traveling on the service road before they'd run into Gavin. Although the route added a few extra miles to any trip, it was the one Palmer had chosen to take to town. He'd driven one last time around the perimeter of the property to double-check that the gates were all locked and secured, and then headed out on his errands.

Rounding the back ridge that bordered the main roadway, he slowed his truck as he approached a police roadblock. Two officers were standing in the middle of the road, checking licenses and asking questions of approaching drivers. Patrol cars were parked on the shoulder. A team of the city's finest was surveying the crime scene, taking measurements and making notes. Soledad's Camry was secure atop a flatbed truck. As

Palmer pulled to a stop, he recognized both men in blue. The oldest of the duo called out his name. Loudly.

"Palmer Colton. Surprised to see you here."

"It's good to see you, too, Officer Linwood. What are you guys doing out here?"

Officer Jay Linwood leaned into Palmer's window. A member of the Grave Gulch police force for as long as Palmer could remember, he was a rotund man with a balding mane and surly attitude. Rarely was he in a good mood when the two men encountered each other. Palmer was genuinely surprised by his buoyant attitude.

"Murder investigation," the man answered. "Found a dead woman on the road out here. Looking for the husband and her baby now," he said unemotionally.

Palmer nodded. Before he could respond, his name was being called a second time. He shook his head, instantly recognizing his sister's voice. Grace was new to the Grave Gulch Police Department and determined to prove her merit.

"You know this rookie?" Linwood questioned sarcastically, eyeing the two of them.

"Since she was in diapers," Palmer answered.

Grace Colton sent her eyes skyward as she came to stand beside the other officer. Linwood winked his eye at her, gave Palmer a nod and moved to the car that had pulled up behind him.

"Where are you headed, big brother?" Grace asked.

"I need to get some errands done. How's it going?"

Grace shook her head. "This one's bad and there's a baby missing. But Melissa has put a gag order on all of us, pending notification to the family."

"I understand."

"Are you coming to dinner this weekend? Mom wants all of us there for Dad's birthday."

Palmer winced. "Is that this weekend?"

"You better show up, Palmer."

"I'll be there," he said with a wry laugh. "How could I miss it? Mom calls to remind me every day."

"Be nice," Grace said. She tapped his forearm as she changed the subject. "You didn't see or hear anything last night, by chance?"

"What would I have heard?" Palmer asked, the little white lie rolling off his tongue. "The house is a few miles from here and it was storming most of the night."

"I told Melissa we should talk to you. The victim was practically shot at your back door."

"You'd be wasting Melissa's time, and mine."

"You don't know that. You might know something and not even realize it. Are you sure you haven't seen any strangers out here?"

Palmer shook his head, dismissing her question. "I need to run," he said. "I'll see you this weekend."

"Stay safe," Grace said.

Palmer grinned. "Love you, too, little sister." He shifted his truck into gear and pulled off down the road.

An hour later, Palmer stood in the children's section of a department store, feeling like a deer caught in headlights. Mustering up the courage to come inside had taken longer than necessary, with him worrying about who he might run into and what he would tell them if they asked. He had thought the chore would be easy, but buying clothes for Lyra was proving to be a challenge he hadn't anticipated. He had a fistful of baby onesies in his left hand and garments on hangers in his right. Everything was pink, pink and pink, and he couldn't help but wonder at what age they started making girls' clothes in some other color. He tossed the whole lot into the cart he pushed.

Minutes later, with the help of a sales associate named Berta, he'd added a crib, a change table, bottles, diapers and enough clothes to outfit half the babies in the state.

"Your baby is one lucky little girl!" Berta exclaimed. "You're going to spoil her with all these gifts. I can just imagine what her mother will say."

"I don't…" Palmer started to object, ready to balk at the idea of being anyone's father. But Berta didn't give him a chance to get in a word, suggesting a half dozen other items to add to the stash in his shopping cart.

"Every little girl needs hair bows," she declared, holding up an assortment of ribbons and headbands.

"Fine," Palmer said, feeling his brow crease with anxiety. "I'll take them. That's fine."

Berta clapped her hands excitedly as if she were earning a commission on the sale. Palmer gave her a smile and a wave, then made an about-face. He paused to check out a display of limited-edition teddy bears when he heard his name being called yet again. He winced, feeling like he'd been caught with his hand in the cookie jar, and turned to face his brother.

Troy Colton was grinning broadly as he walked in

Palmer's direction. "I thought that was you. What are you doing here?"

The two men shook hands and bumped shoulders in a one-armed embrace.

"Just picking up some things for a friend," Palmer quipped, trying to quickly formulate a lie to explain himself.

Troy scanned his cart, amusement dancing across his face. "That must be some friend. Something you need to tell me, little brother?"

Palmer shrugged dismissively. "It's just a few gifts for one of the farmhands. His wife just had a baby and I'm helping them out."

"That's very generous of you."

"What are you doing here?" Palmer asked, slightly desperate to shift the attention off himself.

"I thought I'd pick up a little gift for Evangeline. To celebrate her new job goals."

"New job? She won't be working for the district attorney's office anymore?"

Troy shook his head. "No. She's decided to go into social work. She wants to help."

"I wish her well. She'll do a great job wherever she lands."

"I think so, too. And I also thought she'd look superb in this," he said, holding up a silk teddy he'd selected from the lingerie department.

Palmer chuckled. "So, exactly who are you buying a present for? Evangeline or you?"

"Trust me, I plan to enjoy it, too."

"I just bet you will." Palmer shook his head, his expression smug. He changed the subject. "You don't have to work today?"

Troy took a deep inhalation of air, filling his lungs and holding it briefly. "It's my lunch break. I needed some time to clear my head. There's a lot going on."

"I saw Grace on the way here. She said she's working a murder investigation?"

"It's more complicated than that. You haven't heard, have you?"

Palmer's gaze narrowed. "Heard what?"

There was a moment of hesitation as Troy tossed a look over his shoulder. "It's about Soledad de la Vega."

"Soledad? What about Soledad?" Palmer tried to keep his tone even. "Is she okay?"

"She's missing. The woman murdered last night was Soledad's best friend, Annie. Annie's daughter and Soledad haven't been found. The husband is a person of interest, but we haven't been able to find him, either. When I leave here, I'm going to meet Melissa at Soledad's apartment. We're hoping we'll find something there that'll help us locate her."

A wall of silence seemed to rise thick and heavy between the two brothers. Palmer's eyes feigned concern as he tried not to show his hand. He suddenly had an overwhelming need to get back home to check on Soledad and the baby, to make sure both were well and safe. He felt his knees begin to shake, emotion sweeping through him that was both unexpected and surprising.

"I'm sure they'll be fine," he muttered.

Troy eyed him with a raised brow. "That's it? You're not worried?"

"Of course I'm worried. Why wouldn't I be worried? There's just nothing I can do, right?"

Troy nodded. "We're going to find them. And I'm sure she'll be fine."

"I'm sure," Palmer said. "I trust Grave Gulch's finest will do an exceptional job."

"I'm sure you do. Are you sure there's nothing you want to tell me?" Troy prompted. His fingers trailed down the side of the shopping cart.

Palmer gave his brother a stern look. "What's with all the questions? I'm beginning to feel like one of your suspects."

"Probably because of that dopey expression on your face. You look guilty of something. Do you want to talk about it?"

"There's nothing to talk about."

"I saw how you looked at Soledad at the engagement party, remember? You don't have to pretend with me. It's okay if you're worried. I know this is probably a shock for you. It only makes sense that you'd be worried, Palmer. We're all concerned."

"I'm not… I'm just… It's…" Palmer was suddenly feeling completely out of sorts.

Troy tapped him on the arm. "Hey, we Colton men are notorious for not being honest about our feelings. Trust me, I know." He chuckled, seeming to drift off into thought.

Palmer nodded, ready to be done with their conversation. "I'm good. I'm expected back at the ranch, and I'm sure you need to get back to work, too."

Troy stole a quick glance at his wristwatch. "Yeah, I do need to get going."

"Please, let me know if you turn up anything on Soledad," Palmer said softly.

"I definitely will. And when we find her, you need to promise me you'll let her know how you feel about her."

"See, there you go," Palmer chided. "Trying to make it more than it is."

Troy laughed. "It's your lie. Tell it any way you want to."

"Goodbye, Troy," Palmer said with a slight shake of his head.

He watched as Troy gave him a wave and headed for the front of the store. When his brother was finally out of his sight, he grabbed two of the plush toy bears and tossed them on top of the pile in his cart. He took another deep breath to calm his nerves and headed toward the women's department, thinking the day couldn't possibly get any more challenging.

Palmer was certain he'd broken several traffic laws trying to get back to his home, and to Soledad and the baby. He was grateful that traffic was light and the police barricade cleared. He didn't know if he could take running into one more person that he knew. Most especially with the truckload of paraphernalia he was hauling. It wasn't his nature to lie so wantonly; answering the pointed questions he'd gotten this day had him telling many tall tales.

His experience in the women's department had tested every ounce of his fortitude. He'd added T-shirts and shorts to the cart, two-piece pajamas and another pair of sweats. But it was the lingerie section that had done him in and he still couldn't explain it if someone asked.

Bras didn't scare him. He'd grown up with sisters, making slingshots with the garments when he and his brother were bored. As a child, Grace had routinely danced around in nothing but her underwear. He knew how to navigate lingerie, having stripped a few women out of theirs. He hadn't, however, known how to contend with the inquisition that had come as he'd randomly selected items he'd thought Soledad might need.

He could barely remember the sales rep's name, but she clearly remembered his, stepping up to him as he selected tank tops he thought Soledad might like. The saleswoman was an employee of the department store, but they had often run into one another in social settings. She was an attractive woman, though not at all Palmer's type. The woman's smile filled her face as she bent to look at his selections with a curious eye.

"Palmer Colton," she cooed, her voice oozing what he imagined it would if she moonlighted as a phone sex operator. "Isn't this a pleasant surprise?"

"Hey. How are you?" His mind raced as he tried to remember if she were a Chelsea, Stacey or Mary. He was grateful when she straightened and he could see the name tag pinned to her blazer. "It's good to see you again, Ms. Robbins."

"Please, call me Stacey. I would hope you and I are on a first-name basis by now." She laughed suggestively.

Palmer chuckled politely, although he wasn't in a jovial mood. "Well, it's good to see you again, *Stacey.*"

"I see you're enjoying a shopping spree. Special occasion?" As her gaze narrowed, she rested her palm on the edge of the shopping cart.

"I'm just helping out a friend."

"A close friend?"

"Just someone who needs a helping hand."

She paused, clearly waiting for him to expound on the comment.

The moment, unmistakably awkward, had Palmer wanting to tell her to go away. He obliged her instead.

"She and her children lost everything in a fire," he mumbled.

"Oh, my word!" Stacey exclaimed. "That's horrible."

"They've been devastated," Palmer added. "I just want to make things easier."

"I understand completely." She drew her fingers to the strand of beads around her neck, twirling them anxiously. "How can I help? Because I'd really like to help."

"I just need to get some clothes for her. Clean undergarments, casual wear, that kind of thing."

"Well, those tank tops you're holding are sheer perfection. The fabric is butter-soft against your skin and they can be worn with or without a bra comfortably. They are wonderful layering pieces."

Palmer dropped them atop the merchandise he'd already selected. "I appreciate the recommendation," he said.

"I would also suggest the matching panties," Stacey said. "I absolutely love them. What size is she?"

"Small, I think. She's very petite."

"Small it is." Stacey dropped a half dozen matching colors on top of the tank tops. "How about bras? Do you know her measurements?"

Palmer suddenly imagined his hands cupping Soledad's breasts, the image causing his heart to palpitate and his stomach to twist. Heat rained in his lower extremities and he shifted from side to side to stall the rise of nature threatening to publicly embarrass him. "I don't," he said, shaking his head vehemently. "I think this is enough."

"If I can make a suggestion?" Stacey mused, her brows quirking questioningly.

"Please…"

"Maybe buy her something pretty. You know, to pick up her spirits. We just got these adorable teddies in," she said, holding up a sexy little satin-and-lace set. "I bet this would brighten her day and make her feel very special."

Palmer felt his cheeks flush with heat as he imagined Soledad wearing the set, in his bed, beneath him. It was suddenly too much and he was past ready to be out of the store. He nodded. "Thank you," he said, almost snatching the garment from her hands. "I appreciate all your help."

"Anytime!" Stacey gushed. Her voice dropped two octaves. "And if you need any other assistance," she purred, pressing her business card into the palm of his hand, "don't hesitate to call me. I've written my cell phone number on the back."

With one last nod, Palmer gave the cart a push and

hurried toward the registers. As he stood in line to pay, he whispered a silent prayer that the transaction would happen swiftly and that he wouldn't run into anyone else who knew him.

And even that had taken longer than he would have liked, the clerk who'd finally checked him out wanting to gush over the baby clothes, assuming he was a new father who'd gone overboard to prepare for his newborn.

By the time he'd reached the parking lot with his purchases, he was past ready to be done but had one last errand before he could head home. He'd sat for a few minutes, turning the tracking device he'd found in Lyra's diaper bag over in his hands. A part of him had hoped the man with the dark shades and the damaged fender would have shown up while he was in town, but there'd been no sign of him or anyone else following the tracker. Had Palmer seen him, Gavin Stone would have found himself having an unbelievably bad day, because Palmer would have done whatever was necessary to help the man into jail so that Soledad would feel safe again.

Despite the many distractions as he'd shopped, Palmer had still been mindful to keep an eye out for anyone or anything that didn't feel right. Anything that would have triggered his radar and put him on edge. He'd looked around the parking lot one last time, driving slowly up and down each aisle as he'd pretended to look for an empty spot, studying each vehicle instead. As he'd finally pulled out of the lot, he'd driven to the back of the building and the oversize brown dumpsters that serviced the shopping center. He'd pulled up in front of the recycle bins and shut down his truck.

He'd still palmed the small device in his hand, his mind racing as plans formulated in his head about the lengths he would go to just to protect Soledad. He'd debated just how far too far might be.

With one last glance around, he'd stepped out of his truck and leaned in to gather up the empty cups, fast-food bags and stacks of junk. He tossed it all into one half-full dumpster and then headed for the ranch.

Now, turning into the driveway and toward the house, all he could think about was getting back to Soledad.

Palmer had barely been gone an hour before Soledad was stir-crazy. Being locked away in the bedroom felt as bad as running through the forest in the middle of the night. Every creak and squeak fueled her anxiety, and she was feeling slightly claustrophobic waiting for him to return.

Lyra lay in the center of the bed, doing what Lyra did best. She snored softly and clearly didn't have a care in the world. Soledad wished she could say the same. She pulled open the bedroom door and Jack bounded in, his exuberance steroidal. He ignored Soledad completely, barely letting her pet him on the head before he jumped onto the bed, sniffing and licking the little girl's toes and then settling down beside her.

"Aren't you something," Soledad muttered.

Jack dropped his head to a pillow and closed his eyes, dismissing Soledad with a slight grunt.

She laughed.

Exiting the room, she moved from window to window, peering out in search of Palmer's truck. She wanted to believe that everything was well and that he'd be back without incident. But that wasn't what she was feeling. Every horrible thing she could imagine had run through her head.

She was petrified that Gavin would ambush Palmer, then her, and then disappear with Lyra. She imagined Gavin strangling her or shooting her, or worse, tying her to a stake in the desert for the buzzards to feed on.

Her imagination had devolved into the realm of nightmares with no happy endings for any of them. Imagining Gavin taking a pitchfork or a blowtorch to Palmer had her feeling exceptionally anxious, most especially because Palmer had shown her nothing but kindness since she'd landed on his doorstep. Envisioning Palmer's demise had her nerves on edge. She was anxious for him to return home, to be back safe and secure with her and Lyra.

Soledad debated whether she should call to check on him. Then she imagined he might be put off by her calling when there was no emergency. She tabled the idea, figuring instead that she'd wait at least another hour before sending him a text message if he hadn't returned by then. Until then, she'd have to rein in her doom-and-gloom conjectures.

Soledad took a seat at the counter. With pen and paper in hand, she began to outline Rachel's cake design and to lay out her prep plans. Thinking about business, and what she needed to accomplish, was enough to keep her mind off everything else. She sketched and jotted notes until she felt better about what had to be done.

Time passed and that hour had come and gone, and there was still no sign of Palmer. By hour three, Soledad was beginning to think she needed to be afraid. She pulled the cell phone from the pocket of her pants. She hesitated. *I'm overreacting*, Soledad thought to herself. *This is ridiculous!* Considering everything she had asked him to do, she knew he'd more than likely be gone most of the afternoon. She hadn't thought that one through. Or considered that he might have had his own personal errands to run that she wasn't privy to. Maybe even meeting up with a female friend, someone he wasn't interested in her knowing about. Someone who had his attention, maybe even his heart.

Soledad shook the thought from her head. She was bordering on complete delusion and needed to get a handle on the wealth of emotion consuming her. She palmed the burner phone and began to dial the number committed to memory, assessing the risk versus the necessity. Necessity won out and she tapped her toes as she waited for her twin sister to answer.

"Hello?"

"Dominique, it's me."

"Soledad! Where are you? You've had us worried to death. Whose number is this?"

"I can't tell you. I just want you to know I'm okay."

"¡Dios mío, chica! Dad has practically hired the entire US military to search for you. The police won't tell us anything. Stanton hasn't been able to get any information from any of his family. What is going on?"

"Gavin killed Annie. Now he's looking for me."

Dominique gasped loudly. "No. Oh, Soledad. I'm so sorry."

Soledad's eyes misted with tears. "But you can't say anything to anyone, Dom. Not even Dad. It's not safe. Gavin is dangerous and I wouldn't put it past him to try to get to me through my family and friends."

"You need to come home. You know our father would never let anything happen to you. He will keep you safe."

"I know, but I can't risk putting anyone else in danger. This is for the best. I will call you in a day or two to let you know if there's been any change. Meanwhile, tell Dad not to worry, please. I really am doing okay. Lyra and I are fine."

Dominique inhaled swiftly. "That poor baby. I can't even imagine."

"Once the police find Gavin, I'll be able to come out of hiding. Until then, I just don't feel safe to do so."

"This is just too much, Soledad. You need to tell the police so they can protect you."

At that moment, the door flung open and Palmer stepped through the entrance. He and Soledad immediately locked eyes and held on. The intensity of the moment shifted every ounce of air in the atmosphere. Soledad felt something deep in her gut explode, a wave of heat so intense that she began to perspire, moisture puddling in intimate places. It knocked the breath from her and she gasped. Loudly.

"Soledad? You okay?" Dominique questioned, concern ringing in her voice.

"I'm good," Soledad answered. "I have all the protection I need right where I am," she concluded, and then she disconnected the call.

Chapter 7

Palmer was surprised by the wave of relief that flooded his spirit when he stepped through the door. Laying eyes on Soledad felt like Christmas morning when you still believed in Santa Claus and laid your eyes on your wrapped presents. He was tempted to rub his eyes with his fists to make sure he wasn't dreaming, but he didn't need to. Soledad blessed him with a smile, and just like that, everything he'd gone through earlier at the shopping center was forgotten.

He smiled. "Everything okay?" he asked, trying not to let any anxiety filter through his words.

Soledad nodded. "I took your advice and called my sister to let her know I was okay. I didn't want my father sending out the cavalry looking for me."

"I'm sure the only thing that will stop him from doing

that is his laying eyes on you. But I'm glad you let them know you're safe."

"I am, too."

"Where's the baby?"

"Asleep in your room."

"I guess I don't need to ask where Jack is. There was a time he'd meet me at the door and pretend to be excited that I was home."

Soledad laughed. "I'm sure he's still excited."

"Clearly not as excited about me as he is about Lyra."

"That's true. In fact, I don't think Jack is going to let anyone get between the two of them without a fight."

"Let's hope it never comes down to that," Palmer said. He shook his head. "I'm going to drive around back and start unloading the truck. I think I got everything you needed. But if I didn't and you need anything else, we'll have to order it online and have it delivered. Shopping was painful!"

"Was it that bad?"

"Too many nosy people." He threw up his hands in frustration.

Soledad laughed again. "Grave Gulch definitely has that small-town vibe. Everyone knows everyone and everyone wants to know everyone else's business."

"Well, I'm not used to that many people wanting to know mine."

"Sorry about that."

"Nothing for you to be sorry about."

She blessed him with another bright smile. "Can I help you unpack the car?"

"You can stand at the door and keep out of sight.

I stopped and picked up Chinese food for dinner. I'll hand you the food and I would really appreciate it if you would fix me a plate. I haven't eaten anything since I left this morning and I'm starved. I'll eat once I get everything else out the truck, but you feel free to dig in whenever you want."

Soledad rolled her eyes. "That's it?"

"I've got the rest covered. Besides, most of my men will be punching out for the day. They might pass the house on their way out and I don't want anyone to see you."

Palmer gave her a grin of sorts and turned, moving back out the front door. As she watched him walk away, Soledad felt her eyes mist, tears pressing against her lashes. She wiped the back of her hand across her face as her own smile pulled full and wide, something like joy brimming at the edge of her spirit.

Hours later, Palmer stood in the doorway of his guest room. After a quick meal and casual conversation about his shopping experiences, it had taken the two of them very little time to transform the space. He was still in awe that a room that was once part library, part bedroom now looked like a full-scale nursery.

The bright white crib was set up in the corner where a bookcase had once stood. The freshly washed animal-print linens the salesclerk had suggested decorated the tiny mattress. The addition of the changing table and assortment of stuffed animals pulled it all together. Even he was impressed—and that was sometimes hard to accomplish. Soledad had packed away the diapers and baby clothes, and little Lyra had been officially moved in. Under different circumstances, Palmer would have found that amusing. Now he wasn't so sure.

He stood watching as Soledad set the baby down for the night. She'd had sweet potatoes for her evening meal, preferring them over the peas he had tried to feed her. Now she suckled on a bottle of warm milk, her eyes closing and opening as she settled in for a night's sleep. He watched Soledad, who watched Lyra, in awe of them both. Jack nudging his leg pulled him from the reverie.

"I have to take the dog out and check on the animals," he said softly. "It's time for Pharaoh to get his evening meds."

Soledad shifted to give him a look. She nodded and smiled, then turned her attention back to the baby.

She was a natural when it came to mothering the little girl and Palmer found himself wondering why she didn't already have any children of her own. He hadn't thought to ask her when the two had talked about his own disinterest in fatherhood, but, clearly, he thought, Soledad would make a magnificent mother—and a great wife...to some other guy.

Out in the barn, Pharaoh was resting comfortably, faring far better than he had days earlier. Palmer ensured the horse had fresh bedding, a dose of the medicine the veterinarian had left and a bucket of oats to feed on. He sat with the colt for a good while before tossing a wool blanket on his broad back. The Arabian nuzzled his side and Palmer took that as a good sign the horse was getting better.

Making his regular rounds, Palmer stopped to inspect the fence that had been repaired. He also rode over to the south pasture to check on the cattle. His herd was sizable and seemed to be milling around contentedly together. A few calf stragglers that had strayed from the pack cried out, their mothers mooing in response to guide them. Palmer whistled for Jack, and within a few short minutes, the Bernese was by his side.

"Gather, Jack," Palmer commanded, and the dog shot across the fields to maneuver the dawdlers back into place.

After one last check of the gates, Palmer felt comfortable that all was well and headed back to the house. Usually, the ranch was his happy place, his regular routines giving him a sense of accomplishment and joy. He was proud of what he'd built, and everything about the land and his animals satisfied his sensibilities. This particular night, though, all he wanted was to get back to his home and the woman who was suddenly an anomaly in his life. And nothing about that made an ounce of sense to him. Nothing truly had made sense to him since the night Soledad had turned up in his barn.

Soledad stood with her hands on her hips, assessing her situation. Lyra had gone to sleep easily, seeming to like her new surroundings. Palmer had outdone himself, buying out half the department store to make them comfortable. She had no idea how she'd ever be able to repay his generosity. He'd made it clear that he didn't expect to be reimbursed, but she knew she could never not repay his benevolence.

There were still dozens of dry goods in shopping bags for her to sort through, but they would have to wait. She needed to start prepping the cake she'd been contracted to bake, though she was finding it difficult to focus on anything but her situation and Palmer Colton. She kicked herself for being so scattered thinking about a man who was clearly gun-shy. Not that she was interested in a relationship with him—or anyone. Because she wasn't. Or, at least, that was the story she told anyone who asked. She didn't have time to build a relationship with anyone while she built her business. The bakery was currently thriving and usually that would require every ounce of her attention. Any man would have to take a back seat. Now more than ever, though, since she had to reprioritize her life-goals list to place Lyra at the very top.

Soledad sighed softly. She couldn't help but think that maybe she'd made a mistake. If only she had listened to Palmer that first night and gone straight to the police. What if she hadn't overreacted, her concerns more responsive than reactionary. Maybe she'd gotten things overwhelmingly wrong... If only she had chosen differently, she and Lyra could be home, settling into their new routines with each other. She had a lengthy list of if-onlys, what-ifs and maybes, and alternate scenarios with Gavin dropping off the face of the earth. Then she remembered something her father had often said. *If a toad had wings, it wouldn't bump its ass when it hopped.* There was no room for what-ifs. She had to deal with the here and now and the choices she had made.

She had always believed that everything happened for a reason. Sometimes that reason was easy to see and sometimes fate put a man like Palmer Colton in the way, not caring if it made sense or not. She was overthinking everything and that had never served her well in the past. She needed to shake off all that was clouding her head and to stop thinking about Palmer Colton.

Palmer's kitchen was a dream come true. There was enough space for multiple people to cook and prep food comfortably. The Sub-Zero refrigerator and freezer and the Viking gas range were top-of-the-line. Double convection ovens as well as dual sinks would make her tasks easy and Soledad was grateful for it. She had just laid out her ingredients when Palmer and Jack came bounding through the door.

"Hey there," she said, greeting him warmly.

"Hey. You're getting started."

"I have a lot to do before tomorrow."

Palmer moved to the center island, leaning against the counter. He scanned the foodstuffs Soledad had begun to prep. "What are we making?" he questioned.

She gave him a bright smile. "We?"

He shrugged. "Usually, I'd be on the sofa watching CNN until I fell asleep. I thought I might give you a hand instead. Unless I'd be in the way?"

Soledad shook her head. "Not at all. I'd appreciate the company. I spend a lot of time in the bakery after hours working alone, so this will be a nice change."

"So, what are we making?"

"My famous carrot cake with a buttercream filling. I

don't do the usual cream-cheese frosting. It'll have three tiers and be decorated with a stained-glass design."

"Stained glass?"

"It's one of my specialties and I can knock it out fairly quickly."

"Then I'll just sit here and watch you work. If you need help, I'll be close by to give you instruction." He smirked, looking slightly dopey.

Soledad laughed. "The man has jokes."

Palmer laughed with her. "So, walk me through what you're doing," he said, seeming genuinely interested.

"The first thing is to actually bake the carrot cake."

"Easy peasy!"

Soledad's face lit up, amusement dancing in her eyes. "Really?"

He shrugged his broad shoulders. "My mother used to say it all the time. Whenever I thought anything felt like a challenge, she would say it was easy peasy."

"So did mine," Soledad responded. "I haven't heard that in forever." Her smile was wistful as she thought back to the matriarch of her family. Her mother had died five years ago, and the loss still stung. It had left a massive hole in her heart that nothing would ever be able to fill. She and Dominique had moved forward, finding a new normal that revolved around their father and helping him through the devastation. She missed her mother.

"I'm sorry for your loss," Palmer said as if reading her mind. "I remember your father speaking very fondly of her."

"She was the love of his life. They were so happy together. I had hoped to have that for myself someday."

Palmer's brow creased. "You don't anymore?"

"I'm now a single mother. I'm not sure many men are interested in a ready-made family."

"You'd be surprised."

"I would be. The men I've met recently are more interested in their own good time."

"That sounds like a story."

"One day maybe," she said.

The conversation paused as Soledad combined grated carrots and brown sugar together in a bowl. She added raisins and then set the mixture aside. In a second bowl, she beat the eggs until they were lemony yellow. Then she whisked in vanilla, oil and white sugar.

"Did you add enough vanilla?" Palmer questioned lightly. "I'd probably add a bit more."

Soledad giggled. "I'm pretty sure I have enough."

"It's your cake, but if it doesn't taste good, don't say I didn't warn you," he teased. "I'm a professional, so I know these things."

She rolled her eyes skyward, shaking her head slightly as he asked, "How long have you been doing this?"

"Since forever. I have always loved to bake. Cookies, cakes, pastries. I would make doughnuts every weekend in high school, and Dominique and I would eat until we were sick. In college, I really wasn't sure what I wanted to do with my life. It was Annie who convinced me to open the bakery. It was the best decision I've ever made. I leave work every day happy and I'm excited to go in the next day." There was a moment of hesitation as Soledad thought about her friend. She missed Annie!

Palmer gave her that moment before responding, understanding the pang of loss she was feeling. He nodded, then moved the conversation forward. "That's how I feel about the ranch. I love everything about this cowboy lifestyle."

"Did you always know you wanted to be a rancher?"

"I was hooked the first time my father put me on a horse and taught me to ride. I was eight, maybe nine, at the time."

Soledad smiled, amused that they had both discovered their passions at young ages and had both seen their dreams to fruition.

They paused again as Soledad added crushed pineapple to the egg mixture. She reached for a third bowl and added flour, baking soda, salt and cinnamon. She combined the wet and dry mixtures, then threw in the carrot combination. Her batter was complete with the addition of chopped walnuts.

"That came together fast," Palmer commented as she split the batter between three cake pans she had earlier greased and dusted with flour.

"That's what happens when you know what you're doing. But you know that, being professional and all." She slid the cake pans into the hot oven and set the timer.

Palmer laughed, amused by the hint of snark in her voice. "I, for one, am glad you perfected that doughnut recipe. I admit I'm a fan. I regularly stop at the bakery to get a dozen of your square doughnuts with your signature honey glaze. And the ones with the raspberry filling are to die for."

"The raspberry ones are my personal favorite. The filling is actually my mother's recipe." She grinned, excited to discover that he liked her pastries.

"I've also enjoyed the pecan pie and that twelve-layer chocolate cake with the caramel and nuts. And the cookies! All the cookies are to die for, but the pecan brittle with chocolate glaze are my all-time favorites. I get very excited when you have those in rotation."

Soledad giggled. "How often do you come by the bakery?"

He gave her a wry smile. "Truth?"

"Why would you lie?"

He shrugged. "I wouldn't, but I feel kind of awkward telling you this now." He chuckled softly.

Her forehead furrowed, confusion washing through her. "So, what is it? Have you *never* been to the bakery and you've been sending someone else to pick up your sweets?"

He shook his head, then answered. "I stop by a few times a week. I keep hoping I'll see you there, but you're never out front. Then, of course, I can't leave without buying something, and I try to buy everything because it's all so good." His face was suddenly flushed, color firing his cheeks a deep shade of red.

Soledad felt herself blush, as well, flattered by the compliment. There was an awkward pause that billowed between them. She dropped her gaze to the confectioners' sugar she'd poured into a bowl and took a deep breath. "Why didn't you talk to me at the engagement party the other week?" she asked, still not lifting her eyes to meet his. She prayed the question sounded nonchalant and that curiosity was the only thing he read into it.

Before Palmer could answer, a shrill cry echoed out of the new baby monitor on the counter. Lyra was not happy and wanted them to know it.

Soledad's eyes widened. "Do you mind checking on her?" she asked, finally throwing him a look. She had begun to prep the fondant for her cake, and her hands were full as she kneaded the sugar paste against her palms.

"No problem." Palmer slid off his wooden stool and headed down the hall toward the guest room.

As he left, she mumbled under her breath, *"Saved by the baby!"*

Watching Palmer walk away, Soledad suddenly had new appreciation for the handsome rancher. She realized his rough-and-tough exterior was actually a facade for his soft interior. He was shy and far more introverted than she had realized. She appreciated his effort to come out of his shell to let her in to know him. She imagined that he didn't often have women in his space, ruling his kitchen and practically taking over his home. Had the roles been reversed, she couldn't say with any surety that she would be as accommodating or as pleasant about it.

She moved to the ovens to check on her cakes. It was clear that Palmer didn't use his kitchen often, despite his skills with a scrambled egg. His appliances still had their installation labels, and she didn't think he had ever used his picture-perfect double ovens.

His voice suddenly cooed through the baby monitor

and Soledad's smile lifted sweetly as she eavesdropped on his conversation with Lyra.

"Hey, you," Palmer said, his tone soft and fluffy like cotton candy. "What are you crying for?" He leaned over the crib, untangling the blanket from around Lyra's chubby legs. He reached to pick the baby up into his arms, rocking her gently until her tears eased, leaving her with the hiccups. She pulled a tight fist into her mouth, chewing on her fingers. Jack sat staring up at him, his tail wagging from side to side. The dog barked.

"Easy, boy. I won't drop her. I promise."

Jack barked at him a second time.

Palmer shook his head. He carried Lyra to the changing table and laid her on the platform. She was wet and needed a diaper change. He reached for one of the Huggies he'd purchased. He continued to coo and make faces at the little girl, even blowing bubbles against her belly until she laughed. Minutes later, she had a dry bottom, her tears were gone, and she lay in his arms suckling a bottle of warm milk he'd collected from the kitchen.

Although navigating babies was not his thing, he was fairly decent at the job, he thought. Desiree had given him more than his fair share of practice with his nephew Danny. He thought about the little boy who had given the family a scare when he'd been kidnapped several times. Thinking they might not find his nephew had been devastating. Palmer never wanted to know that feeling again, and the thought of Gavin running off with Lyra felt too similar for any comfort.

Palmer smiled down at the little girl, Lyra's bright eyes dancing across his face as she studied him. She smiled back and a puddle of milk trickled onto her chin. He gently wiped the drool away with the cloth towel tossed over his shoulder.

"You've been through a lot, haven't you, little lady?" His voice was a loud whisper as he stared into her blue eyes. He brushed his hand lightly over her head and tousled the wisps of blond hair. "I'm so sorry about your mommy. My mommy died when I was a little boy, too. But it's going to be okay. I'm not sure what's going to happen, but I don't want you to worry, because that new mommy of yours is a pretty special lady. She is going to love you so hard! And I know she will do everything in her power to make you the happiest little girl in the whole wide world."

Lyra kicked her legs in response and smiled again, another puddle of milk rolling onto her chin.

"We really need to work on that," Palmer said as he dabbed the moisture away. "Try to swallow before you smile at me, kiddo."

Lyra tossed the bottle aside and stretched the length of her body. Lifting her to his shoulder, Palmer gently patted her back until she burped. Loudly.

"That sounded like an old man burp. That's not pretty, kid. Boys will think it's funny when you're nine. But it won't be cute when you're nineteen."

Lyra burped again.

Palmer chuckled softly. He nuzzled his face against her neck, inhaling the sweet scent of baby powder. "Old Jack and I will always be here if you need us, okay?

Don't you ever forget that," he whispered against her cheek.

Palmer felt his heart swell and the wealth of emotion surprised him. His concern for the baby's well-being was tangible, building like bricks on a wall. He instinctively knew he would fight tooth and nail to keep her from harm, and nothing and no one would keep him from protecting her.

He sat her on his lap, one large hand supporting her belly and the other gently caressing her back. Together, they were comfortable in the small recliner that decorated the room.

Lyra suddenly screeched, throwing herself toward Jack, who'd dropped his head onto Palmer's thigh. She grabbed two fistfuls of fur and held on, attempting to chew on the animal's ear. Jack licked her face, washing away remnants of milk with his tongue.

"Eww!" Palmer exclaimed, frowning. "Dog drool. Now you need a bath, little girl." He shook his head, holding her upright as she clawed at his dog and the dog nuzzled her in return. He felt a smile, full and expansive, lift his lips and chuckled again. "Something tells me you two are going to be trouble together."

Chapter 8

Soledad's eyes misted with tears as she tried not to cry into the royal icing she was preparing for the cake. Eavesdropping on Palmer as he'd tended to Lyra had pushed her to the edge of emotional overload. She was surprised by his tenderness with the baby, most especially knowing his disinterest in having children of his own. But he'd been so sweet and funny and entertaining that it had served to remind her of all the good that could be found in people if one just took the time to look.

For a man who was not interested in being anyone's father, Palmer played the role quite well. Had Lyra been blessed with a dad like that, things would be vastly different. Annie would still be alive, her little family at home and happy. Soledad would be in the bakery put-

ting the finishing touches on the next day's orders…
and Palmer Colton would only be a fleeting fantasy.
She couldn't help but wonder if they would ever have
become friends if she hadn't shown up needing to be
rescued. She suddenly thought of Gavin and how hor-
rific he had been as a father and as a husband, and her
stomach flipped remembering that he was still out there.
Still a threat to their safety.

It had gone quiet in the other room, just a low hum
echoing out of the speaker. Then Palmer began to sing.
He was a pitch-perfect baritone, his voice thick and rich
like sorghum molasses. Soledad stopped what she was
doing to listen as he serenaded Lyra. It took her a moment to realize he was singing "Can You Feel the Love
Tonight?" from Disney's *The Lion King* and singing it
quite beautifully. By the time he finished, happy tears
were streaming down Soledad's face and she'd ruined
a batch of her icing.

Palmer woke with a start. Lyra lay asleep on his chest,
the two of them still sitting in the oversize chair that
adorned the room. The little girl actually snored, and
her soft snorts made Palmer smile. He took a slow, deep
breath. As he blew it out, his chest falling, Lyra jumped
ever so slightly. Palmer tapped her gently against her
back.

He looked around the room, not knowing what time
it was or how long he'd been asleep. So much for being
a helping hand in the kitchen, he thought. He could
only begin to imagine what Soledad must be thinking

about him. Jack was sprawled across the queen-size bed, alone. There was no sign of Soledad.

He shifted forward in the seat, then stood slowly. Moving to the crib, he laid the infant down gently, then draped a cotton receiving blanket over her. He stared down at her, bemused that she could slumber so peacefully. He wondered if she had always been an easy baby or if there had been days and weeks of endless screaming and hours of no sleep for her parents. He brushed the pad of his finger across her forehead, taking a wisp of hair out of her face.

She was a cute little thing. And if she were his, there was no way he'd ever let her out of his sight. How her father could put her at risk baffled him, and then he thought of his own sperm donor and things he had done. Not everyone was meant to be a parent, Palmer thought, and too many folks should never have had kids.

Jack suddenly nuzzled his hand for attention.

"You need to go out, Jack?" Palmer questioned. "Come on, then," he said as the two eased out of the bedroom and headed for the kitchen.

It was dead quiet in the front room. Soledad's carrot cake sat on the counter and it was exquisite. The three tiers had been covered in fondant. She'd piped a floral design in black royal icing, the detailed outline showcasing her talent. He wasn't sure how she'd finished the areas of color that gave the cake its stained-glass effect, but he was duly impressed with her work. He imagined her friend Rachel would be, as well.

Soledad lay on the sofa, her back propped on a mound of pillows. She'd wrapped one of the wool blankets over her torso and was sleeping soundly. Palmer found himself staring, awed by how beautiful she was. Her hair was loose, the length of it framing her face. The warm temperature in the room complemented her olive complexion. She was glowing, and looked as angelic as Lyra when she slept. Jack nuzzled his hand again, more persistent about going outside.

"Okay, dog. Okay," Palmer muttered, tearing his eyes from the young woman. "You're a nuisance, do you know that?"

Jack panted, clearly disinterested in Palmer's opinion. When Palmer opened the door to let him out, he took off running, disappearing into the darkness.

When Palmer turned back around, he was surprised to find Soledad sitting upright, staring at him. She pulled a hand to her eyes and rubbed the sleep away.

"I'm sorry," he said softly. "I didn't mean to wake you."

"I didn't mean to doze off," she answered, giving him a slight smile. "You and Lyra were napping so peacefully I didn't want to wake you. I sat out here to catch my breath and that's all I remember."

"I hadn't planned to fall asleep, either," he said. "I think the stress of the past forty-eight hours finally caught up with us both."

"I'm actually surprised I was able to relax," Soledad said with a soft sigh. "I feel safe here."

Something in her words suddenly had him thinking about the future and what time would eventually bring to them. What would happen when it was all over, and they went back to their own circles? When she no longer needed his protection, and they went back to being passing acquaintances? He was glad she felt safe, but he couldn't let himself forget that it was only temporary. That he couldn't keep either of them forever. A wave of melancholy hit him in the chest and he blew a wistful sigh past his lips. He shook the thoughts from his head and changed the subject as he moved to the refrigerator. "I'm hungry. Can I get you something?"

"What are you having?"

"I have some sliced turkey in the fridge. I can make us sandwiches," he answered.

Soledad nodded as she threw her legs off the sofa. "A turkey sandwich works for me. Do you have any cranberry sauce?"

He grinned. "That's the only way to eat a turkey sandwich."

"It would be sheer perfection if you also had some stuffing."

Palmer laughed. "You're a foodie after my own heart. Tell me you also like grilled cheese."

"I'll have to make you my very special grilled Swiss on rye with bacon and tomato."

"Okay, that does sound good, but not as good as my four-cheese grilled cheese on toasted garlic bread. Or my grilled Brie with ham, caramelized onions and apple compote."

"I do my grilled Brie with candied bacon and apricot jam."

"It sounds like you and I are going to have to have a grilled-cheese runoff to find the best sandwich."

Soledad laughed. "You'll lose. You know that, right?"

"Says you, but I'd put my money on me and my favorite cast-iron grilled-cheese pan. I bet you don't have a pan specifically for grilled cheese."

She giggled. "You might have me beat there."

"The pan is important to the artistry of grilled cheese. Much like your cake pans are important to your cakes."

"Touché!"

He grinned, the smile full and wide. She made him laugh, her quick wit fueling the smart quips. He liked that she didn't take herself, or him, too seriously. He suddenly realized he was going to miss it when she wasn't there anymore, the thought like a punch to his midsection. He took a deep breath and held it.

Palmer suddenly cocked his head to the side. His mood shifted from relaxed to tense in the blink of an eye as he tossed her a look. "Did you hear that?" he breathed loudly as he hurried to the door.

Soledad whispered back, "Hear what?"

As Palmer pulled open the door, the noise was clearer. Jack was barking, making a loud fuss about something. He clearly wasn't happy. And then the dog cried out as if something or someone had caused him pain.

"Bedroom. Now!" Palmer snapped as he shut off the lights, darkening the room. The hall gave off just enough illumination for them both to still see. He reached for the rifle that rested by the door where he'd last placed it and rushed out into the late-night air, slamming the door behind him.

* * *

Soledad ran quickly to the guest bedroom to check on Lyra. The baby was sleeping, undisturbed by whatever was going on. She debated whether she would stay in place and lock the two of them inside but decided fairly quickly that a good defense was an even better offense. Rushing back to the kitchen, she grabbed the largest butcher knife in his knife collection and braced herself for a fight, her eyes dancing between the door and the windows.

Waiting for something to happen, for anything to bring this to an end, was painful at best. It had her head spinning and she was feeling completely out of control. Soledad paced back and forth, then hurried to the door and flung it open. She stared out into the dark, hoping for a glimpse of Palmer, or Jack, or any friendly face that wasn't wanting to cause them harm. She tilted her head to listen for any sound or noise that would calm her nerves and let her know that all was well.

But calm didn't come, terror taking its place instead. Gunshots rang through the air. *Bang! Bang! Bang!* One explosion after another echoed too close for comfort. The shots sounded like they were being fired from a small-caliber handgun, and knowing that pushed her emotions right to the edge. She heard Palmer's rifle fire once, and then hearing it a second time sent her over the edge into an abyss.

The next few minutes felt like an eternity. Panic washed over Soledad in heavy waves. Her mind was mush, every awful thing she could imagine once again playing out like some dark thriller on a big screen. She cursed. Loudly. The level of profanity was the stuff of sailors and adolescent boys discovering they could use their lengthy list of bad words in a complete sentence.

Unable to fathom who was shooting, or what she needed to do, Soledad slammed the door closed. She backed herself against the counter, prepared to knife any stranger who came through the door.

It suddenly felt like a perfect storm had converged around them. Just as Soledad mentally prepared herself for the worst, the house alarm sounded, a deep, loud siren that screeched like fingernails against a chalkboard. Just then, Palmer came barreling through the entrance, shouting her name. Jack limped in beside him, panting heavily. A streak of bright red blood matted the white fur on his chest. The house phone began to ring, and as if on cue, Lyra started crying at the top of her little lungs.

Palmer moved to Soledad's side, pressing a warm palm to her cheek. "Are you okay?" he asked, his gaze skipping over her face as concern seeped from his eyes.

She shook her head, tears beginning to rise in her eyes. "No. You scared me. I thought you were dead!" She tossed the knife in her hand onto the marble counter.

He smiled. "I don't plan to go down that easy. Besides, I still need to get myself right with God. Maybe go to church a time or two," he joked.

Soledad rolled her eyes skyward, not at all amused at his attempt at humor. She was Catholic and you didn't play when it came to the Father, the Son, and the Holy Spirit. "Was it Gavin? Was it him shooting at you?"

Palmer shrugged. "Probably, but I'm not sure. They were too far away for me to see exactly, but they shot first and I shot back! I think I hit whoever it was. He's bleeding, I know that." He moved to the alarm box and entered in the passcode to stop the siren. Lyra was still crying, her wails having transitioned to a full-scale sob.

The phone had stopped ringing but began again. "That's the alarm service," Palmer said. "I'm sure they've already dispatched the police. You'll need to stay out of sight unless you're ready to come out of hiding."

"No," she answered with a shake of her head.

"Then my bedroom is the safest place. Lock the door. The room is soundproof, so even if Lyra cries, they won't hear you."

Soledad eyed him oddly. "Why is your master bedroom soundproof?"

"I'm a screamer when I orgasm," he said nonchalantly.

Soledad blinked, her lashes batting up and down as she stared at him. "Are you serious?"

He laughed. "No. I just thought it would lighten the moment."

She shook her head. She bit back her snarky response as Lyra's cries got louder, the baby girl on the verge of hysteria.

Soledad shook her head. "My poor baby. I need to settle Lyra down," she said as she scurried down the length of the hallway to the guest bedroom.

Palmer finally answered the phone. "This is Palmer

Colton… Yes…yes…the code is 547893… Yes…there was an intruder… I think I shot him… Yes…thank you." He hung up, his eyes turning toward Jack, who looked like he'd just gone ten rounds in a heavyweight fight.

"Hey, big boy," he said, grabbing a dishrag from the counter and dropping to the floor to inspect the dog's injuries. He swiped at the blood on the dog's fur, grateful that it wasn't his. Jack licked his hand, then lay against the tiled floor and closed his eyes. Giving in to the exhaustion, he began to snore softly.

Outside, the first police car was pulling onto the property. The car lights were flashing, and the siren sounded. Palmer stood as two additional patrol cars followed behind it.

Soledad rushed into the kitchen, to the refrigerator. She grabbed a bottle of milk from inside. Lyra was in her arms, no longer crying. The baby looked around, trying to make sense of the moment. Palmer pressed his hand to Soledad's arm and leaned in to kiss the child's forehead. Lyra grabbed at his chin and giggled.

"Do you need to warm that?" he asked, gesturing at the baby bottle.

Soledad shook her head as she stole a quick glance out the bay window. "I'll run it under hot water in the bathroom. It'll warm quickly."

He nodded. "Just lock the door. I'll do my best to keep them out of the house," he said softly. He gave her a gentle pat against her back, his touch like the sweetest balm. Then he headed outside to meet with the officers.

Loyal Readers
FREE BOOKS Voucher

We're giving away THOUSANDS

of FREE BOOKS

Suspense

Suspenseful Romance

Don't Miss Out! Send for Your Free Books Today!

Get up to 4
FREE FABULOUS BOOKS
You Love!

To thank you for being a loyal reader we'd like to send you up to 4 FREE BOOKS, absolutely free.

Just write "YES" on the Loyal Reader Voucher and we'll send you up to 4 Free Books and Free Mystery Gifts, altogether worth over $20, as a way of saying thank you for being a loyal reader.

Try **Harlequin® Romantic Suspense** books featuring heart-racing page-turners with unexpected plot twists and irresistible chemistry that will keep you guessing to the very end.

Try **Harlequin Intrigue® Larger-Print** books featuring action-packed stories that will keep you on the edge of your seat. Solve the crime and deliver justice at all costs.

Or **TRY BOTH!**

We are so glad you love the books as much as we do and can't wait to send you great new books.

So don't miss out, return your Loyal Reader Voucher Today!

Pam Powers

LOYAL READER
FREE BOOKS VOUCHER

YES! I Love Reading, please send me up to 4 FREE BOOKS and Free Mystery Gifts from the series I select.

Just write in "YES" on the dotted line below then return this card today and we'll send your free books & gifts asap!

➡ YES ⬅

Which do you prefer?

| ☐ **Harlequin® Romantic Suspense** 240/340 HDL GRHP | ☐ **Harlequin Intrigue® Larger-Print** 199/399 HDL GRHP | ☐ **BOTH** 240/340 & 199/399 HDL GRHZ |

FIRST NAME

LAST NAME

ADDRESS

APT.#

CITY

STATE/PROV.

ZIP/POSTAL CODE

EMAIL ☐ Please check this box if you would like to receive newsletters and promotional emails from Harlequin Enterprises ULC and its affiliates. You can unsubscribe anytime.

HI/HRS-520-LR21

* * *

Palmer wasn't prepared when the silver Honda Accord pulled in line with the Grave Gulch police cars in front of his home. He had already given a statement to the first officers who'd arrived on-site. They had confiscated his rifle and were now canvasing the property for signs of the intruder who had fired on him and possibly taken a bullet for his efforts. The line of flashlights waving about in the distance was formidable. Their bright glow against the dark canvas was slightly eerie. But whoever had breached the property had come in on foot, not having the code to unlock the gates, and the officers were walking the fields to make sure there was no body there.

He wasn't surprised when Troy stepped out of the driver's side of the car, but he had not anticipated his cousin Stanton's exit from the passenger side. He groaned, not in the mood for what he knew would come. The two men hurried to his side and it started as soon as he greeted them.

"Detective Colton. Mr. Colton. I'm surprised to see you two. What brings you here this time of night?" he said facetiously.

"We were enjoying a late dinner with Evangeline and Dominique when we heard the call on Troy's police scanner," Stanton answered.

"Are you okay?" Troy asked as the two men embraced.

"I've been better," Palmer answered. "It's not every day someone is shooting at you on your own property."

"No, it's not. Did you see who it was? Was it anyone you recognized?"

Palmer shrugged. "It was too dark. Someone was firing at me and I fired back. Two shots. And whoever it was kicked my dog. But I think one of my shots landed. Either that or Jack bit a good chunk out of him and made him bleed."

Troy laughed. "I was wondering where Jack was. He's usually right by your side."

"He was traumatized. He's in the house, shaking it off."

Stanton shook his head. "Do you think this was personal? Did you piss someone off?"

"No," Palmer said firmly. "I don't think it has anything at all to do with me."

Troy nodded. "You might be right. We heard from Soledad today. She witnessed that shooting last night. She's scared and won't come in. We've had teams out looking for the husband most of the day. We think he might still be in the area and we're sure he's looking for Soledad, too. Someone trashed her apartment before we got there this afternoon."

"You think it might have been him?" Palmer asked.

"I don't think it's coincidental. And I don't think she should go back there until we apprehend him."

"Do you think it was him shooting at me?"

"You never know. There are only two or three homes close to where the murder happened. Yours happens to be one of them. He might have hedged his bet that Soledad was here. Your neighbors reported a strange man pretending to be police coming to question them about her. Did he stop here, by chance?"

"Yeah, as a matter of fact. It was late. I was in the barn, tending to my new horse, when he drove up."

"And you didn't say something?"

"No one asked and I've had other things on my mind."

"Like buying baby clothes for an employee and his family?" There was a hint of sarcasm in Troy's voice.

Palmer's gaze narrowed. The static vibrating in the air between the two brothers had become dense.

Palmer took a deep breath. "Just cut to the chase. Should I be worried?"

"That depends," Troy said smugly. "Are you harboring our witness?"

Stanton laughed, amused by the two brothers as they stared each other down.

There was a moment of pause before Palmer responded. "And if I were?"

Troy heaved a heavy sigh. "Then I have to trust you'll do whatever you need to do to keep her safe. Just don't tell Melissa," he said, his voice dropping an octave as he tossed a look over his shoulder. "Chief Colton is not happy about all this."

"Melissa has a lot on her shoulders right now," Stanton answered. "She'd probably have problems with it, but it wouldn't be personal. I doubt she'd arrest you or anything."

"Oh, she'd arrest him. In a heartbeat. You know Melissa doesn't play when it comes to the law. She'd hem you up on obstructing an investigation without even blinking," Troy quipped.

Palmer shook his head. He knew his brother was

right about their cousin, but he wasn't willing to put Soledad or Lyra in harm's way. Not even for family he trusted. Maybe it was obstruction, but they'd get over it. "Then I guess if I were harboring your witness, I wouldn't go out of my way to let you or my cousin know about it."

"That might be wise," Stanton said with a hearty chuckle.

"Excuse me for a minute," Troy interjected. "Let me find out where they are with their search. I'll be back as soon as I know what's going on."

Palmer watched his brother walk away, seeking the officer who'd taken his initial statement.

"So, are you harboring the witness?" Stanton questioned when it was just the two of them standing together. "Because Dominique is worried sick about her sister."

"I need you to do me a favor," Palmer said, ignoring the question.

"What's that?"

"Come by later today and pick up a package for me. I'll tell you where to deliver it then."

"Is it important?"

Palmer nodded. "Yeah, very important, and I don't feel comfortable leaving the house right now. I'll owe you one if you do this for me."

"I got you," Stanton responded. "Ten o'clock too early?"

"That'll work. I'll see you at ten. Thank you."

The two continued to chat, the conversation casual. His arms folded over his chest, Palmer thought about his brother's question and knew his face had probably given him away. He was good, but not that good. He rarely lied and had never had much of a poker face. Any one of his siblings asking too many questions had always been his downfall. It had been that way since they were children. Keeping Soledad and Lyra's whereabouts a secret was more for him than them, he mused. Admittedly, he didn't want to risk losing them. He hated keeping the truth from his family, but it was well worth the repercussions he knew would come later.

Troy returned minutes later. "They found blood on the south gate. And tire tracks. It looks like someone sped off in a hurry. We'll send a team out at daybreak when they're able to see more. Our forensic experts will also come by."

Palmer nodded. "Do you need anything else from me?"

"No. Unless you have something you'd like to share?"

"I don't," Palmer said smugly. "I can't tell you any more than you already know."

The two men exchanged a look and Troy nodded. "We'll step up our patrols at each of your entrances. I'll order a car to sit at the main gate. Just in case. Meanwhile, they've already put in a call to the hospital and medical clinics to look out for anyone showing up with a gunshot wound. Or a dog bite. I spoke to Stavros personally," Troy concluded. "If he shows up while he's on duty, we'll know about it instantly." Stavros Makris was their sister Desiree's fiancé and an emergency room physician.

"Well, if you need anything more, you know where

to find me," Palmer said. "I'm going to go turn in. I've got a long day tomorrow. I need some sleep."

Troy gave him a nod. "You're good. My guys will be out of here momentarily and you can get back to whatever it was you were doing." He paused. "What were you doing?"

Palmer smiled. "Minding my own business. You?"

The other two men chuckled.

"If you can think of anything else that you want to tell us, you know where I am," Troy said, heading back to his car. "Until then, please don't let anything happen to our witness."

Stanton gave Palmer a fist bump as he winked. "See you at ten, cousin." As he turned away, Palmer called his name one last time.

"Yeah?"

"Tell Dominique she doesn't have to worry. Soledad is safe."

Minutes later, Palmer stood in his kitchen as Soledad peppered him with questions about all that had happened. She wanted every detail of what had been said and who had said it. Palmer obliged her to the best of his ability, understanding that she was feeling out of the loop with everything going on. Answering her queries also helped him to sort the pieces to make sense of it all.

She suddenly went silent, seeming to fall into thoughts that didn't include him. It was only when their eyes connected again that he realized maybe whatever she was thinking did, in fact, have something to do with the two of them. Then again, he mused as she looked away, maybe it was all just wishful thinking on his part.

"Palmer, are you okay?" Soledad asked, the question shaking him from his thoughts.

"My brother knows you're here."

"Your brother the detective? You told him?"

"He asked and I didn't deny it. He also said you shouldn't go home. Someone trashed your apartment. They think it was Gavin Stone."

"He was in my home? Going through my things?" She suddenly began to shake.

"They're going to find him, Soledad. You just have to be patient."

Soledad wrapped her arms around her torso, her head waving from side to side. She blew a soft sigh. "So, what now? Are they going to come arrest me? Or take Lyra away?"

"No, I don't think so." Palmer wanted to pull her into his arms and hold her close. He fought the urge, clenching his fists tightly as they stared at one another.

"This is such a mess," she muttered.

As Palmer watched her, something he didn't recognize crossed her face. She no longer looked frightened or even angry. There was something like a quiet resolve in her eyes, determination and focus gleaming in her stare.

"I'm exhausted," she said. "I think I'm going to call it a night."

Palmer nodded. "Are *you* okay?" he questioned, not sure what else to ask, or if he should ask anything at all.

Soledad shrugged. "I'm not sure what I am besides

tired. I'm just ready for this to be over so Lyra and I can go home."

Palmer didn't like how she was feeling but he understood it. He was as exhausted with it all as she was, yet, deep down, he didn't want her to go. He actually enjoyed having her around. But he couldn't tell her that and he wasn't sure he should even be thinking it.

"Sleep well, Soledad," he said instead.

She gave him the faintest smile as she stepped past him. "You, too, Palmer."

Sleep didn't come quick enough. Soledad lay staring at the ceiling, trying to make sense out of the nonsense that had become her life. She missed her routines, her bakery and her cat. She trusted that Dominique would step in to care for the feline while she was gone, but it wasn't enough. She just wanted to feel normal again, whatever that looked like. She just knew it didn't look like she was a fugitive on the run, hiding out with a man she would have enjoyed getting to know more had their circumstances been different.

There was a part of her that wanted to be angry with Palmer, but with all that he had done and continued to do to keep her safe, she couldn't find enough energy to give him attitude. She instinctively knew that his telling his brother was all about him being honest and upstanding and nothing about him trying to hurt her. She was just bothered by him sharing a secret that was supposed to have been kept between the two of them. She knew that even that thought was irrational on her part.

The more she thought about Palmer, the more Soledad knew he would never purposely cause her an ounce of pain. He would do everything in his power to protect her. She realized that, other than her father, there had been no man before him she could have said that about. And still, in all honesty, she didn't have a clue if he was genuinely interested in her or was just standing by her side because it was the right thing to do. And, if he was nothing else, Palmer was honorable. She had questions for him and wondered if he had answers he was willing to give.

Lying to his family wasn't something Palmer did. He didn't always tell them everything, but he never lied outright. Troy discovering that Soledad was there had been inevitable when the two had run into each other at the department store. His cart full of baby items had been telling, and even he hadn't believed his own explanation.

He rolled from one side of his king-size bed to the other. Jack slept at his feet, lifting his head briefly to give Palmer a look before settling down. Palmer was finding sleep to be elusive, too much spinning around in his head.

Palmer wished things were different and wondered if they would have been if he had asked Soledad to dinner the night of the engagement party. If they could have had a relationship had he not been a coward, given the number of times he'd gone to the bakery hoping to see her. If he'd had a great pickup line or two or three and been smoother, like his brother and cousins. He wished they'd gotten to know each other over bottles of good wine and questionable Netflix movies. He had a lengthy wish list when it came to Soledad de la Vega.

Chapter 9

An hour later, a knock sounded at Palmer's bedroom door and surprised him. Startled, he jumped, thinking something might be wrong. When he snatched the door open, Soledad stood on the other side. Her eyes were wide, her expression anxious. She was wearing his T-shirt, the oversize garment draped like a dress around her petite frame. Her legs and feet were bare, her toes painted a brilliant shade of bright pink. She'd pulled her hair up into a messy bun and her skin was makeup free and flawless. She was gorgeous and he felt a wave of heat shift every muscle in his lower quadrant. She bit down against her bottom lip as she met his stare.

"What's wrong?" he asked, curiosity painting his expression.

Soledad shook her head. "Nothing. I couldn't sleep and I wanted to ask you something. Did I wake you?"

Relief flooded Palmer's spirit and he felt his whole body sink into the calm. He shook his head. "No. I couldn't sleep, either. I've had a lot on my mind."

"Me, too," she said as she pushed past him. She moved to the king-size bed and took a seat, folding her legs beneath her. She carried the baby monitor in her hand. "Do you mind?" she asked, gesturing with her free hand as she set the monitor on the nightstand.

Palmer shrugged. "If you're comfortable, I'm fine." He moved to the other side of the bed and took his own seat, leaning against the multitude of pillows. Extending his legs, he pulled a pillow into his lap. "What's bothering you?"

"At the engagement party, I felt like there might have been a connection between us, but then you wouldn't speak to me. In fact, I thought you were avoiding me. What was going on? I really need to know."

She was staring at him intently, and Palmer's cheeks warmed with color. The temperature in the room had suddenly risen tenfold.

Palmer was a pro at deflection. He changed the conversation. "Do you know you are the only woman who has ever been in my bedroom and my bed?" He shot her a quick look, then dropped his eyes to the bedclothes.

The words had slipped past his lips before he could catch them. It had not been his intention to share that tidbit of information. No matter how true it was. He hadn't planned to explain that his home and that bedroom had been built with his future wife in mind. Even though he no longer considered marriage to be on the table, the space was sacred, never intended for any random woman he'd been inclined to bed.

Soledad blinked, her lengthy lashes fluttering. It looked as if the comment had surprised her, totally unexpected, and the faintest hint of amusement flickered in her eyes. "I find that very difficult to believe."

He laughed. "Why?"

"You're handsome, intelligent, kind, generous…" She paused. "You're what most people consider a good catch," she concluded. "I find it difficult to believe that not one woman has been able to capture your attention and hold it long enough to make it into your bed."

He hesitated, reflecting on her words. Finally, he said, "One woman has."

Soledad's brows lifted. "This woman must be pretty special."

"I think so. It's why she's sitting on my bed in the middle of the night interrogating me."

Soledad's lips rose in the sweetest smile, spreading full and wide across her face. She laughed. "I asked a question. One question is hardly an interrogation."

"It feels like an interrogation."

"That's because I still can't believe there haven't been many women in your life or your bed."

"I've had to be protective of my personal space. That's why I rarely bring any woman to my home. My home is my sanctuary, and I haven't wanted that to be disrupted. And I've been selfish. I like my peace, and when there's someone else in your space, you have to be considerate of their wants and needs."

"Then along came me and Lyra."

He smiled. "You two have actually been a very pleasant disruption. Of sorts."

"And other women haven't?"

He shrugged. "Too many I've known have wanted a long-term relationship. I don't do long-term. I'm always clear about that. I let anyone I date know up front what will and what won't happen, and I typically don't do any relationship longer than a week. It keeps a woman from becoming too attached and then wanting to move in and be married."

"Just to be clear, they call that a one-night stand. And, instead of being a good catch, that kind of makes you a jerk."

"Maybe, but I'm honest," he replied. "You know what you'll get with me from jump."

"And a woman won't get marriage and children?"

"She'll get friendship, companionship and appreciation. I've never been able to promise anything else."

Soledad heaved a deep sigh. She lay back against the mattress, pulling her arms up and over her head. She realized there was still so much about Palmer that she didn't know, but what she was certain of was believing what he told her. She'd dated more than her fair share of men who said what they meant and meant what they said, and she hadn't wanted to believe them. Not believing them, or thinking she could change their minds, had only gotten her heart broken. She wasn't interested in Palmer Colton breaking her heart.

"So, tell me again why you ignored me at the party?" she persisted.

Palmer crossed his legs at the ankles, shifting in his seat. "Because I overheard a conversation you were having with your sister about being thirty and your biological clock starting to tick. It was clear you wanted the dream—the husband, kids, dog and house with the picket fence. I knew I couldn't give that to you, so there was no point in me wasting your time."

The quiet in the room was suddenly stifling. Soledad was trying to reconcile how a man could have convictions so severe that they would potentially leave him alone and unhappy in his old age. Her heart suddenly hurt for Palmer. That he would want that for himself was devastating. Because, she thought, he was a man who deserved so much more.

Rolling onto her stomach, Soledad lifted herself onto her elbows. She stared at him, searching for the words that would make sense of it all, but she had none. The hurt in Palmer's heart had to be unfathomable. She reached for one of his pillows and pulled it beneath her head instead.

Palmer shifted onto his side to face her. He reached out his hand to brush her hair from her face. She was hauntingly beautiful, and he imagined many men had fallen head over heels in love with her. He knew that if he wasn't careful, falling for her would be easy to do. He snatched his hand back, clutching his fingers as if he'd been burned.

"What was your first happy memory as a child?" Soledad asked.

The question was unexpected. He paused to consider his answer before he spoke. "It was my first birthday after my adoption was finalized," he said finally. "I had riding lessons, and it was the best time. There was ice cream and chocolate cake and all my friends. That was a good day."

"Sounds like someone wanted you to feel very special that day."

"My mother made every day feel special," Palmer said as he slipped into thought, memories placing a smile across his face. He suddenly yawned.

"Don't do that. It's contagious," Soledad said as she yawned with him.

"I think I've finally hit my wall," he said. "I'm having a hard time keeping my eyes open."

"I know the feeling." Soledad settled comfortably against the mattress. "I should probably go back to my room..." she said but didn't move.

"Don't leave on my account," Palmer muttered, losing his own struggle to stay awake.

"I wasn't," Soledad said with the slightest giggle.

Palmer smiled, his body beginning to give in to the slumber that was suddenly determined to drag him into a deep sleep. "Good night, Soledad," he muttered. "Sweet dreams."

Chapter 10

Soledad was laughing hysterically when Palmer entered the kitchen later that morning. Lyra was on the family room floor propped against her pillows and Jack was playing his version of peekaboo with her. There were squeals and barks, and a joy so immense that Palmer immediately smiled. The energy in the room reminded him of those days when he, Troy, Desiree, Annalise and Grace were kids, and their home was everything any child could have wanted. When life was simple, and easy, and he couldn't have imagined wanting anything else for himself. Before the days of adulthood and responsibility and the fear of failure existed.

Soledad's grin was canyon wide as she greeted him. "Good morning."

"Good morning. How long have you been up?"

"I only got about two hours of sleep before Lyra woke me up. You were out like a light, so I didn't bother you."

"I should have gotten up when you did. I'm late for my morning rounds."

"Coffee?" she asked, holding up an overlarge mug.

He nodded. "Black coffee, please. And it needs to be superstrong."

"I've got you covered." Soledad filled the mug and placed it in front of him as he took a seat at the counter. She slid a plate of freshly baked muffins toward him, as well. "Did you know you have blueberries growing out by the barn?" she said.

Palmer shrugged. "I know the ranch hands sometimes pick them. I also have apple and pear trees on the other side of the west pasture. I don't bother with those, either. Why were you outside?"

"Lyra had fallen back to sleep and I needed to clear my head. Since the baby monitor was still in the bedroom with you, I knew you'd hear her if she woke up again, so I took a quick walk. No one saw me."

"You sure about that?"

"I don't think anyone saw me," she said.

"You hope no one saw you," Palmer countered. "I don't like you taking risks like that, Soledad. What if something had happened to you?" His words were steeped in concern, his tone reprimanding. "You can't be too careful."

She eyed him with a raised brow. "I appreciate your concern, but I was fine, Palmer."

"This time," he quipped as he took a bite of the blueberry muffin. He suddenly hummed, licking his fingers and grabbing for another muffin. "These are really good."

"I know. It's the fresh blueberries," Soledad said, her expression smug as she giggled softly.

Palmer shook his head, amusement lifting his own smile. The look she gave him was teasing and he couldn't help but wonder if she tasted as sweet as the blueberry treats she was plying him with. Needing a distraction before he did or said something that might get him in trouble, he shifted his attention from Soledad to the dynamic duo on the floor.

Jack was acting like he was still a pup with endless energy. He would bounce and bark, and Lyra would burst with giggles. Palmer couldn't help but laugh with her.

"Soledad, look!" he suddenly exclaimed. Excitement burst across his face and his chest pushed forward with undeniable pride.

She turned to see that Lyra had pulled herself forward and was sitting upright all on her own, without any assistance. The little girl reached for the dog, trying to grab his tail, and then she toppled over, falling like the pins at the end of a bowling lane. Palmer shot Soledad a glance and the two busted out laughing.

Soledad rushed to the baby's side. Lyra struggled to sit upright as Jack nudged her, trying to help. "Look at you, sweet pea. Such a big girl," Soledad soothed.

Lyra responded with a bloodcurdling scream followed by hysterical giggles.

Palmer swallowed the last bite of his muffin, then

moved to the floor to join the trio. For the next few minutes, they all played together effortlessly. Palmer cooed with Soledad, and Lyra bobbed up and down like a windup toy gone awry. He found himself in awe of the ease with which they felt like a family. Like *his* family.

Lyra suddenly fell back against the pillows, clearly ready to be done with them all. "Babababa ba…" she sputtered.

"You want a bottle, don't you, sweet pea? And I think you need a fresh diaper," Soledad said softly.

Palmer wriggled his nose. "I'll grab that bottle. You can have the diaper."

"Chicken."

"Damn right," he returned. "She's like a miniature toxic waste dump. It's downright scary. Jack's not even that bad."

Soledad laughed as she scooped Lyra up into her arms and nuzzled her nose into the folds of the baby's neck. "Stinky butt!" She laid the child on a vinyl pad and reached for a dry diaper.

"Told you."

"Can you still deliver my cake for me today?" Soledad questioned.

"I can't, but I've made arrangements for it to be delivered."

Her eyes widened. "Arrangements with who?"

"Someone I trust. In fact, he'll be here at ten."

"That's in five minutes."

Palmer shrugged. "Okay. Is it not ready to go?"

"It's ready. I just…well…" She shrugged. "This is

especially important to me. I don't want to trust it to just anyone."

"Because it's important to you, it's important to me, and since you entrusted me with getting the task done, I'm going to make that happen."

"But who did you—" Soledad started to ask when there was a knock on the door, interrupting their conversation.

Panic washed over her. She started down the hallway, Lyra held tightly to her chest, when Palmer stopped her. He pressed his hand against her forearm, his fingers teasing her skin. "It'll be okay," he said. "You don't have to hide. It's your delivery guy."

Soledad looked confused as she came to an abrupt stop. She watched as Palmer stepped up to the door and pulled it open. But he was shocked when Dominique de la Vega came barreling into the room, Stanton following sheepishly behind her.

"What the hell?" Palmer snapped, giving his cousin a narrowed side-eye. "Who else did you tell?"

"He only told me," Dominique answered. "We would never do anything to put my sister in harm's way."

Soledad practically threw herself into her sister's arms, the two women hugging tightly. Lyra was clutched between them, looking from one to the other as she tried to decipher what was going on and breathe at the same time.

Palmer and Stanton stood side by side, each giving the other a look. Stanton shrugged his shoulders. "I couldn't not tell her, Palmer. They are sisters. And, besides, she always knows when I'm lying, or keeping something from her. I had to tell her. She wasn't going to stop worrying until she could lay eyes on Soledad."

Palmer gave him an eye roll as he gestured with his head. "Come on in. Looks like you're going to be here for a minute."

Dominique kissed her sister's cheek, then took the baby from her arms. "You've had me scared to death!" she exclaimed.

"Sorry. I didn't want to risk putting anyone else in harm's way. Gavin is dangerous."

"I am so sorry that you had to go through that, but you really need to come home. You know Dad isn't going to let anything happen to you. Right now, you're out here in the middle of nowhere. That can't be a good thing with that psycho looking for you."

"I really am good, Dominique. I feel safe here."

Dominique tossed Palmer a look. "He's not holding you hostage, is he?"

Soledad laughed. "He's been a real champ about the whole thing."

Her sister looked him up and down. "I just bet he has," she said snidely. "Maybe we should give him a cookie for all his hard work. Maybe one of those ones with the cream filling and chocolate icing on top that you make for special occasions?"

The two men exchanged a look. Stanton shook his head, fighting not to laugh out loud.

Palmer was not amused. Their teasing had him feeling out of sorts. When it came to sisters, it was usually him and his brother making light work of the girls, not the girls besting them. Dominique and Soledad had him feeling like he was in a tag-team match with no one to tag him out and he was losing. "I think this would be a good time for me to go make my rounds. I shouldn't be too long," he said, excusing himself from the room.

"I think I'll make those rounds with you," Stanton said, following on his cousin's heels as he moved toward the door.

"That's a very good idea. You two should do that," Dominique called after the duo. She laughed heartily as they quickly made their escape.

When the men were out of sight, Dominique began to walk through the home, taking it all in. "Give me a tour," she said.

Soledad shook her head as she followed her sister from room to room. "You are so nosy."

"I am," Dominique responded. "And he's got a very nice place."

Soledad nodded in agreement. "It's been very comfortable. He's been such a blessing to me and Lyra."

Her sister paused in the guest bedroom. "Isn't this cute. He did all this?"

"He did," Soledad answered. "Palmer went on a full-scale shopping spree to make us comfortable."

"Hmm." Dominique gave Soledad a look as she moved on to the master bedroom. "This is very nice. Have you poked around?"

"Of course not. Why would I poke around in the man's stuff? I'm not trying to get thrown out."

Dominique's expression brimmed with exasperation. "To make sure he's on the up-and-up. That's why." She moved to the nightstand and pulled open the drawer to peek inside.

"Your journalistic claws are showing. You're like one of those writers from a supermarket tabloid going through people's trash to get a story. Don't do that. It's not pretty."

Dominique laughed. "I do whatever I need to do to get the story." She pulled a firearm from the drawer, a Smith & Wesson .45 semiautomatic pistol. After checking to see if it was loaded, she slid it back where she'd found it. "FYI, he keeps one in the chamber," she said.

Soledad was still shaking her head.

Dominique suddenly grinned, pulling a blue box from inside the drawer. "'Trojan Bareback Lubricated Condoms. Size large,'" she read, waving the container at her sister. "And it hasn't been opened. So, either he goes through them quickly or he doesn't use them often. It should be interesting for you to find out."

Soledad felt her face flush with color. "You need to stop invading the man's privacy before you get me evicted. Put those back."

Dominique laughed as she slid the box into the drawer and closed it. "You'd be amazed what you can find out about a man by going through his things."

"I can't believe you," Soledad said as she led the way out of the room.

Dominique was still chuckling, amusement dancing across her face. Soledad laughed with her sister, shaking her head as her twin settled on the couch, cuddling Lyra in her lap. She took the seat beside her twin. "So, why were you giving Stanton and Palmer a hard time?"

"It keeps them on their toes. Stanton never knows what to expect. That's how I keep the romance alive in our relationship." She winked at her sister.

"How are the wedding plans going?" Soledad asked.

"They'd be going better if my maid of honor was around to help me with them."

Soledad sighed. "Sorry," she said as she leaned back against the sofa. "I hate that this is happening. My whole life is on hold. I barely know what day it is, and I haven't accomplished a third of the things I need to accomplish. I'm sure my business is falling apart, and I don't have a clue when I'll be able to get myself back on track or what I'll need to be doing to make that happen."

"What can I do to help?" Dominique asked.

"I'd really appreciate it if you could run by the bakery to check on how things are going. I'm sure they're okay for the time being, but it can't last much longer."

"I'll swing by to see how they're doing. And if you aren't home by next week, then I suggest you close shop temporarily. We can put a sign on the door that says you're away for vacation."

"Actually, that's not a bad idea. I think I should just do that anyway. I only have one big order due this weekend and then nothing after that I need to be worried about. So it would be the perfect time for a vacation."

"Consider it done. What about the employees? Are you going to lay them off?"

Soledad shook her head. "No, I'd rather give them two weeks' paid vacation."

"Can you afford that?"

"I'll pull it from my savings. It's not their fault that this is happening."

"Anything else?" Dominique prompted.

"When they shut down, make sure they take any leftovers to the food bank for distribution. Please, tell them not to let it go to waste."

Dominique nodded.

"Have they made arrangements for Annie yet?" Soledad asked, her voice dropping an octave. "I know I probably can't go to the funeral, but I want to pay my respects and maybe send some flowers."

"I'll make that happen. You just keep your head down, please. I'd hate for you to go to all this trouble and then do something that exposes you. At least let them catch the killer first. Promise me."

Soledad smiled. "I promise. Besides, Palmer's keeping a close eye on me."

"Speaking of the devil… What's going on with you two? You look very cozy together."

Soledad felt herself blush. She shook her head. "It's not like that. He's just been exceedingly kind."

Dominique chortled. "You usually aren't that naive. That man is head over heels for you."

Soledad laughed with her sister. "Now I know Dad dropped you on your skull when we were babies. You've completely lost your mind if you think that. He's just a really nice—"

"Just a really nice guy…" Dominique mocked, reminiscent of when they'd been younger.

"Well, he is!" Soledad exclaimed, tossing up her hands. "And he's been supersweet to Lyra and me."

For thirty minutes, Soledad clued her sister in on all that had happened since arriving in Palmer's barn. The twins laughed heartily, cried, bickered, and their time together felt like it always did. Soledad found it unfathomable that despite how close they were, their routines kept them from each other for long periods of time. So focused on their respective careers, they seldom realized how much they missed each other until they were together again. She was beyond grateful for the opportunity to spend some time together.

Lyra lay sleeping on Dominique's shoulder.

"You look good with a baby in your arms," Soledad said.

"I do, don't I?" Dominique answered, her expression telling. "I can't wait to have Stanton's babies."

"They'll be cute babies."

"So, what about you? Are you ready for this responsibility? Lyra's a doll, but even dolls can be a handful."

Soledad shrugged. "Honestly, I don't have a clue what's going to happen. Annie's attorney has her codicil naming me Lyra's guardian, but I'm sure Gavin is going to fight that with everything he can if it comes down to it. I just know that I promised Annie I would take care of her daughter, and I won't break that promise."

"Well, you know you'll have all the support in the world. I know Dad will be over the moon when he finds out. He can't wait to be a grandfather."

Soledad trailed her hand down Lyra's back, her touch whisper soft. "Palmer doesn't want kids. He doesn't want to be a father and says he's not interested in marriage."

"He told you this?"

Soledad nodded. "He survived some childhood traumas and, because of them, decided he never wanted children. The level of hurt he was made to endure just breaks my heart."

Dominique stared at her sister. "You do *like* him, don't you?"

Soledad stared at her sister, considering the question. Yes, she did like Palmer. She liked him more than she'd realized, and admitting it would force her to acknowledge feelings she was trying desperately to ignore. "Does it really matter?" Soledad said with a shrug. "There's no way I'd ever consider being in a relationship with a man who didn't want a family with me. Being a wife and mother has always been on my bucket list. I'm not willing to give that up for anyone. And now that I'm a mother by default, I could never be with a man who isn't willing to accept Lyra. Going forward, she and I are a package deal."

A wave of sadness went through Soledad and her twin reached out to give her a hug.

"You do know those two are a package deal, right?" Stanton asked from the passenger seat.

Palmer shot his cousin a look as he maneuvered his truck across the fields. "What two?"

"Soledad and her sister. If you marry one, you automatically get the other by default. Whether you want her or not. It's some twin thing they have going on. It's a good thing they're fraternal, because I imagine that could be a problem if they were identical."

Palmer laughed, his cousin's expression too serious for the conversation.

"Someone who gets my sense of humor!" Stanton exclaimed. "Seriously, though, those two are super close. You need to be ready for it."

"We're not dating. Right now, I'm just helping her out, and when she goes back home, I hope that we'll remain friends." Palmer said the words but even he didn't believe them. What he was feeling for Soledad was far more than friendship and he found himself hoping that her going home would never happen.

"Then you need to stop looking at her the way you do," Stanton chuckled.

"What do you mean? How do I look at her?"

"Like you're hopelessly in love."

"You're seeing things."

"You get those sad puppy-dog eyes, and you start sweating around the collar. It's so obvious. Everyone saw it at our engagement party."

"No one saw anything they weren't imagining."

Stanton shrugged. "Okay. If you don't believe me, ask your brother. He was talking about it on the ride back last night. How you've been fantasizing about you and her since forever. How you've been too nervous to ask her out and tell her how you feel. He said you're like a walking Hallmark card, the way you wear your heart on your sleeve."

"Remind me to kill my brother the next time I see him." Palmer felt his face flush, knowing his cheeks were tinted a rich bright red.

Stanton eyed him, his expression serious. "Life's

short. If she's the one, don't let her get away. Why spend your life regretting lost love when you can have a lifetime of happiness instead?"

"So, you're an expert now?"

"Look, it took a lot to get me to this headspace. Dominique worked overtime to help me see the error of my ways. That's why I love her as much as I do. She knows what she wants and she's fearless about going after it. She's got fight and I love that she challenges me."

"Well, Soledad and I are on different pages. She wants children and marriage, and that has never been in my playbook."

"Sounds like you may want to rewrite some of those plays, or even get you a new book. Women like the de la Vega sisters don't come calling every day, and the fact that she likes you is half your battle."

Palmer sighed. "Whatever, man. Right now, all I can focus on is her safety. Protecting her and that baby are the best I can do."

"I hear you. But think about it. If I were you, I wouldn't want to lose her."

Palmer shook his head. "We need to get back. You need to make that delivery for me."

"What's the package?"

"A cake for a client's party tonight."

"A cake?"

"Yeah, Soledad had a cake order that she was determined to fill. I was going to deliver it myself, but I don't want to leave her alone or risk anyone else figuring out she's here with me."

"You could wear a disguise. Maybe a wig and hat to conceal your identity?"

Palmer gave his cousin a look, not at all amused by his suggestion. "Would you focus, please?"

Stanton laughed and shrugged. "Have you tasted this cake? Is it any good? You know I really like cake."

"I swear, cousin, if anything happens to that damn cake and you mess this up for me, I will rip you to shreds. Don't even think about showing your face around here again."

Stanton laughed, the wealth of it gut deep. "Sure, you're not in love," he said facetiously. "It's your lie, cousin, but tell it any way that makes you happy!"

When the two men returned, Soledad and her sister were seated at the counter. Soledad was giving Dominique explicit instructions for delivering and setting up the cake for her client.

Dominique rolled her eyes, clearly done with the conversation. "Who worked for free the first summer you were open, helping with every position in that damn bakery?"

"You did."

"Who set up the Pinkney wedding cake all by her lonesome when you broke your foot?"

"You did—but I directed you."

"No, you didn't."

"Yes, I did. I kept calling you to tell you what to do."

"You kept calling to be a nuisance and I still managed to get that monstrosity of a wedding cake onto the table without it falling apart. It was stunning when I walked out of there."

"Because I make wonderful cakes."

Dominique tossed Stanton a look. "It was fifteen tiers and had to be delivered in sections and set up on-site. I earned the salary I wasn't making that day."

"You make that sound like I have never pulled an all-nighter editing one of your articles," Soledad retorted. "Without snacks and coffee."

"You got snacks."

"A stale bag of peanuts from some flight you'd taken does not count."

Dominique shrugged. "You didn't complain then."

"I was hungry."

The two women laughed, enjoying the banter that came naturally.

"Is there anything I need to know or do?" Stanton asked, looking from one to the other.

"No, honey. I think I have it under control," Dominique answered. "My sister just doesn't want to give me my due credit."

"I've got your back, baby," Stanton said as he leaned to kiss his fiancée's cheek.

"You just get your girl and that cake to their destination, in one piece, please. You just do that." Palmer gave his cousin a narrowed stare.

Jack suddenly barked and they all turned to look at the same time. Lyra had taken a nosedive into a mound of pillows and was struggling to right herself. Soledad noticed how Palmer made it to her side in three swift steps, lifting the small bundle into his arms.

"Did that bad doggy push you?" he said, snuggling the infant. "You have to be easy with the baby, Jack. You can't bowl her over like one of your play toys."

Soledad chuckled. Amusement danced across her face as she watched Palmer with the baby, the tenderness he showed the little girl like a warm blanket. "Don't yell at Jack. He didn't do anything. She keeps trying to grab his ears, and when she misses, she falls over. When she hits her target, she tries to drag the poor dog. She's going to be a terror when she starts walking."

Palmer was cooing and making silly faces at the baby. Lyra was giggling as she grabbed at Palmer's face, trying to chew his chin. The two were quite a pair, and watching them, she couldn't help but smile.

Soledad and her sister exchanged a look, the duo having a silent conversation that no one else was privy to. Doing that thing twins did when they shut out the world and it was just them. Dominique's eyes lifted, her brow furrowed. Her expression was inquisitive and the slightest smile pulled at her lips. Soledad responded with her own wide-eyed stare, batting her lashes rapidly.

Watching the man and the baby together, Soledad realized Palmer Colton was a natural, despite his assertions that fatherhood was not for him. In that moment, Soledad couldn't help but wonder if she'd ever find a man like Palmer, who was both tender and protective of her and that baby girl. Would there ever be someone who looked at her like he sometimes did? Would she want him as much as she found herself suddenly wanting Palmer? As if reading her mind, Dominique reached for her hand, the two interlocking their fingers and holding tightly to each other.

Chapter 11

Staring out the large bay window, Soledad watched as Dominique and Stanton drove away with her cake delivery. She stared until she could no longer see the car, and she was still staring minutes after. An air of melancholy had filled the room, no hint of the laughter that had been there just an hour earlier. Watching her, Palmer felt as if he'd taken a punch to his gut, unable to catch his breath and make things well.

She caught him staring, noticing his reflection in the glass, and she turned to meet his gaze. He opened his mouth to speak, but she held up her hand, stalling his words. "Please, don't ask me if I'm okay, because I'm not. I'm not okay," she snapped, shaking her head vehemently. Her tone was short and riddled with emotion. "I'm so over this. I want my life back."

Palmer nodded politely. "Are you ready to go to the police?" he asked.

There was a hint of hesitation before she answered. "No. I'm sure if I do, they're just going to put me in hiding somewhere else and maybe even take Lyra from me. For all I know, they might even put me in jail for taking the baby. I can't let that happen. I still feel safer here. With you."

Palmer reflected on her comment as Soledad turned back to the window, her forlorn expression like a knife in his heart. He understood why she felt the way she did and knew there was little he could do to make her feel better. What surprised Palmer was that he found himself wishing that Soledad wanting to remain in his home could be more about her wanting *him* and less about her simply feeling safe. He released the breath he'd been holding, allowing the warm air to blow softly past his lips.

"Why don't I make us some dinner?" he said, moving to the refrigerator. "I don't know about you, but I'm hungry."

Soledad turned back around and gave him a smile. "Thank you," she said. "You've been so kind to me, and I realize I probably sounded ungrateful just then. But I hope you know how much I appreciate everything you've done for me. I'll probably never be able to repay you for everything, but I hope I'm able to come close."

"You don't owe me anything, Soledad."

"And there you go being sweet again. Which is why I'm going to make you dinner." Her smile widened. "Grilled cheese?"

Palmer laughed. "Grilled cheese works for me."

* * *

An hour later, Soledad and Palmer stood side by side in the kitchen, prepping their evening meal. Lyra was sound asleep and Jack lay beneath her crib, keeping a watchful eye out for any threats.

As Soledad cut vegetables for a salad, Palmer slid their favorite sandwich together, layering three different cheeses with fresh spinach on a thick crusty bread. He topped off the bread with a light garlic-butter spread and then laid it in a warm cast-iron pan.

Palmer had turned on the stereo, and as they worked, someone's jazz played softly in the background. The music was soft and easy, and filled the space with warm energy. The conversation between them was casual, the two chatting comfortably together. Soledad discovered he had a penchant for old black-and-white films and country music. He learned she liked roller coasters and NASCAR racing. Both enjoyed a good James Patterson novel and were members of the mile-high club. Time had revived the laughter in the home, the two chuckling together like old friends who knew each other's darkest secrets. They were comfortable with one another, and that spoke volumes to Soledad.

After checking on Lyra, they sat to eat, and their conversation continued. The discussion was heated, the two debating the popular television series *The Blacklist*.

"How can you not like Raymond Reddington?" Palmer questioned. "The man is ultracool."

"The man is a criminal who wears nice suits and has a poetic tongue. But he's still a criminal."

Palmer laughed. "I see watching television with you is going to be interesting."

"Especially if you won't even acknowledge when you're wrong." A slow smile spread across her face.

Shaking his head, Palmer began to clear away the dirty dishes. "I'll wash if you dry."

"I can do that," Soledad responded. "I hate washing dishes. That's what a dishwasher's for."

"It's two plates, Soledad."

"Two or twenty. What difference does it make?"

"You're funny."

"I'm told you like women with a sense of humor."

Palmer gave her a look out of the corner of his eye. "And who told you that?"

"I have my sources."

"Sounds like my cousin's been talking out of turn again."

"Maybe. Maybe not." Soledad grabbed the dish towel to wipe the moisture from the plate he passed to her.

Palmer chuckled.

"I'm glad your sister came," he said after a few minutes of silence between them. "I know you hated to see her leave, but it was nice you two could spend some time together. I think it was good for you."

"It was good. I needed that time more than I realized. And I'm sorry again if I was acting like a brat before."

"You're forgiven. I was told you could be a little high-strung."

"You were not," Soledad quipped, her voice rising to a high squeal. Shock registered; she was surprised that anyone would think such a thing about her. A nervous giggle blew past her lips.

"Yes, I was."

"There is no one who would tell you something like that about me. Because I am not high-strung. Not all the time, anyway." She smiled.

"Maybe. Maybe not." He smirked, his wide smile like a beam in the center of his face.

Soledad gave him an eye roll.

Palmer changed the subject. "So, Stanton mentioned Dominique has been working on articles about the Grave Gulch Police Department. How is that going for her?"

Soledad nodded. "She is. But she says her exposé is more about the forensic scientist that duped them."

"Was that Randall Bowe? The subject of that manhunt?"

"Yes, him. Dominique says she's uncovered information she thinks will change public opinion of the Grave Gulch PD. That the full scope of what he did and how he did it is eye-opening."

"I've read a few of her articles. Dominique's a talented writer."

"Yes, she is. She's a stickler for details and she believes in getting her facts right. She has a way with words, and I'm always impressed with her ability to manipulate them into pretty sentences."

"Much like you manipulate dough into cookies?"

Soledad smiled. "Very much like that."

"Speaking of cookies…" Palmer's eyebrows rose, his eyes bright. "Since you now have my secret grilled-cheese recipe, maybe you can show me how to make those oatmeal cookies with the nuts and Craisins that taste kind of like spice cake. I really like those."

"You want them tonight or tomorrow?" Soledad asked.

Palmer moved to the cupboard and began to pull out the flour and oatmeal and any other ingredient he thought she might need. He dropped everything onto the counter. "No hurry," he said. "I don't want you to think I'm rushing you or anything."

Soledad laughed. "I think you're the one that's funny, Palmer Colton. Just too funny."

Palmer laughed with her. "I will own that," he answered. "For your cookies, I will own it and wear it proudly. Would you like to see my stand-up?" he asked as he winked at her.

She eyed him warmly. He turned back to the pantry, beginning to pull out the baking pans. Muscles rippled beneath the T-shirt he wore and his denim jeans hugged his backside nicely. She bit down against her bottom lip, thinking she'd love to see his stand-up—and anything else he was interested in showing her.

Soledad scooped the last of the cookie dough onto a sheet, twelve evenly arranged balls of doughy goodness. She slid the pan into the oven and the mixing bowl into the sink. It was the last batch of three dozen. The first dozen was cooling on a wire rack on the counter, and the second dozen had a few more minutes in the other oven.

Palmer had left the kitchen to answer the cries of a six-month-old. Lyra had begun crying after they had tossed all the ingredients into the bowl and he had yet to return. Eavesdropping via the baby monitor, she knew the little girl now had a dry diaper, a full tummy, and she was currently being lulled back to sleep with an Irish lullaby. Palmer's voice was liquid gold and the sweetest caress to her ears.

The smell of sugar and spice filled the air. Fresh-baked cookies were the best balm and absolutely made her heart sing. She hadn't realized just how much she'd missed her work at the bakery. The art of sifting flour and whipping butter gave her immense joy. Folding in steel-cut oats, chopped nuts and a host of spices that teased her senses brought her immeasurable delight.

The time Palmer had spent measuring the ingredients had been great fun. She found herself enjoying the moments they shared. Soledad had to admit to a few moments of flirtation, the innuendos overt and heated. Palmer was a tease and he seemed to take a great deal of pleasure in making her blush.

She suddenly thought about her sister and the comment she'd made about Palmer being in love with her. Maybe she was naive, Soledad thought, because she couldn't see it. Yes, he was kind and generous and had blessed her immensely. Soledad didn't think him being sweet to her had anything at all to do with his feelings for her. But she liked him. She liked him more than she'd been willing to admit out loud, and the more she thought about him, the more she would have given almost anything for him to return the sentiment. She imagined that what he was feeling had more to do with pity than anything else. And even if it wasn't, nothing could come of it, if Palmer wasn't interested in a family and children.

Leaning across the counter, she reached for a warm cookie and took a large bite.

Lyra had finally drifted off to sleep. She'd eaten and played and been thoroughly entertained. Palmer had made silly faces and strange noises to make the baby giggle and laugh. Amazingly, Lyra had him in full "daddy" mode, and he was still in awe of how easily he'd fallen into the role.

The entire evening had been one of the best experiences he'd had in some time. He couldn't remember the last time he'd laughed as much or as hard or been that happy. But Soledad had him walking on cloud nine and Lyra was the pot of gold at the end of a bright rainbow.

Palmer was reluctant to give it a name. He just knew it was bigger than a schoolboy crush and next to impossible to pursue because he couldn't wrap his mind around the concept of forever. Not even with a woman he wanted as much as he wanted Soledad.

He groaned heavily, a gust of air escaping past his thin lips. The weight of all the emotion he was feeling fell away, leaving him to question what might come next if he opened himself to the possibility. He knew the life Soledad wanted. He just couldn't see himself being the one to give it to her. He knew his attitude about marriage and children sounded irrational, but he couldn't help how he felt, and he had no plans to apologize for his feelings.

He had been here before. Dating women who wanted

more than he was willing to give. He'd always walked away, unconcerned with what anyone thought. As he spent more time with Soledad, he suddenly couldn't see himself walking away from her. But then he remembered they weren't dating, and he had no idea how Soledad felt about him.

"It shouldn't be so hard," Palmer whispered softly, blowing his words into the palm of Lyra's little hand. "Any advice for me, kiddo?" He paused, drawing the pads of his fingers over the roundness of her chubby cheek. "No? I didn't think so." He chuckled softly as he lifted the baby from his lap and lowered her into the crib.

He stood there for a few minutes, staring down at the little girl. Watching her sleep brought him a sense of peace. He relished the peace. Inhaling the scent of cinnamon, nutmeg and sugar, he craved a cookie. One of Soledad's. As he exited the room, he couldn't help but think of the sophomoric joke hidden in that thought.

Hours later, Soledad and Palmer were still noshing on oatmeal cookies and cups of hot caramel lattes. There was little they hadn't talked about; he'd found a level of comfort with her that felt as natural as breathing.

"Why aren't you married already?" Palmer questioned. He took a sip of his beverage.

Soledad shrugged. "I've spent the past two years completely focused on building my brand. The bakery is my whole life and it has required all of my attention."

"So, you're all work and no play?" he asked, wondering what it would take to get her to play games with him.

"Very little play, but then, you know all about that."

Palmer nodded. "I do. This ranch requires everything I have to give."

"So, tell me what you actually do. What's an average day in the life of Palmer Colton, rancher extraordinaire?"

"Not sure that I'm a rancher extraordinaire," Palmer asserted with a grin, "but I am fully committed to what I do. I supervise all the operations that keep this machine running.

"An average day starts ultra early," he continued. "The animals have to be fed and watered, and the stables need to be cleaned. I tend the herds, deciding when to rotate stock, and I make decisions about breeding. Sometimes we will gather semen from the cattle to sell to continue the stronger bloodlines. Then, of course, I tend to any of the animals that might be sick. There's also the maintenance of the outbuildings and ensuring all the fencing is intact. And let's not forget the fields and crops. That's a Monday. Tuesdays I do that and the paperwork, and start over again on Wednesdays."

Soledad giggled. "But you have help, right?"

"And a lot of it. It takes a whole football team to keep this place running. I employ a great group to help me out."

"I really look forward to getting a tour one day. Maybe I can help out somewhere."

"Whenever you're ready. I like to show the ranch off. I'm proud of what I've built here."

"You should be proud. It's impressive." Soledad suddenly yawned. She pulled her closed fist to her lips. "Excuse me. I'm suddenly exhausted."

"You should go get some rest. We can resume this conversation in the morning over coffee and cookies."

She laughed. "I think I'm all cookied out."

"Never! I will never get enough of your cookies."

Soledad's brow quirked as she eyed him.

"I mean your cookie cookies. I mean…you know…" he stammered, feeling like he'd put his foot in his mouth and not the mashup of oatmeal and sweet raisins he'd been eating.

"I can't believe you're actually blushing."

"You've got me feeling like a grade-schooler who told a dirty joke. Or heard one."

She stood up, her head shaking slightly. "Well, just for the record…" Soledad moved slowly toward the guest bedroom. "If you want a taste of my cookies, you'll have to ask me nicely." She tossed him one last look over her shoulder, a wry smile lifting her lush mouth.

Chapter 12

It was still dark out when Palmer's bedside alarm sounded. After depressing the stop button to silence the annoying chime, he threw his legs off the side of the bed and sat upright. He was stiff and felt heavy, needing a few more hours of sleep, but such was not a luxury he could enjoy. Hanging out half the night enjoying Soledad's company had come with a price, and he would have to pay it over the next few hours as he went about his chores.

He was headed to the bathroom when he heard noises coming from the kitchen. Jack hadn't left the room where little Lyra slept, and Palmer couldn't imagine that Soledad was awake if she didn't have to be. He suddenly couldn't remember if he'd set the house alarm, so distracted by Soledad and those darn oatmeal cookies. His heart began to race, anxiety rising with a vengeance. Easing to his nightstand, he removed the loaded firearm from its lockbox, then crept out the door and down the hallway.

As he moved into the room, he lowered his weapon, a smile creeping across his face. Soledad stood staring into the refrigerator. He couldn't help but notice her bra-style top and the boy-cut shorts that complemented the length of her legs. She'd pulled her hair up into a ponytail that swung back and forth behind her. He cleared his throat and she looked up to meet his gaze.

"Good morning," she chimed cheerily. Her tone changed slightly as her eyes dropped to the weapon in his hand. "Everything okay? Should I be scared?"

Palmer nodded. "Everything's good. I heard someone out here and was coming to make sure they belonged." He engaged the safety and went to tuck the weapon into the waistband of his sleep pants when he realized he was standing there in nothing but his underwear. His eyes widened and his cheeks turned a nice shade of embarrassed when he realized Soledad was staring at his bare chest.

"I like your tighty-whiteys." She giggled.

He ignored the comment. "What's got you up so early?"

"I thought I'd make you breakfast before you headed out. I saw you had four hours blocked off on your calendar to volunteer this morning?" She pointed to the planner that rested on the counter.

His brow lifted as he answered. "Yeah. I volunteer with the Grave Gulch Children's Home. It's a group foster facility for boys. I sponsor a program called Rough Riders, where we bring a group of kids here every week for a dude-ranch event."

"That sounds like fun. What do you all do?"

"We give them the full cowboy experience. The kids take horseback riding lessons and go on trail rides. They also learn what's involved in caring for the horses. Throughout the year, we bring in guests to demonstrate rodeo games. Sometimes I'll take them to fish down at the ponds, which I keep fully stocked so everyone can catch at least one.

"We also do nature walks, and the older boys learn archery and rifle shooting and how to handle each responsibly. During the fall and winter months, there are hayrides and cookouts. We sometimes camp in the woods and sit around the campfire just talking. Many of the boys who participate are about to age out of the foster-care system, so I try to give them some direction and hope about what will happen after they leave. We even make them learn how to square-dance!"

Soledad chuckled. "That's very cool. I'm impressed."

"I've enjoyed it. It's been very rewarding."

"Maybe I can whip up some cookies for them?"

Palmer laughed. "I don't know if I want to share your cookies with anyone else."

Soledad tossed him a lopsided smirk. "You need to be nice. They're kids. I'll save my special cookies just for you," she teased.

"I may collect on that," he said.

"I hope you do," Soledad answered, her voice dropping an octave. She bit down against her bottom lip as they eyed each other intently. She finally gave in, her shoulders rising in a lighthearted shrug. "Anyway, I thought, since I kept you up all night, that the least I could do was make you a good breakfast. So, why don't you go take your shower? By the time you get back, I should have the food ready."

"Thank you," Palmer said. "That's very sweet of you." He turned and headed back to his room.

Soledad called his name, stepping from behind the counter to stand at the end of the hallway.

"Yes?"

"I really do hope you'll take me up on that cookie," she said, blessing him with another bright smile. "I really, really do."

As he walked away, he could feel her staring at his backside, her gaze throwing heat deep into the core of his body.

Either one of two things had happened, Soledad thought. If Palmer was not interested in what she had offered, then she had just made a complete fool of herself. Or her suggestive quip had opened the door for them to move their relationship in a whole other direction. Despite it feeling like the former, she was willing to bank on the latter. When she'd said what she'd said, there was nothing for her to lose and everything to gain.

She had spent most of the night thinking about him. Playing their conversations over in her head. Remembering the gentleness of his touch. How he was with Lyra. How he made her laugh. He was magical. There was something special about him that had her wishing for more. She knew that he might not be her forever, but why shouldn't she take advantage of the right now? Soledad firmly believed in fate and knew there was a reason Palmer had come into her life in the way he had. That he knew her, and had been interested, was a bonus—and much for her to consider. She wanted it to be love, but just being honest about that was taking her completely out of her comfort zone.

She refocused on the popovers she was prepping for breakfast. Blending flour, milk, eggs and butter until she had a batter the consistency of heavy cream. She half filled the cups of the pan and popped it in a hot oven.

By the time Palmer returned, crisp bacon, scrambled eggs and hot popovers with raspberry butter were waiting for him.

She gasped as he walked toward her. He was wearing denim. Dark denim jeans with a matching denim shirt, steel-toed boots and a wide-brimmed, brown-leather Stetson. He looked delicious and she suddenly wanted him more than she wanted the meal she'd fixed.

"Wow!" she exclaimed. "You clean up nice."

"As opposed to how I look any other time?"

"As in, you look yummy," she said teasingly. "If I were a jealous woman, I'd wonder who you were all dressed up for."

"I'm glad you're not a jealous woman," he said, "because you'd be sorely disappointed. She's almost eighty. Her name is Grandma Butler and she's one of the house mothers at the foster home."

Laughter rang sweetly.

"Seriously, though," Soledad said, as she passed him a plate of food. "You look very nice."

"Thank you."

"Can you come back just before lunch to pick up the cookies? I'm going to start baking right after Lyra wakes up and I get her settled."

He nodded. "You really don't need to do that, but I'm sure the boys will appreciate the gesture."

"It's not like I have a lot to do. I just want to keep busy, so I don't drive myself crazy thinking about everything."

"Does that include me?" Palmer asked. He avoided her eyes as he took a bite of his popover.

"I like thinking about you," Soledad said softly.

He cut an eye in her direction and gave her a slight nod. "I like thinking about you, too. And I think about you all the time."

"Is this weird?" Soledad queried. "You and me? I know we joke a lot, but…" She let her words trail off.

"It's not necessarily normal. Whatever *normal* is," he said, making air quotes with his fingers.

"I just don't want our unusual circumstances to blind us to what our reality is."

"I agree. All jokes aside, I want whatever happens between us to be about what feels right to us both. And I want it to be for the right reasons." He stole a quick glance at his wristwatch. "I hate to cut our conversation short, but I have to run. Can we talk more later?"

"Of course." Soledad nodded. "I didn't mean to hold you up."

"Thank you for breakfast. Those popovers were good."

He rose from his seat, moving to the sink with his plate. "I'll be back to check on you. And I'll set the house alarm when I leave. In case you need it, my gun is in the nightstand." He paused. "I guess I should ask if you know how to use a gun."

Soledad gave him a smile. "Since I was twelve. Our father made sure Dominique and I were comfortable with a wide range of weapons. I can wield a mean bow and arrow if I need to."

"I'll have to see that for myself one day," he responded, duly impressed.

He continued. "Melissa's got a patrol car positioned at all the main gates, and one of them will do a drive-by every hour. If you need anything, you just call me. I'll still be right here on the property, and I can be back in seconds."

"We'll be fine. Jack will keep an eye out for us."

"Jack will save Lyra. It's the rest of us who might be in trouble!"

Soledad laughed as Palmer sauntered toward the door. There was a moment of hesitation as he stood with his hand on the doorknob, seeming to fall into thought. She took a step forward as he turned around, their gazes connecting across the room. She felt her pulse begin to race, her heart beating rapidly.

Then Palmer hurried to where she stood and pressed a kiss to her forehead, his lips lingering for only a moment as his hand cupped her face. His touch was heated, and she felt her breath catch deep in her chest. Without another word, he hurried back to the door and made his exit.

* * *

When Palmer pulled into the pasture, his lips were still tingling from that kiss. Her skin had been warm and soft as silk, and he only regretted that there hadn't been time to see if one kiss could have become two. He couldn't help but wonder what Soledad was thinking about the brazenness of the act. He only wished he had time to reflect back on the moment for a little longer, but the bus from the children's home was already there.

The boys had exited the vehicle and were milling around in the field, waiting for something to happen. There were twenty of them, ranging in age from ten to seventeen. Most had visited before and were visibly excited to see what would come this visit. The newbies tried to appear indifferent, and Palmer knew that was their way of protecting themselves from disappointment if the day didn't pan out the way they hoped.

Noé hurried to his side as he parked his truck. The man's enthusiasm was corporeal, bubbling up like water in a fountain. Most of the men who worked for Palmer looked forward to helping out during the Rough Rider events. They all felt good about giving back to the community and the kids who simply needed a kind hand to support and nurture them.

"¡Buenos días, jefe!"

"Good morning, Noé. Sorry I'm late."

"Is everything well, jefe?" Concern blanketed the farmhand's face, seeping like mist from his eyes. "Are there problems?"

Palmer nodded. "Everything's fine," he said, a little white lie slipping past his lips. Because everything wasn't fine. In fact, everything was far from fine as he thought about Soledad, wishing he was back at the house with her. He missed her. Missed her laughter and the snarky comments that always gave him pause. He'd kissed her, and truth be told, all he could think about was sweeping her up into his arms, laying her across his bed and ravaging her with pleasure. He thought about the places his hands would lead and his mouth would follow. Fantasizing about her and him together suddenly felt like an obsession he couldn't control, and Palmer hated not being in control. He shook the thoughts from his head and turned his attention back to his friend. "I apologize for being late."

"You are never late. And you don't miss any days. We thought you might be sick when we did not see you yesterday."

"I just had a ton of paperwork to finish," he said, the little white lie catching in his throat. He coughed into his elbow and blamed it on his allergies. "Excuse me," he said. "The pollen is high today."

"¡Salud!" Noé said.

"Thank you."

"Most of the boys have been here before. We will have our regular four groups today."

"That works. I'll take the older boys who already have riding experience to the stable. They're predicting record-high heat today, so it might be a good idea to take the younger boys to the pond. Let them fish and play in the water. We'll have lunch in the old barn on the west side of the ranch."

"Not the one closest to the house?" Noé questioned.

"No. I'm going to move all of our activities to the other barn permanently. I've arranged to have the space renovated. We'll add classrooms and recreational space specifically for our volunteer programs. They'll start the work in the next few weeks, and it should be finished before the summer is over."

"The boys are very lucky to have you, jefe! You are very good to them."

"They just need to know we care, Noé," Palmer said, thinking back to when he'd been in the system and how he'd been desperate to know that someone cared about his well-being and wanted him to be happy. Leanne showing him attention and supporting him had been everything he wanted when he'd needed to feel loved.

The man nodded. "Everyone is waiting for you, boss."

"Give me one minute," Palmer said. "I need to make a quick telephone call before we get started."

"Very good," Noé said. "We will wait."

As Noé walked away, Palmer leaned back against his truck and took out his cell phone. He wanted to call the house to speak with Soledad, to just hear her voice. He was missing her already and feeling completely out of sorts because of it.

Soledad's presence in his life was a distraction, albeit a pleasant one, but still a distraction that was already proving to be problematic. It wasn't like him to show up to anything late, and he hadn't missed a day of work since before he had closed on the property. Now not wanting to leave Soledad's side and being unable to stop thinking about her had him slacking on the job. How quickly things had changed, he thought.

He sighed, slipping his cell into the back pocket of his jeans. He would see her in an hour or so to pick up those cookies. Until then, he would have to settle for the memory of a kiss he wished he had planted on her lips instead.

"You own all this?" one of the boys challenged.

His name was Tyler, and Palmer thought he looked like a miniature version of Jimmy Kimmel but with red hair. Skepticism filled the boy's face as he eyed Palmer with reservation.

"I do," Palmer answered. "This is all mine."

"I don't want no farm," a second little boy interjected. "I plan to live in a penthouse apartment in a big city like New York or Miami."

"That's good," Palmer said. "It's good to have goals. You can accomplish anything you put your mind to."

"I plan to be a race-car driver," a third child added.

"I love your ambition," Palmer answered. And he was proud of them. They were good kids who'd been dealt bad hands, but most of them were willing to bet the bank on themselves succeeding. He admired their perseverance, determination seeming like it was ingrained in their DNA.

"These are some good cookies," another little boy chimed in. "Where you buy them cookies?"

Palmer laughed. "I didn't buy them. A friend made them especially for you boys."

"I like your friend."

"I like her, too," Palmer said as he bit into his own chocolate-chip cookie that Soledad had made with chunks of dark chocolate and trickles of caramel across the top. He found himself hoping that how much he liked Soledad didn't show on his face.

Running back home to pick up the freshly baked cookies had come with its own challenges. Soledad had been playing with Jack and the baby when he'd arrived, the trio dancing around his living room again. The cookies had been packed in a plastic container and waiting for him on the counter. He had only been able to stay for a quick second, Noé sitting in the truck outside waiting for him to return.

Despite his nervousness, Soledad hadn't had anything to say about that kiss or their previous conversation. It was almost as if he'd dreamed it, nothing at all having happened between them. He had rushed in and rushed back out, cookies in hand and thoughts of Soledad in his head.

The boys' conversation shifted to the latest video game and some girl named Paloma. Paloma's "breast game" had all their attention, someone declaring that she'd moved from training bras to ones with real cups and lace. From the gist of the conversation, Palmer surmised Paloma was much older, closer to fourteen and at least three to five years out of their league.

Despite his efforts to keep the conversation on track, it would split off in a dozen different directions as quickly as a random thought crossed one of their young minds. Those thoughts spoken aloud kept Palmer and the rest of the chaperones on their toes.

Grandma Butler chastised two of the youngsters for inappropriate language and Palmer gave her a smile, nodding his head. "Get them, Grandma!" he said.

One of the new kids sat with his hand raised, waving it eagerly. Palmer gave him a nod. "Yes, Charlie?"

"Can I come back here next time?"

Palmer smiled, his head bobbing up and down. "As long as you keep your grades up and do what you're supposed to do, you'll be able to come back every time."

"Cool. I like this place," he said. "I like riding the horses."

One of the older boys rolled his eyes, less than impressed. He scowled, leaning back in his chair, the front legs lifted off the floor. "Man, this place bites," he grumbled. "Why do we have to muck the horse stalls?"

"David, we have this same conversation every week," Palmer said. "Mucking the stalls is necessary to maintain the health and well-being of the horses. If you want to ride, you also have to be responsible for their care. Those are the rules."

The young man shrugged. "Whatever."

"What's happened?" Palmer questioned. "Why are you in a mood today? This isn't like you." And it wasn't, Palmer thought. David pretended to be hard, a coping mechanism to protect his feelings. Deep down, he was a good kid, kind, compassionate and eager to be of help to others. He had rarely been a problem, so his sour disposition and belligerent attitude were completely out of character.

Since David's first visit to the ranch, Palmer had wanted to see him excel. He'd taken the young man under his wing, personally overseeing his training around the property. Palmer saw a lot of himself in David and he knew the right attention could be a spring-board for his success. He asked him again. "Do you want to talk about it?"

David looked away, not bothering to offer Palmer an explanation. His bad mood seemed to intensify when he punched one of the younger kids in the shoulder for stepping on his sneakers.

Palmer stood. "We're not going to do that. Get up," he snapped.

David gave him a defiant stare, visibly debating his options before finally standing.

"Now apologize," Palmer ordered. "We don't resolve any issue with our fists. Not for any reason."

The boy tried to stare Palmer down but gave in when he quickly realized it was a battle he would not win. "Sorry," he muttered under his breath.

Palmer corrected him. "'I apologize. I should not have hit you.' Now say it. Clearly and with conviction, and look him in the eye when you do."

David snarled, wishing he could sit back down and forget the conversation altogether. A minute passed before he finally turned to the boy he'd bullied and re-peated what Palmer had instructed him to say.

"I apologize. I should not have hit you."

The other boy laughed. "You're a punk!"

"We're not going to do that, either," Palmer said, pointing a finger at the child. He shook his head as he turned back to David. "Walk with me," he said, guid-ing the boy toward the door.

Minutes later, the two sat atop the fence that bordered the pasture where the horses were grazing. Palmer knew that David enjoyed riding and that the quarter horse named Majestic was one of his favorites. This was his third or fourth year in the program and he had always been one of the promising students and successes.

"Talk to me, buddy. What's going on with you?" Palmer asked.

David shrugged his shoulders, staring out across the landscape. His eyes swung back and forth, and Palmer sensed he was trying not to cry.

"It's okay," he persisted. "You can talk to me. Did something happen?"

"It's my birthday next week."

"Happy birthday to you!" Palmer exclaimed. "When you consider the alternative, that's a good thing."

"I'll be eighteen. I'll have to leave the foster home and my aunt said I can't come live with her. She's got a new boyfriend and he's got two daughters, so he says I can't stay there with them. I don't have no place to go."

Palmer heaved a heavy sigh. The number of children who aged out of the foster-care system each year was astronomical. Far too many became instantly homeless. Even more were unemployable. And some suffered with mental-health issues that would never be treated. It had become a vicious cycle, and even David knew he was about to become lost within it.

"What does your social worker say?"

"I might be able to stay at the center until the end of the summer, as long as they don't need the bed. Then I'll be able to move into the dorm at the college."

"You were accepted?"

"I got into the University of Michigan, Michigan State and Wayne."

"Dude! Congratulations! Have you decided where you're going?"

"I got a full scholarship to Wayne State. And I like their engineering program. It'll also pay for housing if I can get through the summer."

"That's good news. I'm proud of you."

David shrugged his shoulders again. "I don't know if I'm going to be able to go. I'll need to find a job to support myself. My aunt is the only family I have left, and she just tossed me over for some guy named Larry."

Palmer could sense the boy's deflation, every ounce of his spirit feeling bruised and battered by the hand life had dealt him. As he shared, tears rained down David's cheeks.

Palmer sat staring out over the landscape. His own frustration was palpable. Too many boys would feel like David did. They would commit to the work, turn their lives around and then get kicked down on their way out the door. "Let me talk to your social worker. We'll figure something out. You won't be homeless. I promise."

"You'd do that for me?"

"Yes, I would. Just remember, though, one day, I'm going to need you to pay it forward and do something good for someone else. Understood?"

David nodded. "Yeah!"

"Good. Now stop beating up on the younger kids. You need to be an example for them to emulate."

"Yes, sir."

"We need to head back. It's almost time for your bus to pull out."

"Thanks, Mr. Colton," David said, throwing himself off the side of the fence to the ground. "Thanks a lot."

As the yellow school bus pulled off the property, Palmer and his men watched, waving goodbye at the boys who were waving at them.

Noé gestured for Palmer's attention.

"We didn't have any problems, did we?" Palmer asked.

"No, boss. Just the usual with them. For the most part, all the boys were good today."

"Yes, they were! I was impressed by their ingenuity and the effort they all put into the team-building exercises. It was a good session this week."

"We have new livestock being delivered tomorrow," Noé reminded him. "I've scheduled more hands on deck to help get them tagged. Is there anything else you need me to do?"

"What time's that truck due?"

"Early morning. He came before eleven the last time."

"We'll be ready. Anything else?"

"No, jefe. We are good."

"Then I'm headed back to the house. I will see you in the morning."

"Thank you, boss. You have a good night."

"You, too, Noé. And thank you for all your help today."

As Palmer headed back to his truck, he smiled. It had

been a good day and another successful event for the kids. He thought about David, making a mental note to give his social worker a call first thing in the morning. The young man was headed toward a bright future, and he wasn't willing to let anyone or anything impede his journey. He felt responsible for David in a way that awed him. Palmer couldn't help but think if he had a son he would go to bat for him in the same way. But he didn't have a son, and he didn't want to worry about someone being there for his child if he couldn't be.

He blew a soft sigh, suddenly wondering if he was being irrational about not wanting children. Because he was there and able to do whatever was necessary. Starting his day with Soledad and Lyra had him rethinking every aspect of his life, and he found himself enjoying the experience of family. It took him back to his days after being adopted. And those had been great days! What if he could have what his parents had and not be afraid that it might blow up on him? Palmer suddenly realized he had more soul-searching to do. Until then, he looked forward to his evening, he thought, pulling his truck out of its parking spot. The night couldn't help but be good once he was back with Soledad.

Chapter 13

Soledad was putting the final touches on five dozen cupcakes as Palmer sat at the table and rocked Lyra to sleep. This was the only other order that she was determined to fulfill. Palmer had promised to take it to her sister, who would deliver the order to her client.

The mother of the bride had ordered lemon cupcakes hand-decorated with vanilla-buttercream flowers and leaves. They were layered and tiered, and Soledad was certain each cupcake, individually wrapped in a green, tulip-cut paper baking cup, would make for a stunning presentation. This was one of those custom orders that would solidify her position in the local culinary scene—and bring in a dozen more orders from those present at the party.

Looking up, she watched as Palmer pulled his index

finger to his lips, shushing the dog. Jack had begun to whine for his attention, not impressed that he had rocked the baby to sleep. The dog had apparently wanted to snuggle with the little girl by his lonesome, seeming irritated by Palmer's presence.

"Stop, Jack," Palmer whispered loudly. The little girl shifted against his shoulder, turning her head to stare down at the dog nuzzling her foot. She leaned and reached a small hand out, muttering something that Palmer couldn't begin to decipher.

"You woke the baby, Jack," Palmer said, rising and shaking his head.

Soledad laughed. "Actually, if you just go put her down in the crib, she'll fall asleep. You rocking her to sleep is spoiling her."

"I like spoiling her," Palmer said.

"You do know, then, that you'll have to come over every night to get her to sleep when we go home, right?"

"Or you could just stay here," he mumbled under his breath.

"Excuse me?" Soledad said, her voice rising slightly. "I didn't catch that."

"I didn't say anything." He blushed, turning toward the makeshift nursery to lay the baby down to sleep.

Soledad laughed. She'd already been prepping the cupcakes when he'd come back from his volunteer event. Lyra had been napping, Jack keeping a watchful eye on her. Palmer had lumbered through the door with a rowdy *Honey, I'm home*, and the laughter between them had started all over again.

After a quick shower, he'd taken a seat at the counter

for a quick lesson on the art of cupcake making and then he'd shared the events of his day. As the cupcakes had baked and cooled, they'd eaten a light dinner, still chatting about their day. Everything between them had felt comfortable and natural. Almost *too* comfortable, Soledad had thought.

Although she enjoyed their time together and the banter between them was as easy as breathing, Soledad couldn't help but worry that maybe she was becoming too close to the man. Palmer didn't want a family and she couldn't let herself want a family with someone who didn't want what she did.

Minutes later, Palmer walked back into the kitchen and resumed his seat at the table. "Those look incredible," he said, eyeing the artwork she'd crafted atop each dessert.

Soledad placed one on a saucer and passed it to him. "I made a few extra for us. Tell me how they taste."

Palmer took a big bite, his eyes widening. He hummed his appreciation. "This is really good, Soledad."

"Thank you. It's one of our more popular flavor combinations."

"I think the salted caramel that you make is probably my favorite."

Soledad gave him a look, one hand falling to her hip. "You really did spend a lot of time at my bakery, didn't you?"

"You didn't believe me? I told you I was there almost every day hoping to catch a glimpse of you. How come you never come out front?"

She laughed. "I do sometimes, but depending on

what orders I need to fulfill, I have to be in the kitchen most of the time. Had you *asked* for me, I would have gladly come to the front to see you."

He tossed up his hands. "Now you tell me!"

Soledad shook her head. "Seriously, though, why didn't you ask me out?"

"Because I am painfully shy if I don't know you. And truth be told, I really didn't think I had a chance with you."

Oh, you had a chance! she thought to herself. She smiled and said out loud, "You may have been right." Soledad teased. "It's not like you're my type."

"You have a type?"

"Don't you?"

"Don't change the subject. What's your type?"

"I like my men tall, handsome and intelligent."

Palmer blinked. "You're right. I might not be your type. I'm probably an inch shy of tall," he said smugly.

Soledad laughed, the beauty of it ringing warmly through the room. "So, what's your type?" she asked after catching her breath.

"Beautiful inside, beautiful inside and beautiful inside," he answered.

"You're not hard to please, I see."

"You'd be surprised." He finished off the last bite of a second cupcake and licked the icing from his fingers.

A significant pause swelled thick and full between them as each dropped silently into self-thought. Palmer eventually spoke first, shattering the quiet that had fallen over the room.

"What's going on with us, Soledad?"

She shrugged her shoulders as she placed the last of the dirty dishes into his dishwasher. "I've been thinking about that most of the day. I worry that what's happening is just us reacting to our being thrown together in what looks like an impossible situation."

Palmer nodded. "I've thought that, too. But I also know that I've had a crush on you since forever. But it's like I told you before—I didn't pursue it because I knew we were on different pages. I didn't think I could give you what I knew you wanted for your future."

"And now?"

He hesitated briefly. "And now I think about you all the time. I don't want to leave your side because I'm enjoying your company so much. I want to see where we can take this if we put effort into it."

"I feel the same way…" Soledad responded, her voice trailing to a whisper. Her eyes skated across his face, noting the tiny scar above his top lip. One eye was just a hair smaller than the other and his cheeks dimpled if he smiled just so.

Palmer smiled. "There's a *but* there…"

She shrugged again, smiling back. "But…I can't help but wonder…" She struggled to find the right words to convey what she was thinking, but nothing came. She shrugged a third time.

"You and I are very similar," Palmer said. "We don't do anything that doesn't make sense. We are desperately trying to make sense of all this. Of what's happening. What might happen. Our feelings about everything. About each other. It's a lot. Maybe even too much.

Maybe we should shelve this until another time, after you go back to your life?"

"Is that what you really want?" Soledad questioned, her eyes still dancing over his face. Because it wasn't what she wanted, she thought to herself. She wanted forever, and she found herself wanting forever with him and being afraid that she couldn't have it.

Palmer answered without hesitating. "Not at all," he said. "What I really want is you."

With the stealth of an animal on the African plain, Palmer slipped to Soledad's side. He stood before her, the heat between them rising swiftly, easing them into a dance that had them both panting heavily. He placed one arm around her waist and pulled her to him. Soledad slid her own arms around his neck, still staring into his eyes. Then she stood on the tips of her toes and kissed his mouth with a fervor she had never known before.

As soon as he did it, Palmer knew that kissing Soledad had quickly become his most favorite thing in the world to do. His mouth fit over hers with near perfection. She tasted sweet, her lips sugared from the cupcake icing. When she'd parted her lips and had granted him permission to enter, his tongue had slipped past the line of her teeth to tangle sweetly with hers. He'd tightened his hold around her waist, pulling her pelvis to his, and every muscle in his lower extremities had tautened with a vengeance. In that moment, he knew there'd be no way in hell that he would ever kiss anyone else again.

Soledad suddenly pressed her palms to his broad

chest and pushed him back gently to break their connection. Her breathing labored, she was gasping for air.

"I'm sorry," Palmer apologized, still panting softly. He took a deep breath and held it momentarily before blowing it back out slowly. He was unable to read the emotion that seeped from her eyes.

"N-no," she sputtered. "Everything…everything is… fine." She gasped, inhaling deeply.

Confusion washed through him. "What is it?"

"I can't make love to you. Not tonight."

Palmer felt a slow smile creep across his face. He saw the bewilderment that washed over hers. And he understood it. She could take all the time in the world, because he was willing to wait for her no matter how long it took for her to be ready and things to be fine between them. "Okay…"

"I don't want you to think I'm easy. Because I'm not. I need to make you work for it."

"Okay," he chuckled. "Is that how dating works now?"

"I don't know. I just know it's what my mother always told me and my sister when we were growing up. She'd say, 'Don't just give a man your sugar dish. Make him earn that privilege. He'll work for it if he really wants a taste.'"

"Sugar dish?"

"Sugar dish, cookie jar, goodies… Take your pick."

Palmer smiled at her. "I just want to kiss you, but we can take things as slow or as fast as you want."

"And I want to kiss you, too, but I'm also ready to come right out of my clothes, and I haven't shaved anything since before I got here. The fur on my legs alone might scare you away."

"Fur?" Palmer howled with laughter. "Really?"

"It's not pretty," Soledad said.

He leaned forward and pecked at her lips. His heart swelled full of excitement and anticipation. He couldn't begin to tell her that everything about her brought him pure joy. Even the "fur" she feared he might see.

"And if you keep kissing me, I'm sure I'm going to be embarrassed at some point."

He shook his head. "I doubt there's anything I will ever see that you need to be embarrassed about. You set the pace, Soledad," he said. "We'll make love when you're ready, not one second before. Okay?"

Soledad nodded, her eyes still dancing with his. Her lips parted ever so slightly, warm breath blowing softly. "Kiss me," she whispered.

Palmer slid his fingers into the length of her hair and dropped his mouth to hers, kissing her hungrily.

As if to resist the sensations of his touch, Soledad fell against his body and kissed him back. Sweeping her up and into his arms, Palmer carried her down the short length of the hallway to his bedroom. He laid her gently across the bed, then stood back to stare down at her. She was the most exquisite woman he had ever known. Her hair fell in wisps around her face and there was the faintest dusting of baking flour across her cheek. Her lips had swollen slightly from his ministrations, leaving her with a picture-perfect pout.

* * *

He reached for the hem of his T-shirt and pulled the garment up and over his head. He looked like he'd been pumping weights, his muscles like sculpted marble beneath his taut skin. He had a near-perfect six-pack, his hard body the result of the manual labor he did around the ranch. Soledad's eyes dropped to his narrowed waist and the lines that V'd downward. She bit her bottom lip and the gesture sent a wave of heat into the pit of his abdomen and then rippled up the length of his spine.

Soledad reached for him and her fingers crept slowly against his skin. As he lowered his body to hers, settling in the eave of her parted legs, his mouth reclaimed hers. Every ounce of air felt as if it were being sucked from the room as she slid her hands into the back of his sweatpants and grabbed the round of his ass.

Palmer whispered her name, muttering it over and over again as if in prayer, and then, without warning, Lyra's tiny voice cried out from the baby monitor and Jack barked for their attention.

Soledad shook her head, laughing as Palmer pulled away from her. He adjusted himself in his pants as he blew a heavy sigh.

"Well, it looks like we have our very own personal chaperones," he muttered, visibly flustered.

"I'll go check on her," Soledad said as she pulled herself upright.

"I've got her," Palmer answered.

"Are you sure?"

He nodded. "Jack probably needs to go out, so Lyra

and I will walk him to the door." He winked at her as he turned and headed for the other room.

Soledad tossed him a smile as she slid to the edge of the bed and adjusted her clothes. She'd been one kiss from welcoming him to her most private place, excited to spread herself open to him. Everything about him felt like home, and she had wanted to give him the key and have him claim her. She laughed out loud, pulling her knees to her chest and wrapping her arms around her legs.

She could hear him cooing, trying to calm Lyra down, but her wails moved from the bedroom to the kitchen and back.

Palmer suddenly called Soledad's name, a hint of anxiety in his tone.

He called her a second time. "Soledad!"

"What's wrong?"

"Lyra has a fever. Do you have a baby thermometer?"

Soledad hurried to his side, pressing her hand to Lyra's forehead and cheek. "She is warm," she said as she reached for the diaper bag.

Annie had packed everything she'd thought her daughter would need, including a digital thermometer and children's ibuprofen. Palmer sat with the baby in his arms, Lyra clinging to him like her life depended on it. Twice, Soledad tried to pick her up, but the little girl wasn't having it. She only wanted Palmer, her tears dripping onto his bare chest as he cradled her against him. Outside, Jack was barking to get back inside.

Soledad shook her head. "If you would take her temperature, please, while I go let Jack back in."

Palmer nuzzled his cheek next to the baby's. Lyra clutched his facial hair in a tight fist, still whimpering steadily. Soledad ran her hand down the child's back before going to the kitchen to let Jack back inside.

After securing the door, she warmed a bottle of milk for the baby, hoping meds and a full belly would help Lyra to feel better. Heaven forbid, Soledad thought, that something serious was wrong with Lyra. She didn't want the child to be ill, but if she was, Soledad hoped it was a simple virus or a cold that Lyra could fight off on her own. Anything more serious would put them in the hospital emergency room, where Gavin might find them.

There was a moment of quiet panic as Soledad tried to fathom what she would need to do and how she would do it if something were seriously wrong with Lyra. Would a doctor allow Soledad to be responsible for the baby's treatment? Would the hospital insist on calling her only living parent? Would they call the police? Truth be told, Lyra had always been such a healthy baby that Soledad hadn't considered illness an option she would have to contend with. Now she didn't have a clue what she needed to do, and she was worried that she might lose Lyra.

She moved to the computer, pulled up Google and typed in Lyra's symptoms. The lengthy list of search results suddenly had her even more anxious, her stomach twisting nervously. She suddenly felt as if she were failing Parenting for Dummies, being thrown a curve she hadn't prepped for.

Back in the room, Lyra had finally stopped crying.

She still clung to Palmer, her head resting against his shoulder. She stared at Soledad, but wasn't moved by the woman's efforts to comfort her.

"Her temperature is high," Palmer said, "but it's not high enough that I think there's something seriously wrong. I gave her a dose of that ibuprofen. She should feel better in no time."

"I thought she might want a bottle," Soledad said, handing it to him.

She watched as Palmer shifted the infant in his arms and fed her the warm milk. Lyra's eyes traveled between the two adults, then stopped to linger on Palmer's face.

I like him, too, Soledad thought, amused by the look of awe Lyra was giving him. *I like him, too!*

Chapter 14

When the alarm sounded, Palmer woke with a start, feeling like he'd been run over by a truck. It had been a long night, neither he nor Soledad getting much sleep. When the night had started, he'd imagined that making love to Soledad would have kept him up till the mid-morning, the two of them savoring the sensual exploration that came with the first time. Neither had imagined a sick baby usurping the moment. Lyra had fussed on and off well into the early morning. Then, just like that, she'd fallen into a sound sleep, leaving the two of them to wonder what they'd done right and why they hadn't done it sooner.

Once they'd realized it was going to be a long night, Palmer had insisted they all climb into his bed. The television had played in the background, reruns of some investigative criminal show Palmer was a fan of. They had passed Lyra back and forth between them, depending on whose arms she showed preference for. To Soledad's chagrin, Jack had licked her tears away, but even she couldn't complain when the dog seemed able to calm her down when they couldn't.

Despite it all, what Palmer had found most interesting was how natural it felt to him: waking up to Soledad in his bed, the baby asleep atop a pillow between them and Jack snoring at their feet. The only other time in his life when something had felt so right, so amazingly perfect, was when his mother Leanne had gone above and beyond to adopt him. When he'd discovered the love of family for the first time and that family was all his. It felt like that again, with Soledad and Lyra. It was inexplicable joy, and Palmer realized it was something he'd been missing, and he wasn't ready to let it go.

He sat watching the two of them. Soledad mumbled in her sleep, only a word here or there that he could recognize. Her breathing was steady, her chest rising and falling rhythmically. Her face was flushed, and one fist was clenched tightly around the bedclothes.

He smiled. He'd often heard friends complain about children changing the trajectory of their sex lives, and now he fully understood it. Any other time, he would have made love to Soledad until his body failed him, exhausted from their loving. Lyra had successfully blocked that effort, his erection withering with her cries. But there was still that ache of need and desire through his pelvic floor, that tingling in his appendages as he thought about the two of them together.

Rising, he headed into the shower, needing the spray of cool water to help him open his eyes and get his day started.

When Soledad opened her eyes, Lyra was sound asleep beside her and Jack lay on her other side. The sound of running water told her Palmer was in the adjoining bathroom. As she thought about him, that shower suddenly felt like it was calling her name. It had been an exceptionally long night and Soledad knew it was probably going to be a long day, as well. She imagined that Lyra would sleep until she was well rested. Then she'd be wide-awake and in need of attention.

Soledad eased her body off the bed, careful not to disturb the sleeping child. Jack lifted his head to give her a look, then nuzzled himself even closer to the baby. They were quite a pair, she thought, remembering how Lyra had given her a side-eye when she'd tried to move Jack to the floor. They had claimed each other and refused to be moved from the comfort they found in their affection for one another. Soledad found herself a little envious of their connection.

She suddenly thought about Palmer again. They had been one orgasm from the tide of their relationship shifting. The intimacy between them had been unexpected and everything Soledad had ever wished for. She had wanted him more than she had ever wanted any man in her life and knew the feeling had been mutual. She could feel it in the hardened lines of every muscle that had risen in his body and in hers. In fact, she still wanted him, that desire so intense that it felt like a gulf had opened up in the pit of her stomach, threatening to swallow her from the inside. The heat was so vast that she imagined herself combusting internally.

Nothing about their situation made an ounce of sense, but in the insanity of it, something beautiful was blooming between them. Something so precious that it gave immense value to the future she wanted for herself. And what she wanted for herself was him.

Sliding open the nightstand drawer, she carefully opened that new box of condoms and palmed one in her hand.

Easing off the bed so as not to wake the baby or the dog, she headed toward the bathroom. With each step, Soledad second-guessed her decision. It was a momentary hesitation as she questioned if she was doing the right thing. Instinctively, she kept moving forward, faith in everything that felt right about him and her together guiding her steps.

As she stepped into the bathroom, Soledad dropped a trail of clothes onto the tiled floor. The room was warm and moist, steam from the hot water painting the walls. Palmer stood behind the frosted glass doors, his head tilted back as the water washed over him. He looked startled when Soledad slid the shower door open.

Neither spoke, words unnecessary as they each admired the view. Soap streaked his torso and the patch of pubic hair was lathered with bubbles. His breathing was suddenly labored and she watched as his erection grew, seeming to beckon her to him. She lifted her eyes to his, moisture laced through his lashes.

The prophylactic in her palm spoke volumes. She

watched as he took it from her and sheathed himself quickly. He extended his hand toward her and pulled her forward. As the palms of her hands pressed against his chest, Palmer crushed his mouth to hers in a kiss that stole her breath and had her curling her toes.

They were suddenly an amalgamation of hands and fingers, mouths and tongues. He lifted her against the tiled wall as she wrapped her legs around him. Heat coursed between them with a mind of its own, the magnitude sweeping through the entirety of the bathroom.

When his body entered hers, Soledad cried out, her nails digging into the flesh across his back. The walls of her most private place pulsed with fervor around his male member, welcoming him home. She met him stroke for stroke as he pushed and pulled against her. Their loving was intense and swift, its power like a tidal wave of energy neither could control. It was a sweet dance of give and take, back and forth, round and round. Soledad climaxed first, her entire body convulsing with pleasure as she clung to him. Palmer followed, the intensity of their interaction making her feel like she'd been thrown from a cliff and was flying sky-high. His legs shook as he eased himself and her to the shower floor, collapsing beneath the sheer beauty of the moment.

Palmer sent Noé a text message to let him know he would be late. Again. It was becoming a bad habit that he was going to have to break before it became problematic. He could only begin to imagine what the ranch hands were whispering about him. In the past, they could set their clocks by his punctuality; missing a full day of work on the ranch was completely out of the question. Lately, he'd been late with some regularity, even not showing up multiple days in a row. Heaven forbid his family found out.

He stared at his reflection in the bathroom mirror. There was something in his face he didn't recognize. Something that put a shimmer in his eyes and deepened the dimples in his cheeks. He liked the change, although he would never admit it to anyone aloud. A wide grin filled his face, the smile spreading from ear to ear.

Making love to Soledad had left him exhilarated. The first time had been fast and furious, only about the physical act necessary to release the sexual tension that had grown between them before Lyra had interrupted them. The second time had been more emotional, the sensual act bringing them both to tears. The third time had been about exploration, about discovering each other's bodies and idiosyncrasies. Like finding that sweet spot just behind her ear that had Soledad writhing with ecstasy whenever he nuzzled his lips and tongue against it.

There would have been a fourth time if Lyra hadn't interrupted them again. She was a demanding little thing, he thought, her sweet smile deceiving if you didn't know better. Palmer shook his head, trying to fathom how parents managed to have two, three and four kids when the first never let them enjoy the act of procreation. He laughed out loud as he wrapped a bath sheet around his waist.

Walking into the bedroom, he was surprised to find

Jack lying in the middle of the bed alone. Soledad and the baby had disappeared into another room.

"What? The girls abandoned you and now you want to hang out with me?"

Jack grunted at him, disinterest written all over his muzzle. He jumped from the bed and padded slowly out the door.

"So much for loyalty and appreciation," Palmer muttered. He laughed, moving to the closet to find his clothes.

When he stepped into the kitchen minutes later, Soledad stood in the center of the room, her hands on her hips as she stared at the television set. There was a commercial playing and she seemed to be waiting for something, one foot tapping anxiously against the hardwood floor. She made him smile and he imagined what every day could be for them with her and the baby there.

Lyra sat propped against Jack, who opened one eye to give him a look that dared Palmer to take the little girl from him. His dog had officially become a monster, Palmer thought.

The local station returned to the morning news. There was a clear shot of downtown, the camera spanning the length of Grave Gulch Boulevard toward the police station and town hall. The streets were lined with protesters holding signs and chanting, their voices ringing out in unison. The newscaster's voice narrated over the images.

"Folks also took to the streets in downtown Grave Gulch today to peacefully protest ongoing concerns with local police chief Melissa Colton and what some are calling a clear lack of accountability and leadership within the ranks. Protesters tell us this issue is particularly concerning in light of the recent discovery that forensic scientist Randall Bowe manipulated evidence in numerous cases, resulting in prejudicial outcomes. Bowe is currently wanted for questioning and a warrant has been issued for his arrest."

The camera then panned to two protesters, a robust woman who was the spitting image of Dolly Parton and an African American man who owned a local business on the protest route.

"All police aren't bad," the woman was saying. "My father is a retired police chief. The problem is the good cops lack the support and resources to do their jobs successfully. We have an issue with that."

The shop owner was less enthusiastic. "Corruption within the police ranks is rampant, and until those in charge are held to a higher standard, it's not going to get better. We need a police chief who isn't afraid to push the status quo and demand better from his team!" he admonished.

The camera went back to the line of protesters, capturing their chants a second time. The newscaster continued.

"The Grave Gulch Police Department took to social media today, posting its response to the protests and calls for Chief Colton's resignation. To read their full statement, go to our website."

The cameras shot back to the newsroom and the newscaster. She was an attractive brunette who looked pageant-ready with her overbright smile and bouffant hairstyle.

"New this morning, authorities are looking for a missing Michigan woman who may have been in Grave Gulch prior to her disappearance, and they need your help."

Soledad's picture suddenly filled the screen. It was a promotional photo she'd had taken when she'd opened the bakery. One of the few pictures that she liked of herself. The on-air personality resumed.

"Grave Gulch Police Department said thirty-year-old Soledad de la Vega was reported missing when she failed to show up for work at her local business, Dream Bakes. De la Vega is believed to have last been in the company of Annie Stone, whose body was discovered days ago. Dr. Gavin Stone is considered a person of interest in the investigation. However, Ms. de la Vega's disappearance is considered suspicious, police said. Anyone with information about the whereabouts of Soledad de la Vega should contact the Grave Gulch police. There is currently a five-thousand-dollar reward for information leading to her whereabouts. When we return…"

Palmer reached for the television remote and depressed the off button. Soledad spun toward him, her eyes wild.

"That doesn't make any sense," she started. "Why would they report me missing?"

Palmer shook his head. "I'm not going to venture to guess," he said as he pulled his cell phone out of his back pocket and dialed. The number rang three times before his brother answered.

"What's wrong?" Troy questioned.

"Is that how you say hello?"

"Under the circumstances, I have to be concerned."

"Local police reported Soledad missing. Do you know anything about that?"

"Technically, she is missing. Melissa was afraid that if it didn't look like we were looking for her or concerned about her whereabouts, Dr. Stone would figure out we knew where she was and maybe figure out where she is himself. We don't want to take any chances he'll find her before we find him."

"And the reward?"

"We wanted to make it look good."

Palmer nodded into the receiver, bobbing his head as if Troy could see him. "Any leads on where Stone might be?"

"The investigation is still ongoing. He's got money and connections, which is making our job harder. Melissa thinks he may have left the state, but there have been one or two tips that have come in, saying he's been spotted here in Grave Gulch."

"You people need to find him," Palmer said.

"You just take care of our witness," Troy answered.

"You need to step up the patrols around my property. Just in case," Palmer quipped. "Please," he added.

"Done," Troy responded.

Disconnecting the call, Palmer shared the information with Soledad. She shook her head, suddenly feeling completely out of sorts. She moved back to the kitchen and the sink full of dishes. Frustration pulled her mouth into a frown, and her eyes narrowed as she felt her brow crease with worry.

"I have to ask," Palmer said. "Are you okay?"

Soledad shrugged her shoulders. "I let my guard down. I let myself forget why Lyra and I are here. Then I started playing house with you like this is some fairy tale with a happy ending."

"It can be."

She shook her head. "I'm not safe as long as Gavin is out there. And me just being here puts you in danger, too."

Palmer shook his head, seeming to fall into thought as he pondered her comment. "No, not as long as I'm here and you trust me. Five minutes from now things will feel like normal again and I will still be doing everything within my power to protect you and Lyra. Nothing is going to happen to you on my watch. Nothing."

Soledad took a deep breath and let it out slowly. She finally gave him a quick nod, her gaze clinging to him as if her life depended on it. Because in many ways, it did.

Something in the oven had filled the room with the aroma of cinnamon and sugar. Soledad took a peek inside the appliance, then moved back to the sink. Palmer shook his head as he eased up behind her. He dropped his hands to the curve of her hips and pressed a damp kiss to her neck. She purred in response, then turned her face to be kissed, grateful to be distracted from those feelings of dread.

"Hungry?" she asked.

"For you."

Soledad giggled. "I made cinnamon rolls. They should be ready any minute now."

"The ones you sell at the bakery with the thick cream-cheese icing?"

She nodded. "Yep. Those ones."

"Let me grab a very large cup of coffee," he said as he kissed her one last time. "Or I'll need a nap when I'm finished with breakfast."

"You're going to be late, aren't you?"

"You mean I'm already late, don't you? If someone hadn't been holding me hostage in the shower…"

Soledad laughed. "You are not going to blame me because you got greedy."

"Greedy? If you weren't giving it away, all willy-nilly like. I am a man, after all."

"Willy-nilly?"

Palmer waved his hand in the air. "I am just calling it like I see it."

"And that sounds just like it might be the last time you get to see it," she joked.

Palmer didn't miss the innuendo. He laughed with her, chuckling heartily. Sliding his arms around her torso, he hugged her close, feeling her body settle against his. He kissed her cheeks, the tip of her nose, her forehead.

"It's going to be okay," he whispered softly. "I promise."

Soledad nodded as she lifted her face to his, easing into the vow against his lips. The kiss they shared was furtive, tongues doing a brazen two-step. He snaked a hand beneath her T-shirt, his fingers pulling at the rock-hard nipple that had blossomed beneath his touch. The moment stalled abruptly when Lyra began crying for attention.

Palmer lifted his gaze, amusement in his eyes. "Baby girl," he said, as he shifted himself from Soledad. "We really need to work on your timing, princess."

Feeling completely out of control at having to stay indoors, Soledad was ready to run screaming into the fields and pull her hair out. She was frustrated and ready to take out her anguish on the first person who looked at her the wrong way. Although she loved Palmer's home, the four walls were starting to feel too close for comfort. She wasn't sure how much more she could take.

Beside her, Lyra gurgled and cooed in her baby seat. Soledad was grateful that the child had no clue what was going on or that what was going on was beginning to get to her. Lyra was happy and the smile on her face could melt icebergs. She was a great source of joy, and Soledad still worried that, with everything going on, she wouldn't be able to keep the child safe.

She hadn't wanted Palmer to see how frightened she was. Because it wasn't Gavin who frightened her. It wasn't Gavin who had her heart racing, thinking about what would happen when things were over and her life went back to normal. Gavin didn't have anything to do with her concerns about where things would stand with Palmer when there was no one and nothing for him to protect her from.

Palmer was trying so hard to ease her mind and to convince her that everything was going to be well. He was also doing a darn good job keeping her distracted. Every time he was near, the heat from their bodies merging, she had a hard time thinking straight. Because Palmer Colton was sexy as hell and damn near perfection in bed! Everything about the man made her heart sing. Taking that step with him had been more than she could have ever wished for. He was definitely some bright sunshine on a dark day.

Soledad suddenly thought about Annie. How she and Annie would have huddled together over the details and a bottle of wine. How Annie would have alleviated her fears and encouraged her to take a risk if it meant she would be happy. How Annie would have been thrilled that she'd found someone she could love. Someone who would love her back.

Annie would have also given her a hard time about jumping into bed with a man she hadn't known longer than a minute. Under normal circumstances, what had happened between them would have been more of a one-night stand. Annie would have helped her make sense of everything she was feeling, though. She would have made sense out of the nonsense. Soledad missed her best friend.

Lyra giggled, seeming to read her mind. She made Soledad laugh and Soledad had seriously needed the laughter. The baby suddenly scrunched up her face as if to cry, but pulled her big toe into her mouth. Drool trickled down her foot.

Soledad chuckled. "Okay, kiddo, I'm limber, but I'm not that limber. Why are you showing off?"

Lyra looked at her with wide eyes and the slightest pout. Her face twisted a second time, and then she kicked her legs and pitched her body backward.

"Well, that's not very ladylike. What's going on, sweet pea?"

Lyra went back to chewing on that toe and her clenched fist. Soledad grabbed a cloth diaper and wiped at the spit that puddled over the baby's chin. That was when she saw the beginnings of a new tooth piercing Lyra's upper gum.

"Someone's teething. Look at that! Poor baby! No wonder you had a bad night!"

Lyra gurgled and chewed.

Soledad leaned to give the baby a kiss on her forehead. Everything about Lyra brought her immense joy. She fully understood Annie's commitment to the infant because she now, too, would lay down her own life to keep the child safe. Her love knew no limits and she imagined it was what Palmer's mother felt for him when he'd been adopted.

She suddenly had a light-bulb moment. "I need to bake you some teething cookies," she thought out loud. "In fact, I'm going to bake cookies for you and for Palmer. Palmer likes my cookies."

Lyra didn't look all that impressed, which made Soledad laugh.

Chapter 15

Whether or not Palmer showed up on time, Colton Ranch still operated like an efficient machine. Between the miles of fencing, irrigation systems, corrals for holding the sheep and cattle, the loading chutes and trailers, his crew was quite able to keep things running smoothly. With the new shipment of cattle that had arrived the day before, they now had to be branded with the ranch logo.

Palmer was fortunate in his ranch hands. Between the animals, the land, the machines and dozens of other jobs that needed to be performed, his workers were loyal, giving him 110 percent of themselves. As he pulled up to the site, Noé was already in place, ensuring the branding process went off without a hitch.

Gone were the days of traditional branding, where

an animal was captured and thrown to the ground, its legs tied together and a fire-heated branding iron applied to its hindquarters. Palmer and his crew herded the animals through a chute instead, where they ran into a confined area and could be safely secured while the brand was being applied with an electric iron. By the time Palmer reached the pasture, more than half the cows had been marked.

"Good job," Palmer said, extending his hand to shake Noé's. "I can't tell you how much I appreciate you."

"All the men are doing great," Noé said, gesturing at one of the workers with his hand. "This is a good crew."

Palmer nodded. "Then I'm going to leave you to it. I'll head over to the north fields. We need to finish the repairs on those irrigation pipes. It'll probably be dusk when we get done."

"I'll head over to help when we are done here, jefe."

Palmer shook his head. "No, I need you to move the cattle to the other pasture, so they don't start overgrazing here. Tomorrow we're going to need to cut the hay, so we'll need to check the haying equipment tonight to make sure everything's in good working order."

Noé gave him a nod, then went back to focusing on the job at hand.

Jumping back into his truck, Palmer drove to the other side of the ranch. He parked his vehicle and got out, pulling on a pair of leather gloves as he made his exit. A handful of men, already in place, had started to dig out the ditches that needed to be repaired. Grabbing his own shovel from the bed of the truck, Palmer leaped in to give them a hand.

An hour later his shirt was stained with sweat, his face was streaked with mud, and every muscle in his body hurt. The work wasn't easy and only a select few were able to do it and do it well. These were some of the strongest men he'd ever known, and he was honored to call most of them friends.

Lunch came quickly and they were past the point of readiness when they were finally able to take a break. Most fell to the ground to rest and enjoy packed lunches and bottles of ice water from the cooler in the bed of Palmer's truck. Laughter was abundant and Palmer took a bit of ribbing from the men who'd known him longest. Shortly after lunch, Noé and two of the other men joined them, helping to knock the job out quickly.

Palmer was first to see the young man in the distance. He was coming from the direction of the main road. He was alone and walking at a good pace toward the crew. As he got closer, Palmer saw that he was fairly young, more boy than man, with dark curls, large eyes and a lanky frame. He wore denim jeans, a white T-shirt, and carried a backpack. He wasn't the first stranger to pass through the farmland and probably wouldn't be the last, but given everything going on with Soledad, Palmer didn't trust anyone he didn't know.

Noé seemed to sense his concern as he stepped beside him.

"Do you recognize him?" Palmer asked.

Noé shook his head. "No, jefe. I have never seen him before."

"Do me a favor and check him out. If he doesn't feel right to you, send him on his way."

Palmer watched as Noé met the boy down the road. The two stood in conversation for a brief moment, then began to walk together toward Palmer and the work crew. As tests went, it looked like he had passed the first one. Getting past Palmer's number two in charge wasn't an easy thing to do.

When the two reached his side, Noé gave his boss a nod as he sauntered past, leaving him and the boy standing together.

"How can I help you?" Palmer asked.

He extended his hand. "Good afternoon, sir. My name's Benjamin Harris. I heard you might be hiring and I'm looking for a job."

"Palmer Colton," he said as he shook the boy's hand. "How old are you, Benjamin Harris? You look awful young."

"I'll be eighteen in the fall."

"Have you ever worked on a ranch before? Or done any kind of manual labor?"

"Not really, but I'm willing to learn. My father was a jack-of-all-trades and he taught me a lot before he died."

"I'm sorry for your loss."

The young man shrugged. "Thank you."

"So, why should I hire you?"

"I have a strong work ethic. I'll work hard. I'm a fast learner and I like getting my hands dirty. You won't be disappointed."

Palmer stared at the kid. There was something in his eyes that Palmer recognized. A deep hunger that seeped past his lashes. A look that reminded Palmer of himself at that age. Determined to have his dreams, to accomplish a lengthy list of goals and to be the best person he could possibly be. What he saw in the young man named Benjamin had been the same drive he himself had possessed when he had wanted to make his parents proud.

"What about school?" Palmer asked. "Have you graduated?"

"Yes, sir. This past spring."

"What about college? Are you going in the fall?"

"I don't know if school is what I want to do with my life right now. That's why I need a job."

"Do you know anything about horses?"

"Some. My dad taught me how to ride, but we never owned one."

Palmer turned to eye the crew, who'd just replaced the last length of pipe that needed to be repaired. The trenches were being filled in and the crew was ready to be done for the day. He turned back to Benjamin.

"If you're willing to learn, I'm willing to give you a shot. Be here tomorrow at dawn. The work is going to be dirty. You'll be mucking horse stalls and cleaning stables. Whether or not we keep you will depend on how well you do."

Benjamin grinned. "Thank you, sir. Thank you. I really appreciate it."

Palmer held out his hand a second time. "Call me Palmer."

Benjamin nodded. "Palmer, thank you. And you can call me Ben."

"Well, Ben, aren't you going to ask me how much you'll be making?"

Ben shrugged. "I know it'll be a fair wage. Your reputation precedes you, sir."

As he headed back to the house, Palmer had a lot on his mind. A few times, he thought his head might explode, too many thoughts vying for his attention—Soledad taking center stage with most of them. He had missed her. Even as he'd dug piles of dirt and torn up his hands cinching pipe, she had been on his mind. All he could think of was getting to the end of the day and getting back to her.

There was so much for him to process and unpack. Soledad was his dream come true, but he had to be rational about their situation. Soledad had known what she'd wanted. But had she wanted what had happened between them because she'd desired him or because she'd needed a diversion from the stress of the situation? And why was he suddenly doubtful about them being together, second-guessing if taking that jump had been a good thing? Because, deep down, he knew that what they'd shared was honest and genuine, and everything he had ever wanted. He just wasn't certain that Soledad felt the same way, and that actually scared him more than anything else.

As he pulled in, his cell phone rang. He glanced at the incoming number before he answered the call.

"I could use some good news," he said to the caller, not bothering with "hello."

"So could I. Do you have any for me?" Melissa Colton asked.

"I wish. How are you doing, beautiful?"

"I've been better. I'm sure you've heard about the protests. They're calling for my head on a platter."

"I hate that you have to go through this."

"It may well be the end for me. I know the city council is considering a special meeting to discuss whether or not I am fit to continue in my position."

"Whatever you need from me, you know you have it, right?"

"I appreciate that. Right now, though, I need to know about my witness."

"Obviously, I'm not doing a good job keeping her hidden if you're asking about her."

"Quite the opposite. I wouldn't know where she was if you hadn't told Troy."

"He's such a tattletale."

"He's a good cop. We excuse the rest because he's family."

Palmer chuckled. "So, where are you with finding Gavin Stone?"

"That's why I'm calling. I want you to know I've stepped up the patrols in your area. We've had two credible sightings. He is definitely still in the area, and for some reason, he seems to be focused on that end of town."

"Good. I have something for him if he shows up."

Melissa took a deep breath. "I want to move Soledad and the baby to a safe house. I think it would be best."

Palmer paused, considering the comment. Personally, he didn't agree with his cousin. He wasn't ready for Soledad or Lyra to leave him, and he was willing to do whatever was necessary to keep her there, safe and sound under his watch. He said, "I'll discuss it with her, but I doubt she'll do it. Under the circumstances, she's not very trusting."

"Look, I get it, but I still think it would be in her best interest."

"I don't want to risk her running. I'll see what she says, but if the answer is no, I'll keep a watchful eye on her. You can trust that."

"You just be careful, please. Stone is a dangerous man and there's no telling what he might do if he feels cornered. He's hell-bent on getting his hands on Soledad and his baby, and there's no telling what he might do."

"Does he have a legal claim to Lyra?" Palmer questioned.

Melissa took a deep breath. "Legally, the court would have to consider any claims he may have, since he is her biological father, but Annie was very clear about where she wanted the child to be placed. I highly doubt he's planning to take any legal route to get custody of Lyra."

Palmer sighed, a heavy breath blowing past his lips. "I'll call you once I talk to Soledad. But I wouldn't get my hopes up if I were you," he said.

"Thanks, cousin. Love you!"

Palmer disconnected the call. He didn't have to ask Soledad the question to know the answer. She wasn't going to leave if she didn't have to, and he didn't want her to go. He couldn't keep her safe if she were somewhere else, and he didn't have the heart to tell Melissa that he wasn't so trusting of the Grave Gulch Police Department himself. He knew most of the officers through his family. Some he liked, others he didn't. Trust didn't come just because they wore a badge and carried a gun. Many were a fine lot of officers and most just wanted to do the best job they could possibly do. It was the few who weren't as committed that worried him. The ones who didn't wear a sign that said they might be dirty, on the take or just plain lazy about their responsibilities. So, no, he thought. Soledad and Lyra weren't going anywhere if he had anything to say about it.

From where he sat, he saw Soledad peeking out past the wooden blinds that decorated his windows. He waved his hand so that she would know he was fine. He had one more phone call to make before he went inside, and he was dialing as she blew him a kiss through the glass.

Geoff Colton answered on the first ring. "Where are you, son? We were expecting you here an hour ago."

"Hey, Pop. Happy birthday."

"Thank you."

"I ran into some problems here on the ranch. It's taking me longer to get them resolved than I anticipated."

"I hate to hear that. Do you need us to come give you a hand?"

Palmer chuckled. "No, sir. I can handle it. You just enjoy your birthday party. I'm sorry I can't be there, but I'll make it up to you." And Palmer was sorry, wishing he could be there and wishing Soledad and Lyra could be there with him.

He finally understood what his father had meant

when he'd been a boy, professing that your family was your greatest blessing. How he'd been a stern disciplinarian, ensuring they all stayed on a straight and narrow path. He often found himself sounding like his dad when he spoke with the boys in his program. And his time with baby Lyra brought memories of his father's adoration for his sisters. Geoff Colton was the epitome of what a father should be, and Palmer was discovering just how much he wanted to follow in those footsteps.

There was a rumbling on the other end and Palmer could hear Grace's muffled voice. He didn't have to be there to know that she was fussing, or that his father had covered the receiver with his hand, hoping that he wouldn't hear her complaining.

Geoff cleared his throat. "Your sister is already making faces. Do you want to talk to her?"

"Oh, hell no. Tell Grace there is only one woman who gets to discipline me, and her name is Leanne Colton."

Geoff laughed. "Well, Mom is loving on little Danny. Your nephew is quite the ladies' man."

"I'm sure Desiree doesn't want to hear that."

"Your sister will have to get over it. When you have pretty babies, they grow up to be pretty adults. Danny will be a heartbreaker like his grandpa."

Palmer laughed. "Well, I hate to miss all the fun, but I'll run by the house to see you both soon."

"Not to worry, son. God willing, there'll be more birthday parties for you to celebrate with me. I plan to get good and old."

"I love you, Dad."

"We love you, too, son."

* * *

When Palmer walked through the door, Soledad stood with Lyra in her arms, the two of them smiling brightly. Amusement flitted across their faces.

"What?" he said, eyeing them both anxiously. "What did I do?" He tossed a look over both shoulders in jest.

"We need a taste tester," Soledad announced.

Lyra suddenly flung a biscuit across the room. Jack bounded in that direction and eagerly scooped up the treat.

"Naughty girl." Soledad's scold brimmed with amusement. "Stop doing that."

Confusion danced through Palmer. "What are you three up to?"

"I tried to make teething biscuits for Lyra. But she doesn't like them, and every time I give her one, she flings it across the room for Jack to eat."

"That's not saying much. Jack is a canine vacuum cleaner. He'll eat pretty much anything and everything."

"I think they taste good. There's no accounting for her taste buds. You get to be the deciding vote," Soledad said as she pointed to the plate of cookies on the counter.

Palmer shook his head as he stepped forward to take one. He eyed the cookie cautiously, his brow lifted and his face squinched. "It doesn't look very appetizing. There aren't any chocolate chips or nuts or caramel… Nothing."

"It's a teething biscuit."

He took a nibble and then a bigger bite. A second later, he flung the cookie across the room and Jack happily retrieved it. Lyra laughed robustly, the wealth of it so heartwarming that Soledad and Palmer couldn't help but laugh with her.

"You two are no help at all," Soledad said.

Palmer leaned in to kiss her lips. "They taste like paste with a hint of vanilla."

"Paste? They are not that bad!"

Palmer took Lyra from Soledad's arms. "Oh, yes, they are. Isn't that right, princess?"

Soledad rolled her eyes at the ceiling. "How was your day?"

"Long and exhausting. I need a shower, something to eat and your good cookies." He gave her a suggestive wink.

Soledad felt herself blush, her cheeks warming rapidly.

"Not those cookies," Palmer said teasingly. "Your *other* cookies."

Soledad moved to stand behind the counter. "Well, go grab that shower. By the time you get back, the food will be ready and we can discuss my cookies after Lyra goes down for the night. Considering that food review, I'm not sure you're going to get any more of my cookies."

"Do you see how your mommy does me?" Palmer said teasingly. He nuzzled his face against Lyra's as the little girl grabbed both his cheeks. "She's not being a very nice mommy."

"You're not winning any points, Mr. Colton. You might want to quit while you're ahead."

Palmer sat Lyra in her high chair. He eased around the counter to press himself against Soledad, cradling his body against hers. She was warm and soft and smelled of cardamom and ginger. He pressed a damp kiss to her neck and felt her body jump ever so slightly.

Dessert couldn't come fast enough, Palmer thought. He kissed her one last time, then headed down the hall to the bedroom.

Chapter 16

"No!" Soledad said emphatically. "If Melissa insists, Lyra and I'll take off and find somewhere else to hide out, but I'm not going into witness protection with the local police department."

"I told her you probably wouldn't agree, but I promised I'd ask," Palmer responded.

The two sat side by side on the family room sofa. Palmer was finishing off a bottle of beer and she sipped on a glass of white wine. Lyra had gone down for the night and they hoped with fingers crossed that she would sleep through most of it. Jack had gone out the door ten minutes earlier, racing across the fields toward goodness knew what. He would come in when Palmer made his late-night rounds to check on the animals.

"Unless you'd prefer we leave?" Soledad said. She shifted in her seat to face him.

"Not at all. You are welcome to stay here for as long as you need."

"And that's kind of you, but how do you really feel about us being here?" Soledad questioned.

Palmer paused for a split second. "It would break my heart if you left," he finally said softly. "I want you here, with me." He leaned to kiss her cheek, allowing his lips to linger sweetly against her skin.

Soledad let go of the breath she'd been holding as she waited for him to answer. She took a sip of her wine. "Did she say anything about Gavin?"

Palmer pushed his shoulders toward the ceiling. "They're still looking," he muttered, not bothering to elaborate because he really had nothing new to add to the conversation.

"Maybe he has left town," Soledad said. "Maybe this will be over soon and then things can go back to normal for the both of us."

"What's normal?"

"You'll get your life back and you won't have to babysit me and Lyra anymore."

"Who's babysitting you?"

"Didn't you have a party to go to tonight? You mentioned it the other day."

"Yeah, it was a birthday party for my father. There'll be other ones," Palmer said.

"I hate that you had to miss it. You know you could have gone. Lyra and I would have been fine."

"I didn't want to go. I wanted to spend the evening with you."

"But your family…"

"My family celebrates something every other week. Hopefully, when they have the next party, you'll be able to go with me." Palmer shifted in his seat. Things were different between them now and he knew he couldn't consider a future that didn't include her and the baby. More important, Palmer knew he didn't want to. He frequently wished a quiet prayer that she was feeling the same way.

"Do you think about what will happen with us when this is over, Palmer?"

"I do. All the time. I imagine you'll go back to the bakery and forget all about me," he said facetiously.

"I was thinking the same thing about you and your ranch."

"I could never forget about you, Soledad." Palmer gave her a smile as he slid his empty beer bottle across the table. "You've left quite an impression on me."

"You say that now. But we'll see."

"I'm sure we will," Palmer laughed and then changed the subject. "I'm going to be gone most of the day tomorrow. I have to catch up on some maintenance work. Noé has to take a few days off, so I'll need to step up and act like I own this place."

"One of your employees came to the door today. At least, I think it was one of your employees."

"Here at the house?"

Soledad nodded. "He was a young guy. He wore jeans and a T-shirt, and he carried a backpack. He rang the bell first and then he went into the barn. Later I saw him with the other guys, sitting in the bed of the truck. That's why I assumed he worked for you."

"He was in the barn?"

"Yeah, and then he walked that way." She pointed a finger toward where Palmer and his crew had been working.

Palmer's eyes shifted as he pondered that tidbit of news. He had to wonder who had trespassed and why, although he was fairly certain he knew who it had been. But why, he wondered, was his new employee poking around the property?

"Did he see you?" Palmer prodded.

"No, I don't think so. When he came to the door, he was trying to peek through the sidelights, but Lyra and I were in the bedroom. I only knew he went into the barn because he was coming out of it when I finally came out to see who it was."

"Interesting…"

"Does he not work for you?"

"If we're talking about the same young man, I actually hired him today."

"So, he's new and he was nosing around?"

"I was just thinking the same thing," Palmer said. "I have some questions for him tomorrow. If I don't like the answers, his career here may come to a quick end."

"I didn't get the impression that he was up to anything malicious. Just that maybe he was looking for you."

"Let's hope that's all it was. Because I really liked

him. He seemed like a good kid and I thought he had potential. He reminded me a lot of myself."

Soledad reached her hand out and tapped his thigh. The gesture was gentle and comforting. Palmer dropped his own atop hers and tangled his fingers with her fingers. They sat together for a few minutes, listening to the jazz that played on his stereo.

"I need to make my rounds," Palmer finally said. He pressed a kiss to her cheek.

"Find that babysitter of ours while you're out there," Soledad said. "And I'll go get your cookies ready."

Palmer laughed and kissed her again.

Palmer stood in the center of the barn and looked around. Although Soledad was certain the young man who'd told Palmer his name was Ben Harris had been there, there was nothing amiss or out of place that gave Palmer any pause. They had been able to move Pharaoh back with the other horses the day before, so this barn was empty, housing nothing but old tools and farm equipment. He didn't bother to check the cabinets because he had moved all the guns from the space the night he'd been shot at. Giving any possible intruders easy access to a weapon didn't seem prudent.

Jack suddenly barked as he came barreling into the barn. He was panting heavily, like he'd just run a marathon. Palmer filled a metal trough with water, and the dog drank, practically plunging his whole head into the container. "What's up, big guy? What are you chasing?"

Jack barked again excitedly, spinning around Palmer's feet. He raced to the farmhouse and back again.

"Okay! Okay! We're going back inside. Just be patient. Down, Jack," he commanded.

Jack lay at his feet, feigning patience. He made Palmer laugh as he tried not to jump up and down.

Minutes later, the Bernese was sound asleep under the crib in the guest bedroom. Lyra slept as soundly, out like a light. The kitchen was clean, and Soledad had dimmed the lights. He could hear soft music coming from the bedroom. After double-checking that all the doors were closed and locked, and then setting the alarm, he made his way to the master bedroom.

He stilled in the doorway. Excitement rained through his body like a downpour in the middle of a summer day. Soledad lay naked across the bed. Her head rested against the palm of her hand, her elbow propping up her torso. Her legs were crossed at the ankles and a plate of chocolate-chip cookies rested in front of her pubic area. The smile on her face was pure gold.

"Cookies!" Palmer exclaimed. "May I have one?"

He watched as she bit down on her bottom lip, widened her eyes and gave the slightest shrug of her shoulder.

Palmer reached for one of the treats, pulled it to his mouth and took a bite. He chewed slowly, observing her as she slid her top leg up the length of the other and back down.

He reached his hand down a second time to caress her long hair, twirling a strand around his finger. Soledad trailed her index finger across the back of his hand. Her touch was teasing, and every muscle in his body quivered for attention.

Palmer swallowed the last bite of his treat, then bent to kiss her mouth. Their lips met in a gentle touch, gliding like velvet against silk. Their tongues danced sweetly, flirted nonchalantly.

He finally took a step back. He began a slow striptease, pulling his T-shirt over his head and flinging it to the side. His pants followed, boxers and all, as he slid them to his ankles and kicked them after his discarded shirt. Soledad rolled back against the pillows, apparently admiring the sight as Palmer lifted one knee onto the mattress and then the other.

Picking up the plate, Palmer eased it onto the nightstand. He grabbed Soledad by the ankle and parted her legs. Before she could exhale a breath, he pressed his mouth against her, his tongue darting back and forth over her mons.

He could sense the sheer pleasure rippling through her, every nerve obviously firing sweetly as he gently spread her open like a flower, exposing the petals of her sex as his tongue lashed at her hungrily.

Soledad slid her hand against the back of his head and pushed herself into his face. She moaned, and when he found her most sensitive spot, his tongue wrapping around it as he sucked her juices, she arched her back and he heard her call out his name.

Palmer clutched the round of her buttocks and rolled, pulling her above him, his mouth still locked tightly around her. Her arms flailed as she began to ride his face, thrusting her pubis back and forth against his lips and tongue.

She came quickly, her orgasm hitting with a vengeance. Her body quivered and shook as he held her, refusing to let her move from him as his mouth and tongue continued their ministrations. Then Palmer shifted gears, sliding her downward until she dropped against him, his sheathed dick like solid steel piercing her feminine spirit.

They made the sweetest love, his hands wrapped around her body as he cupped her buttocks beneath his palms and guided her ministrations. He felt her muscles grab his member, her insides pulsing rhythmically around him. It was almost more than he could bear as she leaned forward to kiss his chest, his neck and that sweet spot beneath his chin.

Palmer pumped himself into and out of her, over and over again. He grabbed one bouncing breast and then the other as he fondled the dark nubs that had hardened beneath his touch. Fluids mingled, time stood still and then every nerve in both their bodies exploded in unison. It was pure bliss, paradise on steroids, pleasure beyond belief. As Soledad collapsed against him, Palmer wrapped her in his arms and hugged her tightly against him, vowing to never let her go.

Sleep came quickly to them both, but not before he whispered her name and told her that he loved her. When Soledad closed her eyes, a smile graced her face and joy blessed her heart.

There had to be some law against the things she and Palmer had done in his bed, Soledad thought. In the back of her mind, she swore that she had heard her mother's voice admonishing her to be a good girl because only bad girls behaved so wantonly. Annie's voice had superseded the matriarch's, her bestie praising her and giving her a high five for being able to get both legs up over her head. Him saying he loved her was icing on some very sweet, sweet cake!

Making love to Palmer was truly an out-of-body experience, and Soledad was certain Saint Peter would hose her down, make her recite a decade's worth of Hail Marys and then maybe, just maybe, consider giving her a ticket to enter through the pearly gates.

"We're going straight to hell," she said out loud.

Palmer laughed. "You don't go to hell for great sex, Soledad."

"Well, you definitely don't get into heaven doing what we just did."

"Correct me if I'm wrong, but I think they call that purgatory."

"Exactly. We're going straight to hell. Because what we just did can't possibly be any good for anyone."

He tightened his arms around her, her head resting on his chest.

"Do you regret being with me, Soledad?" Palmer asked. "Because you're starting to make me feel some kind of way."

"No. Not at all. If I had to make the decision again, I would do it each and every time. What about you?"

"I might not do a repeat of that cramp I caught in my thigh, but I would happily give you a repeat performance of everything else."

Soledad giggled. They had made love, slept and then woken to repeat their performance over again. Now, lying together as the sun was starting to find its rightful seat in the sky, both were wide-awake and she was feeling reflective.

"We happened fast. Under extenuating circumstances," Soledad continued.

"Which makes our being together even more special."

"Some people would say we've only set ourselves up for failure."

"What do you say?"

"I don't want us to fail," she said. And she didn't, because Soledad had come to accept that she loved Palmer. She loved him with every fiber of her being and she never wanted to let him go. She lifted her gaze to his, her eyes saying everything that was in her heart.

"Then we won't. But you're doing what I often do. You're overthinking things and you need to stop. Can't we just enjoy being together without questioning every little detail?"

Soledad paused, thinking about his question. "No, of course not," she finally answered. "Where's the fun in that? Especially since that now means we have a daughter to consider and little girls come with a whole other set of problems!"

Palmer laughed again. "I'm going to grab a quick nap. Then I'm going to make love to you one more time before I have to get up and go to work. I'd suggest you do the same." He curled his body around hers, his pelvis against her buttocks, his chest to her back, his arms crossed over her breasts. He cuddled close to her and blew a kiss against the back of her neck.

"Hey," Soledad said minutes later. "I love you, too, Palmer Colton." And then she giggled softly, because Palmer was sound asleep and hadn't heard a word she said.

Soledad jumped, a loud noise in the kitchen scaring her awake. She lay there for a moment, listening. Except for what had dropped in the distance, it was quiet. Eerily quiet. She reached a hand over to the other side of the bed and it was empty. Palmer was gone. And so was the baby monitor that had rested on the nightstand. If Lyra had cried, she wouldn't have heard a thing. She took a deep breath to calm her nerves.

Rising, she grabbed the clothes she'd discarded the night before and threw them on to cover her nakedness. Pulling her hair back, she twisted the lengthy strands into a bun. Still uncertain, Soledad hurried down the hall to the other bedroom to check for Lyra, but the baby wasn't there. She rushed to the kitchen.

Palmer sat at the counter, sipping on a cup of coffee. He was jotting notes onto a sheet of paper. Lyra was in her high chair, gumming one of the teething cookies from the night before. Soledad felt her entire body smile at the sight of them.

"Good morning," she said softly.

Palmer looked up, not having expected her to be there. "Good morning," he answered. "You're up. I was going to let you sleep until I had to leave."

"I heard a loud noise."

"I dropped that big pot trying to put it into the cabinet. I apologize."

"No apology necessary. Are you late?"

He shook his head. "No, right on schedule, actually."

"You must be exhausted. You didn't get a whole lot of sleep last night."

"I got enough. I feel invigorated."

"That probably won't last long. You'll be dragging by lunch."

"Then I'll come home and you can put me to bed."

"Me putting you to bed is why you didn't get any sleep last night," she said with a hearty laugh.

Palmer chuckled with her. "That's what I was counting on."

"Do I have time to grab a shower before you have to leave?"

He nodded. "You do if it's a quick one. I'm going to finish my coffee and read the headlines to Lyra."

"Aren't you a lucky little girl," Soledad said as she moved to give the baby a kiss.

Lyra gurgled, still gnawing on that cookie.

"What did you do to get her to eat that?"

"I smeared a little grape jelly on it," Palmer said. "I thought about peanut butter, but since we don't know if she has any allergies, grape jelly won out."

Soledad shook her head. "Seriously, they were not that bad."

He laughed. "You're right, but with jelly and peanut butter, they are much better."

Chapter 17

Palmer stopped digging the trench to take a quick breather. The sun had finally disappeared behind a multitude of clouds, giving them a few minutes of reprieve. He gulped air and stretched his tired muscles. At the other end of the expanse, Benjamin was still wielding his shovel, breaking the soil and slinging dirt behind him. He'd been shoveling for as long as Palmer, only pausing for water once or twice. Palmer still had concerns about the boy's motives, questions unanswered about why he'd gone to the house and into the barn. He trusted the answers would come, and as he watched him work so steadily, Palmer was impressed with his fortitude and told him so.

"You're doing a good job, Ben," he said as he stepped over to where the boy was working. "You tired yet?"

Benjamin stopped and stood upright. He swept dirt from his hands onto his face as he wiped away the sweat pooling on his forehead. "Thank you, sir. I'm just trying to keep up with you."

"That could get you hurt. You just focus on doing what you can do, son."

"Yes, sir."

"You ready to grab some lunch?"

Benjamin shrugged. "I didn't bring anything to eat, so I can just keep working."

"Don't worry about that. I'll gladly share mine. But you need to take a break. You can't keep pushing your body like that without risking an injury."

"Yes, sir. Thank you, sir."

"Come on. We're done here for the day. I need to make my rounds. Then, after we eat something, I'm going to teach you how to muck the stables. You'll do that for the rest of the day. It's dirty work but necessary."

"Whatever you need, sir."

"And stop 'sir-ing' me. Call me Palmer."

"Yes, sir."

Palmer gave the kid a look, then burst out laughing. "Let's ride," he said, gesturing toward his truck.

Gathering the shovels, Benjamin followed Palmer to his vehicle. They placed the tools in the bed and hopped into the cab. Palmer started the ignition and a gust of cool air rushed out of the vents.

"Air-conditioning!" Benjamin said with a chuckle.

"It can be a workingman's best friend," Palmer said.

Palmer twiddled with the radio dial until the local country station came in loud and clear. A Trace Adkins song billowed out of the speakers, and both men began to bob their heads in time to the music.

"There's nothing like a cool breeze and a good country song," Palmer said.

"Maybe throw in a bottle of pop," Benjamin added.

"A cool breeze, a good country song and your favorite beverage. Sounds like heaven to me," Palmer laughed.

"My father used to say heaven was a good meal, a good woman and good loving. If a man had that, he didn't need anything else."

"Tell me about your father," Palmer said as he drove toward the pastures to check on the cattle. He wanted to know more about the kid, still not sure if he could be trusted. In the back of his mind something about the boy was eating at him. Something that said he needed to be wary, most especially since he had to protect Soledad and Lyra with every resource available to him.

"He was a great guy. He and my mother adopted me when I was a kid. According to my adoption records, they didn't know who my sperm donor was, and my biological mother just abandoned me at the local hospital. They never found her and I was put in foster care for a few years.

"The Harris family was the fourth or fifth family to take me in. I wasn't an easy kid. I had rage issues. But they were great. My mom was so patient with me. I remember how she used to just sit and hold me and sing to me until I calmed down. She died when I was twelve years old. She had breast cancer. After that, it was just me and my dad. He became my mother and my father.

He was the best. He said that they had once wanted to adopt more children, but never got the chance, and when my mom died, he thought it best that I get all his attention, so I never had any siblings. It was just me and him. He gave me a good life. A really good life."

"If you don't mind me asking, what happened to him?" Palmer asked, cutting his eye toward the young man. "I know you said he died recently."

"He was murdered. You know that serial killer Len Davison, who's been in the news for getting away with murder because of that dude who threw away all the evidence?"

Palmer nodded. "Yeah, Randall Bowe."

"My dad was one of his victims. I didn't have anyone after that, and now I'm here."

Palmer released a heavy sigh. "I'm sorry that it's been hard for you, kid. I was in foster care, too. I was five years old when my family adopted me. I'm blessed to still have them. I know everyone's not that lucky and I don't take it for granted."

Palmer felt the young man staring at him. "You were lucky," the kid said, his tone almost wistful.

Palmer smiled. "We were both lucky. Don't ever think differently. We had family who loved us. Not all the kids in foster care will have that."

Benjamin muttered something under his breath.

"Excuse me?" Palmer said. "I didn't catch that."

Benjamin shook his head. "It was nothing. I was just agreeing with you." He changed the subject. "Do you have any kids?"

Palmer shook his head. "No. I really wasn't interested in having kids, but…well…" He hesitated, suddenly realizing that, since Lyra and Soledad, everything he had thought he'd wanted and everything he'd believed about himself had changed. He was a different man and life had taken on a whole other meaning. It had happened so quickly that he hadn't even seen it coming. "No," he concluded, "I don't have any children yet." He took a deep inhalation of air, allowing the wealth of emotion he was feeling to envelop him.

"I thought you had a wife and kid," Benjamin was saying. "I saw them at your house when I was there."

Palmer's brow creased. "When were you at my house?"

"Yesterday, when I walked in from the road. One of the work crews pointed me toward the house, but no one answered when I rang the bell. I looked in the barn for you, but when you weren't there, I kept walking until I ran into you."

Palmer nodded his head as he took the information in, but didn't respond. Why had Benjamin been looking for him?

"You're not upset with me, are you?" Benjamin continued. "I know I was trespassing, but I didn't mean your family any harm. And I don't think she even saw me. I just wanted to ask about a job."

"No, it's fine," Palmer said finally. But it wasn't, something still laying a brick wall of doubt around him. He ignored the comment as he pondered the ramifications of Ben's admission, his answers feeling ready before the questions were even asked.

The two had finally made it to the other side of the

property by the ponds. Palmer parked the truck and gestured for Benjamin to follow him. He grabbed a picnic basket from the rear and began to walk. Two massive rock formations bordered one side of the watery pool. The landing at the top of each was flat and Palmer climbed up a set of steps that looked like they'd been carved into the towers. He took a seat. Benjamin climbed up after him and they settled down to enjoy their lunch.

"This is pretty cool," Benjamin said as he looked out over the water, enjoying the view.

"This was one reason why I purchased the property. The previous owner was a friend of my father's, and my brother and I would come play here when we were little. This spot here has become my personal sanctuary when I need to think and clear my head. Because I have been where you are now and I understand how you feel, I thought you could use a space like this. You're welcome to come sit anytime. And if you ever need someone to talk to, I'm here for you." Palmer gave the young man a compassionate smile.

"Thank you," Benjamin responded. "I appreciate the kindness. You know when you're a foster kid that people aren't always kind to you."

Palmer nodded. "It's a broken system, and sadly, there are some who are so broken themselves that all they know how to do is hurt others."

Seeming to fall into thought, Benjamin shifted his gaze back over the landscape.

Palmer carried on. "You were blessed to have been spared the hardships of the foster system. I'm grateful every day that I was showed so much love by my adoptive family. Just as I'm sure you appreciate yours."

"Yeah," Benjamin said, "it was a blessing."

Palmer flipped the lid open on the lunch basket he'd carried to the top with them. Soledad had packed him two sandwiches and he passed one to Benjamin. The bread was homemade. It was a focaccia topped with fresh rosemary, olive oil and flaky sea salt. She had layered the bread with Genoa salami and provolone topped with thinly sliced onion, lettuce, peperoncino and tomatoes, then drizzled with olive oil and vinegar.

Benjamin took a bite, chewing slowly. He suddenly hummed his appreciation. "This is really good," he said.

Palmer grinned. "One of my new favorites."

He pulled a penknife from his back pocket and sliced an apple in two. There were also three cookies, one of which he gave to Benjamin. "These were made special just for me. I can't share them as generously."

Benjamin laughed. "I wouldn't share, either. They're even better than the sandwich."

The men continued to chat easily. The more Palmer learned about Benjamin, the more he saw himself and the more he wanted to help the kid.

"There's a program I sponsor every month for children in Grave Gulch group homes. I'd like it if you'd think about volunteering and helping out. I think you'd be an inspiration to them. Especially the older boys who are looking for role models."

"Me? A role model?"

"Of course. Why not?"

"Why would anyone want to look up to me?" Benjamin asked.

"Because you're doing the work to better yourself and it's important that other kids see that the hard work is necessary for success."

"You sound like one of those pamphlets they give you when you age out of the system."

"I don't know about all that. I was actually thinking I just sounded a lot like my father," Palmer said with a soft chuckle.

Soledad listened as Palmer told her about his day. He was excited, his new employee having made quite an impression on him. She found his exuberance heartwarming. They were falling into an easy pattern with each other. Their love language felt natural and easy as the fresh air blowing through the trees outside. She felt confident in the decisions they would make together, and she trusted him with her and Lyra's lives. She reached for his hand and squeezed his fingers.

"I think he just needs to know there are people out there who care about him," Palmer told her. "He's carrying a lot of baggage. I also get the impression there's something else weighing on his spirit. He may still be mourning the loss of his father. Or having a difficult time processing his dad's death."

"It's so heartbreaking. It's almost like he's had two families stolen from him." Soledad shook her head. "That may be a lot for you to take on. Are you certain you can handle what might get thrown at you?"

"I'm not sure, and I won't know until I'm in the situation. I just know I want to try." Palmer raised Lyra to his shoulder and gently patted her back. She'd polished off a full bottle of milk and the burp that erupted from her sounded like a truck backfiring.

"Whoa!" Palmer exclaimed. "That one was award worthy."

"She's going to give the boys a good run for their money." Soledad snickered as she rose from her seat, removing the used dishes from the kitchen table. Dinner had been a large salad topped with sautéed shrimp. It had been a quick and easy meal. "So what's on your agenda tonight?"

"I have some paperwork I need to finish. Then I'm all yours. Why? What do you have in mind?"

"Shall we Netflix and chill?"

"You've been dying to say that, haven't you?"

Soledad giggled. "Yeah."

"Just don't pick a romance movie and I'll be good. Give me something with a little action in it. Maybe a drama."

"Check. Action and drama. I think I can handle that. Meanwhile, I want to go pick the last of those blueberries. I'd like to make a tart."

Palmer tossed a glance over his shoulder to the clock on the wall. "Most of the men have gone for the day. I don't think there's anyone still around. If you want, I can do my rounds early just to be sure."

"I think I'll be good. And I'll be careful. It shouldn't take too long. They're past ready to be picked, so it should be quick."

"Do your thing, honey. I'll watch Lyra while you do."

"I love it when a plan comes together." Soledad went to the cupboard to take out a large ceramic bowl.

Palmer moved to the front door, the baby still in his arms. He looked out and, when it was clear, gestured for Soledad to head for the barn.

Hurrying across the walkway, Soledad slipped into the barn and out the far door.

The bushes on the back side of the barn were sizable, each shrub loaded with berries. Soledad began filling her bowl with the ripe fruit, excited as she began to plan how she would use them. That tart, more muffins, maybe even a cobbler or scones. Her bowl was almost full when she suddenly felt like she wasn't alone. She looked up and around, but saw nothing. A tight knot formed in the pit of her stomach. She couldn't help but wonder if she would always be afraid that Gavin was lurking somewhere in the wings, determined to do them harm. Afraid that the wrong move or a bad choice would take Lyra and Palmer from her.

Fear was a funny emotion, she suddenly thought. There was little she'd been afraid of as a child and even less as an adult. Now the slightest noise could leave her shaking like a withered leaf, her own shadow giving her reason to pause. She took a deep breath and held on tighter to the bowl.

Just as she was moving back toward the barn door, it flung open and Palmer stepped through. Lyra, cradled high in his arms, squealed excitedly at being outside.

Soledad pulled her hand to her chest, breathing a sigh of relief. "It's just you."

"Were you expecting someone else?" he teased, his eyes shining sweetly.

"No. I just…well… It was like…" She faltered, suddenly unable to explain what it was she was feeling.

"You okay?" Palmer asked. Concern washed over his face.

She shook her head. "I've been better. I think I'm ready to go back inside."

"It's okay," he said as he shifted to her side. Reaching for the large bowl, he passed her the baby and wrapped an arm around her waist to guide her back toward the house.

They had just made it to the steps of the farmhouse when Benjamin called out his name. Palmer turned abruptly, surprised by the young man walking hurriedly in their direction. "Go inside," he snapped, his voice a loud whisper. He gave Soledad a gentle shove. "And lock the door."

As she and the baby stepped over the threshold, the door closing securely behind them, Palmer turned.

Benjamin stopped in front of him at the bottom of the stairs.

"What's going on? Why are you still here?" Palmer asked.

"I missed my ride. I went back to the pond to sit and think about some things and I lost track of time. I was walking out to the main road to hitchhike home when I saw you. I didn't mean to interrupt you and your friend." He gestured toward the house and Soledad, who was standing behind the closed door, eyeing him with reservation.

"If you want, I can give you a ride," Palmer said. "Just let me get my wallet."

"I don't want to be any trouble."

"It's not a problem," Palmer said as he turned, took the steps and bounded into the house. But it was a problem, because something still didn't feel right, and Palmer always trusted his gut.

Soledad could feel the young man watching her intently through the glass door. He seemed innocent enough and Palmer was willing to vouch for him, but that knot in the middle of her belly was only getting tighter. There was just…something about the way he looked at her that made her uncomfortable. She took a step back from the door and out of his view.

"I shouldn't be too long," Palmer said as he kissed her cheek. "I feel like there's something going on with him and I'd like to try to figure out what it is. Will you be okay?"

Soledad forced a smile to her face. "We'll be fine. I have the alarm, the dog and your gun. Besides, I doubt Gavin is planning to just come out of the shadows without some kind of fanfare. He likes attention too much. But if he does, he'll regret it."

"I'm sure he will. But I'll still lock the door and set the alarm. Just to be safe, you and Lyra should hang out in my bedroom until I get back."

"Lyra and I are making a blueberry tart. We'll be fine."

Palmer kissed her again. "Just keep that burner in your pocket in case you need to call me or 9-1-1 for help."

Palmer dropped Ben off downtown, on the corner of Market and Holland streets. Home was a friend's sofa, and the friend, a young woman named Hadley, hadn't finished her shift at the local McDonald's. Palmer learned that Hadley had also been a foster kid until she hadn't been, returned to her mother when she'd been fifteen.

Palmer couldn't put his finger on it, but something about Benjamin was starting to bother him. The kid just showing up at his front door was problematic, despite the young man's assertions that he meant no ill will.

On the ride to town, they'd had a lengthy conversation about boundaries and him being respectful of them, but Palmer couldn't say with certainty that Benjamin understood or even cared. He sometimes talked too fast and had an explanation for everything Palmer threw at him. There was also something in his demeanor that gave Palmer pause whenever they talked about family. He couldn't help but wonder if the boy was dealing with issues bigger than Palmer was prepared to handle.

After some thoughtful consideration, the more he reflected on what he knew about the kid, the more uncertain Palmer suddenly felt. He turned his truck onto Grave Gulch Boulevard and headed for the police station.

The path leading into the building was crowded with protesters. Their chants for police reform and Melissa

Colton's dismissal were loud and caustic. Store own-
ers had begun to board up their neighboring buildings,
fearful that the protests would turn violent and agita-
tors would destroy their town. Watching it on television
had been one thing. Seeing it up close and personal was
something totally different.

The main entrance to the building was gated. Inside,
a receptionist at the front desk would point visitors to
where they needed to go. The receptionist's name was
Mary and behind her stern business demeanor was a
sweet, bubbly personality. She was well-liked by everyone and greeted Palmer warmly.

"Mr. Colton. How are you?"

"I'm well, Mary."

"So what can I do for you today?"

"I was hoping to see Troy. Is he here, by chance?"

"I believe he is," she answered. "Let me call him
up for you."

"Thank you, Mary."

Minutes later, Troy came from the back of the building. He looked frustrated, despite his efforts to hide
his emotion. "Hey, what's up? What brings you here?"
Troy asked, extending his hand to shake his brother's.

"I'm headed home, but I need you to do me a favor,"
Palmer said, dropping his voice slightly as the two
stepped outside.

"What's going on?"

"I need you to run a background check on a new
hire for me."

"Something out of sync?"

"Something, but I can't put my finger on it. He says

his father was murdered and was one of the Len Davison victims. I like the kid and I want to believe him, but I need to be careful with Soledad and the baby."

Palmer handed his brother a Post-it note with Benjamin's personal information written on it.

"Do you have a picture of him?"

"No. Do you need one?"

"That would have been nice."

Palmer shrugged. "He looks like he could be Zayn Malik's little brother."

"Zayn who?"

Palmer laughed. "He was a singer in that boy band One Direction."

"How do you know this?" Troy asked, his incredulous expression spurring Palmer to laughter. "When do you have time to follow a boy band?"

"Seriously, how have things been going here with you?"

"Busy."

"Busy is good, though, right?"

Troy shrugged. "Depends on how you look at it."

"You sound frustrated."

"I am. The protests are starting to wear on my nerves. I get it. People have the right to express their frustration. In fact, it's their civic duty to bring attention to issues the community needs to be aware of. But the timing right now couldn't be worse. I'm afraid the protests are going to distract my officers from closing these cases. We have a serial killer to find, a murderer to catch so Soledad can go home, and Bowe is still out there wreaking havoc. It's a lot and it doesn't help that they're gunning for Melissa when she's been working her ass off to do right by this department and this city."

"How can I support you? If I can, I really want to help."

"You're letting me vent. I can't tell you how much that means to me." He shrugged.

"Well, anytime you need an ear, you know I'm here, right?"

"Yeah, but I need to get back to work." Troy gestured with that piece of paper. "I'll run this and give you a call when I find out something."

"Thanks, and you stay safe out there, please!"

Chapter 18

Soledad split the last slice of blueberry tart in two, taking a sliver for herself and plating the other for Palmer. It had been two days since she had picked the fresh berries, and the sweet treats she'd made had finally run their course. She and Palmer had also had their fill of blueberries. What they hadn't had their fill of was each other.

Everything about their time together was beginning to feel like forever. Enjoying everything about Palmer was as natural as breathing. Where days earlier she'd had doubts about the two of them, she could now see them having a brilliant future together. Or maybe it was just wishful thinking? Whatever it was, Soledad thought, she planned to enjoy every bit of it for as long as she could.

She carried the dessert plates on a wooden tray into the family room and took the seat beside Palmer. He sat with Lyra on his chest, the little girl having fallen asleep right after dinner. "I'm going to go put her in her crib," Soledad said as she gently took the child out of his arms.

"I'll find us a movie while you're gone," Palmer responded.

"Let's not do a movie," Soledad said. "I'd much rather we chat and cuddle. I know you have to be up bright and early in the morning, and that way we can get to bed early."

"That sounds like you're trying to seduce me," Palmer teased.

"Do I need to try?" Soledad teased back. "I thought seducing you was as easy as dropping my clothes."

Palmer laughed. "Says the woman who is clearly sex-crazed!"

She laughed. "I am not. Just because we've made love every day…"

"Two and three times per day…"

"…doesn't make me sex-crazed."

"If you say so, but I'm good with going to bed early, if you are."

Thirty minutes later, the tart demolished, teeth brushed and pajamas on, Soledad and Palmer were cuddled together in the center of his bed, catching up on the day.

"It was a good day today," Palmer said. "We're finally finished with the irrigation repairs. Fencing is complete and I'll be able to finalize the renovations on the large barn this week."

"I had a good day, too," Soledad said. "I've created two new cupcake recipes and tested four bread-pudding recipes. I think tomorrow I may try my hand at making a banana pudding."

Palmer made a face. "Banana pudding?"

"It'll be some of the best banana pudding you will ever have. I put rum in the cream and I make my vanilla wafers from scratch."

"Why does that sound like we need to order groceries?"

"Probably because we do," Soledad said with a giggle.

"You're missing the bakery, aren't you?"

There was a moment of pause as Soledad considered her answer. "I am. I really am. I've been thinking that maybe I just need to go back to my life. That may bring Gavin out of hiding and they'll be able to arrest him."

"It may also put you at risk for him to do you harm."

"At some point I may very well have to take that risk. I'd rather do it sooner than later. I don't want to get so comfortable that I make Lyra and myself targets because I've done something silly, believing that I'm safe."

Palmer nodded. "Well, if you think you're ready, we can put a plan in place. We can think about security for you and the baby. Maybe a team at the bakery? Definitely at your apartment?"

Soledad agreed, though hearing him talk about her going home suddenly felt very final and not something she wanted to consider. And definitely not as she lay content in his arms as they traded easy caresses. But they had not discussed her staying, and she didn't think it was her place to ask. But she wanted to stay, to make his home her home. She was excited to wake up with him in the mornings and go to bed with him at night. She liked that they could agree to disagree when they didn't share the same opinion about things. She loved that he so willingly supported those things that brought her joy. She blew a soft sigh.

Palmer captured her lips, kissing her sweetly. He tasted like minty toothpaste. His kisses became more intense, his touches passionate. Their bodies responded in kind to the ministrations, and soon they were making love as easily as they breathed. Both believed their bodies were meant for each other, and they swayed across the mattress, perspiration puddling in secret places, panting softly and whispering sweetly in one another's ear.

Palmer had rigged a pulley system to lift the oversize beams to the open loft of the barn. As he yanked on the thick rope, he was joined by Noé and Benjamin, both standing behind him and pulling in unison. The work was hard, and care needed to be taken to ensure no accidents happened. Palmer appreciated the teamwork, the guys coming together to get the job done. And he trusted Noé, even if he wasn't as confident about Benjamin.

As the last beam fell into place, the two men cheered, sounding like a squad at a homecoming event.

"It's been a good day, guys. I hope you two know how much I appreciate you."

"*¡Gracias, jefe!*"

"Thanks!"

Palmer gave them both a nod. "Noé, if you'd please go pass out payroll, then dismiss the crew. We're going to call it a day."

"Yes, boss," Noé said. He took the stack of envelopes Palmer passed to him, jumped into the pickup truck and headed for the pasture where a crew was herding cattle.

Palmer handed Benjamin a single envelope. "You've really impressed me these past few days. And I'll be honest. I've had my doubts about you. But you've worked hard, taken the advice given to you and stepped up when you were needed. I appreciate having you here. Good job!"

"Thanks, boss! I sometimes get ahead of myself, so it means a lot to me that you were willing to give me a chance. And I apologize again if I overstepped. I just wanted to make a good impression."

Palmer nodded. "As long as you're honest with me, we can make things work," he said.

"Thank you." Benjamin peeked into the mailer and quickly counted his money. "Wow!" he exclaimed. "Wow. I wasn't expecting this."

"You earned it. Keep up the good work and there'll be more where that came from. You have a good night."

Benjamin left the barn. When he was out of sight, Palmer checked his phone for any missed calls. He was still waiting to hear back from his brother since Soledad was talking more and more about going home.

He hadn't been able to express how he felt about that and it bothered him. He didn't want her to go. Although there wasn't anything they still felt uncomfortable talking about, he wasn't ready to consider that she might not want to be there with him anymore. That would have broken his heart. So much had changed between them. With *him*. He wanted something different and he hadn't yet verbalized that to himself, so telling Soledad wasn't something he was prepared to do.

Fatherhood was actually a consideration. He adored Lyra, had grown to love caring for her. She would need a father, and for the first time in his life, he felt capable and ready to be that for her.

Palmer was putting away tools and futzing around when Benjamin came strolling back into the space. He looked anxious, moisture beading his brow.

"Hey, what are you still doing here? I thought you'd left."

"I did. I was hoping to catch a ride with Noé, but he didn't have any more room. I was wondering if you might be able to give me a ride home. I hate to ask, but I'm supposed to meet my roommate tonight before she heads to work, and if I have to walk, I'm not going to make it in time."

Palmer looked at his watch. He had planned a date night for him and Soledad. Since a sitter wasn't possible, Lyra and Jack were going to be their third and fourth wheels, and he was hopeful that both would go down early for the night.

A private event planner was currently in the small barn by the house, transforming the space into a light-filled wonderland complete with white linens and gold chairs. Dinner had been ordered from Soledad's favorite food truck and staff had been hired to serve and clean up. He was planning to wear the only tuxedo he owned, and a flower delivery would be arriving soon with a few dozen white roses. There would be a scavenger hunt after dessert, and if all went well, Palmer planned to make love to Soledad well into the next morning. Leaving the ranch to give anyone a ride had not been on the list of things he needed to do.

"Hey, it's not a problem," Benjamin said, seeming to read his mind. "I can walk. Really. And my roomie will understand. Since I have a job, she's thinking about letting me live with her permanently so that I can go to school."

"That's great news. It's good to hear."

Benjamin smiled. "Thank you. I'll get out of your way."

"Look, I have something planned myself tonight, but if you can give me a few minutes, I can give you a ride." Palmer sighed, his jaw tightening as he clenched his back teeth together. He wanted to help the kid, but he couldn't shake the feeling that something was amiss. Giving him a ride took him off the property and far from his family.

Benjamin's smile widened. "Thank you. I really appreciate that. I can't tell you how much this means to me."

"Not a problem. Hop in the truck. I need to stop by the house first and then we can take off. That good?"

"It sure is! Thank you again."

Palmer made a quick stop to let Soledad know where he was headed.

"You've had to give him a ride practically every day since he got here. That's not cool."

"I need to talk to him about it. He's been doing so well that I don't want to make an issue of it when it's really not that big a deal. I'll be back in plenty of time to get dressed and escort you to dinner."

Soledad shrugged. "Well, just be careful, please. I don't know what you've got planned, but I'm excited about dressing up and spending the evening with you." And she was, a new dress hanging against the bedroom door. Palmer had excellent taste, and she was excited to wear the purchase he had gifted her earlier in the day.

He kissed her lips. "You know the routine. Lock the doors and set the alarm. There's no reason for anyone to come into the house. For anything."

She gave him a salute. "Yes, captain," she said teasingly.

"I'm serious, Soledad. Don't do anything to put yourself at risk."

Palmer quickly walked from the house to the small barn to pop his head in and check that things were going smoothly. The party planner was gone, so he knew setup was complete. The catering people weren't due for another hour, so he had some time.

As he passed by his Ford F-150, Benjamin was on his cell phone, seeming to be in a heated conversation with someone. Minutes later, satisfied that everything was on track, Palmer jumped into his truck and took off for the main road.

"Everything okay?" he asked, sensing that Benjamin's mood had shifted drastically.

"Sorry, my roommate is just tripping."

"Anything I can help with?" Palmer asked.

"No," Benjamin answered, shaking his head. "I just need to show her I can be responsible and take care of myself. I still don't know if it'll work out, but if it means I'll have a home, I want to try to make it work."

"I'm proud of you, Ben. I want you to know that. This isn't easy and you can easily get distracted. I'm proud that you're focused on doing what you need to do."

"Really?"

"Why wouldn't I be?"

He shrugged, his shoulders rolling forward as he fell into thought. Minutes passed before either spoke again. They were parked in traffic, an accident keeping them from their destination. Palmer kept watching the clock, time not being a good friend to him.

Benjamin broke through the quiet. "I've made some bad choices. Some of them I can't take back," he said, his voice a loud whisper. "But I'm not really a bad person. At least, I'm not trying to be."

"You're still finding your way. Your confusion now is not a bad thing. You'll get my age and still be learning about yourself. Trust that."

Benjamin turned to stare out the window, his brow creased with thought. For a split second, Palmer thought he might cry, but he didn't, seeming to pull himself together.

"Are you sure you don't want to talk about it?"

Benjamin shook his head, words catching in his

throat. Before either man could say anything more, Palmer's cell phone rang, his brother's image popping up on the screen.

"Sorry, I need to take this," Palmer said as he answered the call. "Hey, what's up?"

"I think you've got a problem."

"What do you mean?" Palmer felt every nerve in his body bristle with tension.

"What's the deal with this kid? Is he working for you?"

Palmer shifted his cell phone to his other ear. He shot Benjamin a look, the boy still staring intently out the window. "Yeah. Why?"

"Benjamin Harris is Benjamin Harris Monroe. Monroe is his legal last name. He is eighteen years old, but he was never adopted by anyone named Harris. In fact, he bounced from foster home to foster home, starting when he was five years old. He was labeled problematic, has been arrested four times for various misdemeanors and has one felony conviction for assault. His last place of residence was a group home in Detroit before being incarcerated at the juvenile detention center here in Grave Gulch. He aged out of the foster-care system six months ago."

"Well, that's definitely not the story I was told."

"There's more," Troy noted. "He has no connection to Len Davison. There was no father who was a victim of Davison's, but he does have a connection to Dr. Gavin Stone. Stone volunteered at the detention center as part of his own community service for assaulting a woman three years ago. He took a plea deal that gave him community service in exchange for his record being expunged once completed."

"Are you sure about that?"

"I just spoke to Benjamin's parole officer. Dr. Stone vouched for him and wrote a letter of recommendation for his release from the detention center. They would seem to know each other very well."

The traffic inched forward a single car length. Palmer had broken out into a sweat, perspiration like a faucet left running. A quiet rage suddenly swept through him. "Troy, hold on," he snapped as he dropped his cell phone into his lap. Abruptly making a three-point turn, he aimed the truck in the opposite direction and sped off back toward the ranch.

"I think we have a bigger problem," Palmer suddenly snapped as he pulled the phone back to his ear. "Send units to my house now!"

Soledad loved that Lyra always slept when she needed her to. She was the best baby, and even in the short time they'd been with Palmer, the little girl had grown exponentially. Her mother would have been very proud.

Stepping out of the shower, Soledad peeked into the nursery as she made her way to her room. Lyra was sleeping peacefully, and Jack had taken up his guardian position beneath the crib.

The dress that lay across the bed had been in a box lined with tissue paper. An exquisite off-the-shoulder, midi-length dress with ruched mesh, it was the most stunning design she'd seen in a long time. And it fit her figure like a glove. She couldn't begin to explain how excited she was to wear it, even if their date night only started and stopped in the kitchen. She just knew that it wasn't a meal she had to cook or dishes she had to clean, and the entire evening was devoted to her and Palmer. The flurry of activity that was happening in the barn only served to heighten her excitement, and she couldn't wait to see what he'd been up to.

She didn't want to admit it, but tension had risen between them. It was like a layer of frustration that neither was willing to address. Despite wanting a future together, they'd been reluctant to express what that future might look like when she was free to go home. Would they start to date like normal people did? Would they bounce from his place to hers and back? Would there be mornings when they didn't wake up to each other, or nights when they went to bed alone?

Soledad knew Palmer cared about her. He'd even told her it was love. But did he care about her enough to want to marry her? Or would his love for her fade into a casual friendship with benefits? Most important, was he still opposed to being a father, and would he turn his back on Lyra when he no longer felt responsible for her?

Suddenly, once again, Soledad had more questions than answers, and even as she admired her reflection in the pretty dress, there was still far too much that she didn't know about how Palmer was feeling when it came down to their relationship.

The sound of glass breaking in the kitchen startled her from her thoughts. She reached for the remote for the bedroom stereo and lowered the volume. She stood as still as stone. Jack had jumped from where he rested and he eased his way to the door, moving as if he were hunting prey. The sound of rubber-soled shoes on the hardwood floor moved the dog to growl. Instinctively, Soledad knew someone was in the house and it wasn't Palmer who had come home.

She hurried into the bathroom and turned the shower back on. Leaving the door partially closed, she moved to the crib and lifted Lyra into her arms. The baby barely noticed as she rested her head on Soledad's shoulder and continued to snore softly.

Soledad tiptoed to the bed and set the infant down in its center. She had to think fast and, knowing that there was nowhere for her to run, fast meant putting up a good fight to protect the little girl she loved with every fiber of her being.

She grabbed a fire poker from the fireplace and stood behind the door. Seeing his shadow before she saw him, she knew she was cornered. There was nowhere to run, no escaping the inevitable, and so she braced herself, prepared to give Gavin Stone the worst day of his life.

Palmer was shouting, his calm having dissipated into thin air. "What did you do? What does he have planned?" He didn't care about the traffic laws he was breaking as he zigzagged between the cars to get back to his ranch.

"I don't know," Benjamin shouted back. "He just asked me to get you out of the house. He said that woman kidnapped his daughter and he just wanted to get her back."

Palmer was ready to commit murder himself, his frustration level miles high. He had let his guard down and put Soledad in danger. If anything happened to her, he thought, he would never forgive himself and he would make it his mission to destroy everyone who'd had anything to do with her being harmed—starting with Benjamin.

"I trusted you!" Palmer snapped. "Did he send you to spy for him?"

"He wasn't sure where she was and he needed me to confirm if I saw her."

"So you came and asked for a job?"

"Yes, and I'm sorry!"

Rage washed over Palmer's face. "You'll be sorry if he does anything to her. He killed his wife. Did you know that? Soledad's hiding because she witnessed him commit murder."

Shock registered in Benjamin's expression. He had no words as his gaze dropped to the floor, apparently struggling to make sense of what Palmer was telling him.

Palmer took a hard right turn into the southern entrance of the Colton Ranch property. He barreled straight through the closed gate, not bothering to wait for the metal fencing to open. He depressed the accelerator, speeding up the F-150 as he barreled down the dirt road, turning left toward home.

His heart was racing and he was finding it difficult to breathe, but all he could think of was getting to Soledad and the baby as quickly as he could. In the distance, he heard the sound of sirens and wished a silent prayer that they all could get to them in time.

Chapter 19

As Gavin moved into the room, his eyes focused on the baby lying on the bed, Soledad swung the fire poker with every ounce of energy that she possessed. Due to the height differential, she missed his head, striking him in the shoulder instead. Gavin bellowed in pain, which was just enough of a diversion for Jack to lunge for his neck. As he struggled to get the dog off him, he managed to fire off a shot from the gun in his hand, the bullet missing Soledad and shattering the dresser mirror instead.

Soledad grabbed the baby and ran, Jack racing them both to the front door. A second shot zoomed past her head. Flinging the door open, Soledad bolted onto the front porch and down the steps. With nowhere else to run, she headed for the small barn beside the house to hide, hopeful that Palmer hadn't made too many changes and the bales of hay would still afford them a modicum of shelter.

As he neared his home, Palmer saw Soledad bolt across the yard toward the barn. Though the siren sounds were getting closer, there was no sign of any of the patrol cars.

Gavin Stone came limping out of the house and off the porch, clearly determined to give chase. Palmer just missed hitting the murderer with his truck, throwing the vehicle into Park as Gavin jumped out of his way.

Then everything seemed to happen in slow motion, like a scene in a bad movie.

Palmer grabbed the Glock he kept in the glove box and threw himself from the truck. Gavin fired his weapon as Palmer ducked behind the rear of the vehicle. As he did, they exchanged fire, both determined to bring the fight to an end.

Palmer didn't know when or how, but Jack was suddenly standing between them, baring his teeth at Stone. Palmer watched as the man raised his gun arm.

Palmer shouted and Jack shifted gears, turning toward him.

In that split second, Palmer lost focus, his firearm wavering. Gavin aimed and fired, and from out of nowhere, Benjamin threw himself between the two men, taking a bullet that wasn't meant for him. As both men watched the boy's body fall, Palmer fired once and then a second time, hitting his target squarely in the chest with both shots.

The moment was surreal, everything seeming to happen in slow motion. Palmer felt his stomach pitch with tension, and concern for Benjamin rose with a vengeance. The kid has purposely put himself in the line of fire and saved his life. Seconds later, his body was flooded with relief.

He stood tall as Gavin Stone fell to the ground.

The shooting finally stopped. Lyra was crying. Jack was barking. Outside, it sounded as if sirens were surrounding the building. Voices shouted and Palmer was screaming Soledad's name. But in that moment, all Soledad could see were the miniature lights that sparkled around the room. There was a dinner table set for two, with white linens, gold-trimmed dinner plates, crystal wineglasses and flickering battery-powered candles. It was the most amazing presentation that she had ever seen.

Soledad came out from behind the hay bales in the loft. She had scaled the ladder with Lyra in her arms, determined that Gavin would never get his hands on the baby. Retreating to ground level proved to be more of a challenge, and she'd just planted her bare feet on the wooden planks when Palmer barreled into the barn. Melissa Colton and his brother Troy were both on his heels.

It was only when Palmer pulled her into his arms that Soledad realized tears streamed down her face. Her pretty dress was torn down the side and dirt covered her face and hands. But Palmer Colton kissed her like she was the prettiest girl in the whole wide world.

"I was so scared," he muttered against her lips as his eyes skated easily back and forth over hers. "Are you okay?"

She shook her head. "I didn't know what to do. I just knew I had to fight and keep Lyra safe."

Palmer kissed her again, pulling his hand through her hair as he wrapped his other arm around her and the baby.

"Where is he?" she asked, still shaking.

"He's dead," Palmer muttered. "You never have to worry about him again." Something dark and sad spilled from his eyes.

"What?" Soledad questioned, concern wafting like a cool breeze between them.

"I shot him," Palmer said, his voice a loud whisper. The magnitude of everything that had happened suddenly hit him. He'd killed a man and he didn't take that lightly. Whether or not he'd find atonement for that sin was yet to be seen. He tightened the grip he had on Soledad and the baby.

Melissa interjected. "The ambulance is transporting Mr. Monroe to the hospital now. EMS says it doesn't look like the bullet hit any vital organs, so they anticipate he'll survive his injuries."

Soledad looked confused. "Who's Mr. Monroe?"

"Benjamin Harris," Palmer said matter-of-factly, filling her in on the connection between him and Gavin.

"I'm so sorry," she whispered. "I know how much you wanted to help him. You put a lot of faith into him succeeding."

"I did and I'm still processing how I got that wrong."

"He'll be charged with conspiracy," Troy added. "I imagine he's going to do some time in an adult jail this time."

Palmer shook his head. "He saved my life. He didn't have to do that, but he did."

His brother shrugged. "He'll still be charged. What he did was criminal."

Soledad brushed her palm against Palmer's back, gliding her hand up and down the length of his spine.

"I need EMS to check that you and the baby are okay," Melissa said. "Then you and Palmer will need to come down to the station to give us statements. I'm glad that you're all right, Soledad, and you can have your life back."

Soledad smiled. "Thank you. And thank you for supporting my decision to hide out here."

Melissa grinned. "I don't know anything about that. I'm just happy we were able to find you safe and sound."

They all watched as Melissa turned and exited the barn.

"Do you two need anything else from me?" Troy asked.

Palmer shook his head for a second time. "I think we're good."

Troy glanced around the barn. "It sure is pretty in here. Looks like a great place to ask someone to marry you."

Palmer shook his head yet again and snapped, "Go away!"

Troy chuckled heartily as he gave Soledad a wave and made his way out of the building.

Palmer pulled Soledad back into his arms. He kissed her and then bent his head to give Lyra a kiss, too. The baby was staring in awe, completely mesmerized by the lights.

"My date-night plans were ruined," Palmer said. "I don't even know if the caterer has been able to make it onto the property with all the police cars out there."

"You outdid yourself."

"Well, my brother was right about one thing," he said. "I was determined to have a pretty place to ask you to be my wife." He reached into his pocket and pulled a stunning diamond ring from inside.

Soledad's mouth fell open and her eyes widened. Surprise seeped from her eyes.

Palmer dropped to one knee, taking Soledad's hand into his. "Soledad de la Vega, I love you. I am so in love with you that I almost lost my mind at the very thought of something happening to you. I never want to lose you. Or Lyra. You and that beautiful baby girl have become my entire life, and I want to spend every day from now until eternity making you happy. Will you marry me? And will you allow me to adopt Lyra, so that she is officially our baby girl?"

Soledad pressed her hand to Palmer's face, her eyes dancing a beautiful two-step with his. He loved her. He wanted her. And he wanted the life she envisioned for herself and for Lyra. She smiled. "Oh, hell yes!" she exclaimed. "I didn't know if you would ever ask."

The Grave Gulch Police Department was buzzing with reporters hoping to get an exclusive interview with

Soledad. News of the shooting that ended the hunt for Annie Stone's murderer had broken on the evening news. Both Soledad and Palmer had endured hours of questioning by numerous detectives until they'd been satisfied that the case could be closed. Dominique and Stanton had rushed to the home and were waiting there with Lyra until they returned.

The magistrate had also granted Soledad temporary custody of Lyra pending a formal hearing and the reading of Annie's last will and testament. There was no doubt from anyone involved that her mother's last wishes were for Lyra to remain in the care of Soledad.

Soledad held tight to Palmer's hand as Troy walked them to a side exit. They paused when he was stopped by K-9 detective Brett Shea.

"Sorry to interrupt, partner," the man said. He gave Palmer and Soledad a look, apologizing for the interruption. "We've gotten a tip on Randall Bowe. It's credible and I'm headed to check it out. I thought you might want to take the ride with me."

Troy nodded. "Let me grab my stuff and I'll be right there." He turned to his brother. "I'll check on you two tomorrow unless you need something else?"

Palmer shook his head. "We're good. I need to go feed my woman and we need to check on our baby girl."

"That's important."

"Is he new? I don't recognize him," Palmer said, gesturing after the officer who'd just rushed out the door.

Troy nodded. "That's Brett Shea."

"He's intense," Soledad observed. "He obviously takes his work seriously."

"He was recently transferred here from Lansing. He's fighting some demons and he's got trust issues. One of his best friends was arrested for a crime he didn't commit. Brett struggled because he couldn't help him, even though he knew he wasn't guilty. The friend served some time, but was eventually exonerated."

"That's horrible!" Soledad exclaimed.

Troy nodded. "I often think that when the department is able to regain Brett's trust, I'll know we've won back the community's trust, as well."

Palmer nodded. "You be safe out there, big brother."

"We Coltons don't go down easy," Troy said with a wink.

The couple watched as he hurried after his partner, one more case needing to be solved.

Soledad lifted her gaze to Palmer's. "Can we go home? I want to dance cheek to cheek in the barn, under the pretty lights."

Palmer laughed. "Soledad, I adore you. And for you, my darling, whatever you wish for is yours. There's only one problem with that wish, though."

"What's that?"

"I can't dance."

Soledad laughed. "I still love you!"

* * * * *

COMING NEXT MONTH FROM

ROMANTIC SUSPENSE

#2147 COLTON 911: TEMPTATION UNDERCOVER
Colton 911: Chicago • by Jennifer Morey

Ruby Duarte and her daughter are finally free of her ex—but his followers are still a threat. Damon Jones seems like a friendly local bartender, but he's secretly undercover and determined to take down a dangerous ring while keeping Ruby safe. But will his lies ruin any chance they have at a future?

#2148 COLTON K-9 TARGET
The Coltons of Grave Gulch • by Justine Davis

When he came to Grave Gulch PD, K-9 handler Brett Shea never expected to land in the middle of a criminal catfishing case. Annalise Colton may be a part of the family that seems far too entwined in Grave Gulch's police department, but she's also at the center of his current case—and Brett finds himself falling for her even if he's not sure the Colton family can be trusted.

#2149 FIRST RESPONDERS ON DEADLY GROUND
by Colleen Thompson

Determined to expose the powerful family that destroyed his mother's life, paramedic Jude Castleman knows he stands little chance of success. Then widowed flight nurse Callie Fielding comes up with a high-risk plan to find the justice they crave...if their own unstoppable attraction doesn't lead them into danger.

#2150 A FIREFIGHTER'S ULTIMATE DUTY
Heroes of the Pacific Northwest • by Beverly Long

Daisy Rambler's new job in small coastal Knoware, Washington, is a new start for her and her sixteen-year-old daughter, away from an abusive ex. When her daughter goes missing, local hero and paramedic Blade Savick comes to the rescue—but more danger lurks around the corner...

HRSCNM0821

Love Harlequin romance?

DISCOVER.

Be the first to find out about promotions, news and exclusive content!

Facebook.com/HarlequinBooks

Twitter.com/HarlequinBooks

Instagram.com/HarlequinBooks

Pinterest.com/HarlequinBooks

YouTube.com/HarlequinBooks

ReaderService.com

EXPLORE.

Sign up for the Harlequin e-newsletter and download a free book from any series at **TryHarlequin.com**

CONNECT.

Join our Harlequin community to share your thoughts and connect with other romance readers!
Facebook.com/groups/HarlequinConnection

HSOCIAL2021